The Biker Below th

Graeme Woolaston has an Englis
was born in England, grew up in Scotland, lived for
years in England as an adult, and now lives again in Scotland, where he celebrates his ethnic origins by drinking large quantities of English beer and Scotch whisky. When sober, he works as an arts administrator in Glasgow. He is the author of *Stranger Than Love* ('fascinating and incredible . . . a substantial and memorable book' – *TWT*, Houston, Texas) and *The Learning of Paul O'Neill*, also published by Millivres Books ('I urge *Rouge* readers to buy this book. It is written with consummate skill and has a complexity rare in modern gay fiction' – *Rouge*, London).

The Biker Below the Downs

Graeme Woolaston

Millivres Books
Brighton

First Published in 1995 by Millivres Books (Publishers)
33 Bristol Gardens, Brighton BN2 5JR, East Sussex, England

A CIP catalogue record for this book is available from the British Library

ISBN 1 873741 25 1

Typeset by Hailsham Typesetting Services, 4-5 Wentworth House, George Street, Hailsham, East Sussex BN27 1AD

Printed and bound by Biddles Ltd., Walnut Tree House, Woodbridge Park, Guildford, Surrey GU1 1DA

Distributed in the United Kingdom and Western Europe by Turnaround Distribution Co-Op Ltd., 27 Horsell Road, London N5 1XL

Distributed in the United States of America by InBook, 140 Commerce Street, East Haven, Connecticut 06512, USA

Distributed in Australia by Stilone Pty Ltd, PO Box 155, Broadway, NSW 2007, Australia.

For Chris

and David

and Peter

PART ONE

JOHN'S STORY

CHAPTER ONE

All day I had been walking on the high Sussex downs.

I say 'high' because, in that landscape, I had begun to think again as the Sussex man I was for three years when I was a student, a quarter of a century ago. But to our Scottish eyes the downs aren't, of course, 'high' at all; they wouldn't be seen even as hills in our broken, jagged country.

That August afternoon I was on holiday, in Sussex because in Edinburgh it was the time of the Festival, the annual extravaganza of the arts which for three weeks turns our city into the most uninhabitable in Britain. My work takes me frequently into the north of England, to auctions and book fairs – I am joint owner of a second hand bookshop – but once a year I travel south for pleasure, to spend ten days or a fortnight in a specific county, driving around from Norman church to timber-framed steading to cathedral close. This, however, was my first visit to Sussex in nearly ten years, and only the third since my student days in Brighton.

All through the afternoon I had been happily aware of how different the southern climate is from the Scottish. On the downland chalk paths I had felt sufficiently alone and comfortable to walk stripped to the waist. The sensations of sun and breeze on my torso were both rare and nostalgic, for it has to be said that in Edinburgh you don't often feel like taking your shirt off out of doors.

Not that I would be seriously tempted to exploit such an opportunity even if it existed; not at forty-four. I'm in as good a state of preservation, I suppose, as most men of my age – I still have a full head of hair – but nonetheless, the waistline is a number of inches greater than it should be, my chest hair is greying, and there is flabbiness where, in a happier state of things, there would not be flabbiness.

As I descended back to my car I put on my shirt again; the population of Sussex has a right to be protected against the sight of excessively pale middle-aged Scotsmen. But as

I turned an abrupt corner of the path, between high hawthorn bushes, I found myself just yards from two ascending walkers who were also stripped to the waist, and one of whom was a young woman. She hurriedly pulled a tee-shirt over her head, but as we passed our eyes met and we shared a brief smile of complicity. She had guessed, perhaps, that her modesty had been unnecessary; it was her companion who – though he seemed too thick to realise it – might have had more reason to cover himself if he was shy. Nonetheless she was very pretty, and her breasts were full and firm; there was a time when I was far from indifferent to such attractions, and I hope I will never be wholly so.

I drove back to Westhurst, the village where I was staying, renting what had been described as a 'holiday cottage' – in reality, a modern detached house at the edge of the village.

Just as I was getting out of the car I heard an approaching sound which I'd heard a number of times when I was indoors, and which was unmistakable: the noise of a powerful motor-bike with a faulty silencer. I lingered over the process of locking up the car, out of curiosity, since I knew the motor-bike would stop next door, and I had yet to see either it or its rider. A few moments later it came round the corner of the village street, fast, and, as I had expected, more or less rocketed to beside where I was standing, stopped abruptly enough, I might have thought, to send its rider over the handlebars, had its side-stand kicked down, and disburdened itself of its rider who, as if he couldn't switch off speed in himself as easily as he switched off his engine, nearly collided with me as he headed towards his front gate.

A few inches apart, we looked at each other.

Beneath his helmet he had a blue scarf covering the lower part of his face, so all I could see of his body was his eyes. They were deep, dark brown, gazing at me at first with a still frankness in which I read the uncorrupted honesty of youth. Then their expression changed. I saw he was amused; I could guess that behind his visor and scarf he was starting to smile as he moved on without a word to open the gate.

What had made his reaction change was that I had not been able to stop my own eyes from glancing down over him and pausing a moment before they went back to his face. He was in black leather from his helmet to his boots. If I say that all I saw of him was his eyes, then I suppose this was literally true. But his leather jeans left no doubt about what he had enclosed inside them as he zipped them up. And if there is one thing I cannot resist in the great pantomime of sex, it is a male crotch defined in black leather.

I watched him go up the path to his front door. His jeans didn't sag, as leather trousers are liable to do, at the back. They fitted him with perfect smoothness – the seat polished, no doubt, by his biking; the leather gleamed around the curves of his arse as splendidly as where it took its shape from the containment of him at the front.

As he disappeared indoors it was my turn to be amused by his amusement. My unsuppressible betrayal of interest in him hadn't offended him, which I took as confirmation of a pet theory of mine: that no-one dresses in black leather if they object to being looked at.

And his bike was hardly less attractive than himself. It was a shining blue-and-white 550cc Kawasaki, fitted with a full fairing and panniers. It was a bike for riding on a motorway, or better still an autobahn, rather than the country roads of Sussex. Before I turned towards my own front door I admired it with envy for the young man who could own both such a body and such a bike.

You see, I was a biker myself, when I was younger. I know the transforming joy of riding as if you can feel the turning of the earth below you, so smooth is the speeding of your machine. I sold my last bike when I gave up teaching and bought myself into my current business, but I still hanker after that sensation, like someone who was once hooked on a drug and knows it could seduce him back at once if he ever let it.

Indoors, I had a bath and a snooze. In the evening I

drove down to Chichester for dinner, and afterwards strolled round the Cathedral precinct. Back in my 'cottage' I drank a fine malt whisky while reading a new gay novel with some scenes set in Brighton; for my holiday reading I had brought with me two or three books with a Sussex connection. As usual, I was in bed before midnight and soon fast asleep. If I had any premonitory dreams, I remembered nothing of them on waking.

I was with the novel again over breakfast – I refuse to read newspapers on holiday – when to my surprise there was a loud rapping at the front door. Since I knew no-one in the whole county of Sussex, I was expecting no callers.

It was a postman, holding a large parcel.

'Sorry to trouble you, guv,' he said, 'but this is for next door and I can't get any answer – you couldn't take it in for them, could you?'

'Next door?' I asked.

'Yes' – and he indicated the house of my biking friend. 'You wouldn't mind looking after it, would you, guv, and dropping it round to them later on?'

Guv? I wondered if the man had been watching too many Ealing comedies. But 'guv' was perfectly willing to accept the parcel, and yes, he'd be happy to take it round in the evening, when no doubt they'd be in. Or someone would be, anyway. Apart from the biker I had seen no-one coming or going next door.

I decided I would visit some of the flint churches of the downlands, most of which are too remote and too lacking in wealthy patrons to have been horribly 'restored'. It was a splendid day: out of doors, of perfect weather, and inside, of repeated architectural delights. I stood in half-a-dozen country churches, breaking off only to lunch in one of those English pubs which also give their country a claim to high civilisation.

I totally forgot about the parcel sitting on the table in the hall at home.

But there it was, when I got back. At first I was disappointed that the Kawasaki wasn't parked outside, but then remembered that I had only seen it in the street once, and my neighbour's house, like my own, was equipped with a double garage. No doubt the bike had been put away for the night.

What gave me grounds for this belief was that from my kitchen, at the back of the house, I could hear loud music coming from next door's garden. There was a high fence between our gardens – Sussex people, living so closely together, value their privacy – so I couldn't see who was playing the music, but I could hazard a guess. The music was of a kind that, shall I say, a young person might wish to listen to.

So, after a quick wash, I picked up the parcel and went round to my neighbour. I rang the doorbell.

Nothing happened.

I tried again.

Nothing happened.

I knocked loudly.

Still nothing.

Clearly there was no-one inside the house, and the music at the back was drowning out my attempts to be heard. I was about to give up when I saw there was a gate by the side of the house which gave access to a path to the back.

I tried the gate, and it opened. I called out, 'Hallo?'. No answer. I took a few paces down the side of the house, and called out again, 'Hallo? Excuse me?'

Still no answer. Two or three more paces, and I was round the corner of the house and standing in its garden.

And there, in the centre of a large and very green lawn, was the portable stereo which was obscuring my efforts to make myself known; and next to it, stretched out on a sunbed, was its young owner.

He was wearing rather less than when I had first seen him. In fact, if you exempt a pair of sunglasses, he was wearing nothing at all.

And still he hadn't heard me. Heaven knows how long I might have stood there admiring his beauty – for, believe me, he was beautiful – had there not been a more alert living presence in the garden, which now jumped up barking and ran towards me, stopping a yard or so away to bark more and more emphatically. It was a Golden Retriever, and though no doubt it was an excellent friend to man, at that moment I could have wished it in hell – since of course the boy sat bolt upright, pushed up his sunglasses, gaped at me, and within a couple of seconds was off his sunbed and had pulled on a pair of football shorts.

He blushed as he came towards me. Maybe I was blushing too. It was an awkward moment for both of us.

He spoke to the dog first: 'Oh, shut up, Rex. Shut up! Down, boy!'

The dog fell quiet, but remained alert. 'I'm sorry to have disturbed you,' I said, 'but' – and I explained about the postman and the parcel.

The boy said nothing, but merely looked at the parcel.

'Are you Mr Carson?' I asked, suddenly wondering if, to compound my *faux pas*, I had come to the wrong house. To my surprise he laughed: 'Oh, no, but he lives here. Yes, I'll take the parcel for him. Thanks for bringing it round.'

I handed it to him. He blushed again, and lowered his eyes – which weren't as dark brown as I had first thought: 'I'm sorry I was – like that,' he said, indicating the sunbed with his free hand.

'Oh, it doesn't matter,' I said at once, trying to sound as if I ran into nude young men every other day. 'I think *I* should be the one to apologise, for walking in on you.'

He didn't disagree.

The dog was still watching me. Since it had cut short the time I had had to admire my young friend naked, I decided the wretched creature could at least provide me with an excuse for lingering another half-minute. For even in his shorts, which were of the modern baggy kind that prudishly conceal their wearer's form, the boy was stunningly attractive. He was short – shorter than I remembered from our first encounter – with black curly hair; lean, almost skinny, but with just enough definition of his muscles to prevent that; a slight growth of hair on his chest suggested he was about twenty.

'He's a lovely dog, isn't he?' I said, with total insincerity.

'Yes, he is,' the boy conceded as if reluctantly. 'But he's not much use as a guard-dog. Thinks he's a kitten, that one. Pat him and see – he'll be all over you right away.'

This sounded a less than inviting prospect, but nonetheless I patted the dog; and sure enough, at once he wagged his tail and panted. Setting aside my prejudice I could see he really was a friendly and very handsome animal; I dropped on one knee to pat him more easily – and also, of course, to give me a fine angle from which to look up at the no less handsome animal who owned him: 'Rex, did you say his name was?'

'Yes. He's Mr Carson's dog.'

The remark puzzled me, but before I could work out what it meant the boy asked: 'Are you on holiday?'

I nodded: 'That's right.'

'Mr Carson told us the place next door was let out in the summer.'

It was the second time the boy had used that strange formality, but once again he didn't give me time to reflect on it: 'You from Scotland?'

I laughed as I stood up. 'Yes. Well, I'll leave you in peace again.' But as I started to move away I half-turned back: 'By the way, that's a great bike you've got.'

'Sorry?'

'The Kawasaki – it's a very fine bike. What speed do you get out of it on the open road?'

To my astonishment the boy burst out laughing.

'Oh, not me – that's not *my* bike. That's Andy's.'

'Andy?'

'Yes. You wouldn't catch me on a motor-bike – too flaming dangerous for me, I can tell you.'

I was completely lost: 'But didn't I see you yesterday . . .?'

The boy's smile changed. It became knowing; his eyelids drooped slightly: 'No. It was Andy you saw.'

It took me a second or two to grasp the implication. So there were *two* of these delightful creatures?

'Andy?' I asked; and then, before I could check myself – though it was none of my business: 'Is he your brother, then?'

The character of the boy's smile intensified.

'No. He's my boyfriend.'

I was astounded. I know the young are franker than our generation ever was; and this was Sussex, not Scotland; but even so . . . Then I realised that the boy knew about *me*. He wasn't being 'out'; obviously Andy had told him about how I'd eyed him up almost on their doorstep the previous afternoon.

'Oh, I see – I see,' I said, virtually mumbling with surprise. Then, idiotically: 'Well, that's nice.'

The boy looked away: 'He should have been back by now. He's up in London today. Traffic must be bad on the A23 again – it always is on a Friday.'

'Right,' I said, still talking like a fool.

The boy turned to me and smiled again, but now more diffidently: 'Just as well he's late, maybe. Otherwise you might have found us *both* in the nuddy.'

I couldn't think of any appropriate response to this.

'The thing is,' the boy went on, 'we thought we were safe here – no-one can see us, on either side.' He pointed to left and right: 'See?'

I followed his indications. Sure enough, to one side a line of trees hid the garden, and to the other – 'my' side – the houses were not only built at a slight angle, but Mr Carson's, whoever he was, had been extended at the back. The garden was closed off at its end with the same high fence which separated it from mine, and beyond there was open country. As a result the lawn we were standing on wasn't overlooked by any window.

'Yes, you're right,' I said. 'You've got perfect privacy.'

'It never occurred to us somebody could walk in.' He laughed, and blushed again. 'Just as well you're not the vicar.'

From what I know of Anglican vicars, the sight of a naked boy would have come as no novelty to him; but I didn't say anything.

'It was Andy got me into it,' the boy added. 'I mean, sunbathing in the buff, and all that. He uses the nudist beach a lot – in Brighton, that is.'

His continuing embarrassment was obvious. I had to set him at his ease: 'Don't worry about it,' I said quietly. 'You've every right to do what you like in your own garden.' I went on more loudly: 'I'll let you get back to it, then. But' – I started to move – 'tell Andy what I said about his bike.'

The boy smiled: 'I will.'

As I left the garden I was sure he would, but there was an ambiguousness about the thought. I could easily imagine how they would laugh together over that old guy next door, the old lech whose eyes had popped out of his head when he saw one of them in leather and the other flashing his dick to the sun.

But as I opened my front door, I had to smile. I could see the joke myself.

That night, in bed, I jerked off happily to the memory of the nameless boy – picturing that firm little arse I had caught too brief a glimpse of, and his thin torso, and the droplets of sweat glistening among his chest hairs. I tried to work Andy into the fantasy, but he was faceless to me; and you can't – or at least, I can't – get off on an image of a helmet and a set of leathers.

It was a pleasurable ending to the day; I rolled over well content, and was rapidly fast asleep.

CHAPTER TWO

I wasn't always, of course, a middle-aged wanker – to speak bluntly about what I've just described. As I've already hinted, when I was a young man I was more or less bisexual, and as a student I had casual sex with both men and women – the encounters with men, I have to admit, distinctly guilt-ridden. The two serious relationships I had at that time were with women; the second broke up a few months before my Finals, and after that – I've no idea why; the development of sexuality is a mystery to us all – I became more and more one-sidedly gay, to the extent that I hardly slept with women at all, and after the age of twenty-three, never.

I was a student in Brighton, at what was then the still-new University of Sussex. I chose an English university for two reasons. Firstly, it would take me only three years to obtain a degree there, as opposed to four in Scotland, and I was in a hurry to become a wage-earning adult. Secondly, Brighton was about as far away from Edinburgh as I could get without falling into the English Channel.

You must not imagine that I disliked my parents. I never felt any emotion for them which could be described in such strong terms. And I have every reason to believe that they reciprocated the sentiment.

My father was an Edinburgh advocate – what in England would be called a barrister – well known in Parliament House, the seat of the Scottish supreme courts. *His* father was a Sheriff Clerk, an altogether humbler figure in our Scottish legal system; indeed I have never entirely understood how my grandfather managed to finance my father's progress into the exclusive world of the Bar. Perhaps because of financial problems, and then because of the war, my father remained single till he was thirty-five, when he married an advocate's daughter.

It must sound like a calculated career move; my mother's father is said to have *nearly* become a High Court judge. In fact it was an almost perfect love-match. My father and mother were devoted to each other, so much so that I cannot recall ever hearing them exchange a cross word. I believe the only failing my father had in my mother's eyes was that he was a pipe-smoker; and out of deference to her feelings, throughout all their married life he smoked at home only in his study, and never in any other room of the house.

I was their only child, born three years after their marriage. Since my mother was just two years younger than my father it is possible that she was advised against a second pregnancy so late in her thirties. But I believe the truth is that they didn't want to have a second child. Indeed, I sometimes wonder why they even had *me*, except to make their marriage seem more complete. They were so content with each other's company they had no need of children; I was more or less an intruder.

Again, you mustn't imagine that my father was unkind or cruel or even, in his own way, unloving. He was just incredibly *remote*. When I was ten, he was already forty-eight; by the time I was in my teens, he was in his fifties. In those days – the 1960s - Edinburgh was still a backward and reactionary city, and within that city the Faculty of Advocates was more backward and reactionary yet; I suspect that if the ghost of Robert Louis Stevenson had wandered into Parliament House about 1965, he would have felt perfectly at home.

By the standards of the Faculty my father was a liberal man – which means that by everyone else's standards he was remarkably conservative. It wasn't that he forbade me to listen to the Beatles, or banned *Ready, Steady, Go!* from his television, or any nonsense like that. It was rather that he gave out – quite unintentionally, I suppose – unmistakable signs of pain that a son of his should *want* to listen to the Beatles, or *want* to follow the latest developments of Mersey beat. To him it must have been as foreign as Japanese kabuki, and a taste for it no less inexplicable.

Moreover, by then he was serving on a variety of public commissions and Boards of Enquiry, with the result that his conversation began to be scattered with the names of people I read about daily in *The Scotsman;* and as if that wasn't intimidating enough, at the age of fifteen I found myself one evening sitting at dinner between the Secretary of State for Scotland and the Lord Provost of Edinburgh.

My father's one touch of radicalism was that he was by far and away the most single-minded anti-Christian I have ever known. He so detested Christianity that even when I went to primary school he took me aside, at the mature age of five, to warn me not to believe a single word I was ever told in Religious Education, and I suspect that only his ingrained love of order prevented him from having me withdrawn from RE classes altogether.

Since in those days the Church was far more influential in Scotland than it is now, this may be one reason why he was never appointed to the Bench. But it is also possible that he had no ambitions in that direction, since it might have badly disrupted his married life. He was content with the life he had, with the woman he loved and, I suppose, to some extent with his increasingly long-haired son.

But it was an impossibly stifling world for any teenager; and in 1968 I fled to Sussex, and didn't return to live in Scotland for nine years.

My degree was in English. In 1971 life was easy for new graduates, and I had no problem obtaining work to teach English as a Foreign Language, at first in Morocco and then in Cairo, and finally in Greece, in the early years of restored democracy after the fall of the Colonels' regime.

These were, indeed, the most carefree years of my life. Those countries meant for me what Berlin meant for the young Christopher Isherwood: boys. All inhibitions about my homosexuality fell away from me amongst the Arabs, for whom I developed a life-long affection, and under the skies that looked down on Socrates and Alexander – on the subject of Greece, I can wax disgustingly romantic whenever I choose.

Why, then, did I return to grey old Edinburgh? The truth is that after six years abroad I had met enough expats to know, beyond a shadow of doubt, that I had no desire to become a permanent ex-pat myself; they made even the Faculty of Advocates seem progressive and forward-looking. Moreover, by the late Seventies Scotland had begun to change dramatically, and I backed a hunch that it would go on doing so. In this I wasn't wrong. Now, in the Nineties, Scotland has transformed itself into a liberal and open society, and the Scotland I grew up in has simply vanished without trace. Bloody good riddance to it.

I did a year's teacher-training in Edinburgh (which was hell) and then taught for seven years, at first in a brutal Catholic school but subsequently, far more happily, in what officialdom quaintly calls a 'non-denominational' school, and everyone else calls a Protestant one.

I will never forget the day I knew I could no longer go on being a schoolteacher.

There was a boy in Sixth Year, called Jonathan. I had taught him in his Fourth and Fifth Years, after which, having obtained a good pass in English in his Highers (the university qualification exam in Scotland) he gave up the subject.

He had always been good-looking – blond and lean - but in that final year at school he achieved perfection. He became far more than good-looking; he was beautiful. Every movement he made was graceful; he seemed incapable of slipping into an ugly posture or adopting an ugly expression. He let his hair grow as a thick, shining fall of blond waves till he looked like an incarnation of Sebastian from *Brideshead Revisited*: truly *la jeunesse dorée*.

That year I volunteered to become an Assistant Housemaster. The Headmaster was delighted; he had more than once suggested to me that I wasn't playing my full part in extra-curricular activities. Poor misguided idiot. He made no connection between my sudden enthusiasm for school sports and the fact that our House Captain was Jonathan.

As an Assistant Housemaster I was sometimes obliged – obliged! – to join our boys in the changing room before a rugby or a football match, supposedly to inspire them with appropriate enthusiasm, and again afterwards, either to congratulate or console, depending on circumstances.

It was madness. 'Playing with fire' is a cliché; but that's what I was doing. Jonathan was in both our rugby and our soccer teams.

One freezing afternoon in March we had a football match against another House. Fifteen minutes into the second half Jonathan did something neither I nor anyone else had seen him do before: he blatantly fouled an opposing defender, so crudely that there could be no protest against his inevitable and instant sending-off. He walked towards the sports pavilion without, quite evidently, the least contrition.

I could feel my heart beating faster and faster, as if I myself was a seventeen-year-old schoolboy and not a thirtyfive-year-old teacher. I waited three or four minutes and then turned to Callaghan, the Housemaster, who was beside me on the touchline: 'You're going to have to excuse me,' I whispered urgently. 'I'm dying for a slash.'

He laughed.

'You should have gone at half-time,' he said, without taking his eyes off the pitch.

Now it was my turn to walk to the pavilion, trying to keep my pace moderate, trying not to show the turbulence which was making me almost giddy with anticipation. When I got there I didn't go into the staff toilet. I went into the Boys changing room.

I had timed my arrival to perfection. Jonathan was under one of the showers.

I leaned against the tiles by the entrance to the cubicles. Jonathan turned: 'Mr Paterson,' he said. He showed no surprise at my being there. He must have known he would be in for a ballocking from either myself or Callaghan.

'Well, Jonathan,' I said. 'What was all that about?'

'Sir?'

I straightened up: 'You can tell me when you've finished showering.'

I knew, because I had been in the changing room before

the match, where Jonathan had hung his clothes. I sat down on the bench near his place. It was barely a minute before he turned off the water and came walking towards me. He wasn't, of course, embarrassed by my presence; already in my short career as a sports enthusiast I had regularly seen him and the other boys naked.

But I had never been alone with him before. Nor had I sat scarcely a yard from him as he began to dry himself.

'I suppose you're going to tell me,' I said, 'that the fact that the boy you crocked was Douglas Hamilton was pure coincidence?'

He stopped with the towel at his shoulders.

'Sir?'

I laughed: 'Jonathan, what on earth do you think we talk about in the Staff Room? The latest proposals for the Standard Grade curriculum?' He smiled uneasily. 'No,' I went on. 'I'm afraid the affairs of our senior pupils are much more interesting.'

I hadn't intended any pun on the word 'affair', but perhaps Jonathan misunderstood me; for whatever reason, he dropped his towel to his middle and began rubbing it across his stomach.

'You know, then, sir?'

'Of course I know.'

The movements of his towel became slower, but he said nothing.

'I know,' I went on, 'that you've broken up with Sarah Greene, and now she's going out with Douglas Hamilton. Correct?'

He stopped drying himself.

'Yes, sir.'

'And that's why you kicked the legs out from under him back there?'

'Yes, sir.'

I hadn't expected such directness: 'You *admit* it?'

The towel went to his chest as he resumed drying himself: 'Yes, sir.'

'Well, you should be ashamed of yourself. Surely you realise that as House Captain' – I went on about how he would miss the two remaining matches of the football season because he'd been red-carded, and what kind of example was that to set to the rest of the House, and so on; but it produced no discernible effect. I wasn't surprised. Even to my own ears it sounded like standard schoolteacher claptrap, and I suspect that in addition my tone of voice gave away that, really, I didn't care a fig about him being suspended. No, let me be crude here, as crude as any pornographer would be: what I cared about was how he was hung.

He was wonderfully, unashamedly naked beside me – ballock-naked, to use the vivid but accurate slang. I hadn't been so close to a naked boy as young as him, alone, since I left Greece.

You might think that a seventeen-year-old boy, in the mid-Eighties, could not be so innocent as not to realise the sexual charge of the situation. No Greek or Arab of his age could have been so naive; but Jonathan was a Scot, and I knew he had no such thoughts. It redoubled his attractiveness. He was bonding me to him in an illusion of male camaraderie: for him, he was just a football player in a changing room beside another man, with no need to be self-conscious about being undressed.

My tension grew as I saw he would soon be finished drying. In a few moments he would pull on his boxer shorts and begin to mar himself. To delay him I changed the subject, and my tone of voice.

'You know, Jonathan, you really have no reason to worry about attracting another girl.'

He looked at me, partly amused and partly surprised: 'Sir?'

'You really haven't, Jonathan. You're a very handsome young man. If girls aren't falling over you now, they will be soon. Believe me.'

He laughed, and – how little of the coquette there was in him! – he blushed. I laughed in turn: 'And moreover – I hope you haven't forgotten your Shakespeare sonnets?' He looked puzzled. 'Do you remember the line, "but since she prick'd thee out for women's pleasure"?' The four-hundred-year-old pun made him laugh more loudly, but obviously with some embarrassment: 'Sir,' he said again, with a slight protest in his voice.

My madness could no longer be held back from overflowing. I slid along the bench to be next to him. I leaned forward and touched the firm muscles of his stomach with the back of my hand, drew my hand slowly down to his still-damp pubic hair, and very gently, so that my fingers just brushed against his penis, let it fall away from him.

He looked down at me not with shock, nor disgust, but sheer disbelief. I think that at that moment he was genuinely wondering if he'd imagined what had just happened.

'*Eisai polu horaios*,' I said to him softly – 'you are very beautiful', in the language descended from that of Athens in the golden age. And since now I had nothing to lose – my career, if Jonathan so chose, was in ruins – I put my hand behind him and ran my open palm down over the smoothness of his arse.

Then I jumped up and looked him straight in the eye. He still hadn't reacted, or couldn't react, to what I'd done.

'You'd better get dressed,' I said briskly, 'and come and join us on the touchline. I'll tell Mr Callaghan I've spoken to you and he doesn't need to say anything more. OK?'

He was, I'm afraid, stupefied. He said simply, 'Yes, sir', as if nothing had taken place between us which was in any way unusual between a pupil and a schoolteacher.

But as I left the changing room I knew my teaching days were over. It wasn't that I expected Jonathan would go to the Headmaster; I was certain he would be too ashamed to say anything about the incident to anyone. And even if he had, I would have no problem convincing the Headmaster, who was one of the stupidest men I had ever met, that the boy was grossly misrepresenting a harmless piece of intermale horseplay: all I had done, of course, was lightly slap his behind as a jokey telling-off.

The truth was that I had assaulted one boy and I might assault another. I couldn't leave myself open to a repeat of such a temptation – even in a classroom, alone with a boy, my hand might wander to his clothed backside, inside the shiny seat of his trousers. I could end up in court; in theory I could end up in court for what had happened already.

I had a gay friend, Sandy, who was talking about buying a second hand bookshop in Candlemaker Row, and who was having difficulty raising all the necessary capital. I went to see him; we went to see lawyers; and in August, instead of returning to school, I became an equal partner in the business.

I had borrowed much of my share of the money from my father, who was by now retired. I was to repay him in instalments, and did so for nearly two years. Then, one sunny April morning, he was sitting in his study smoking and reading Horace, when the pipe fell from his mouth, the book fell from his hands, and he slumped sideways, dead.

Within little more than a year my mother had followed him; I believe she died, quite simply, of a broken heart. I was the sole heir to my parents' estate, and since my father had, of course, become a man of some means, I found my own financial position transformed. I sold their house when the property market was booming, sold my own small flat at a profit, and moved to the handsome first-floor flat in the New Town where I still live.

Sandy and I remain partners in the shop, which has prospered as the area around it has been revitalised; we have extended it twice, into back premises and into a basement which was previously used for storage. It was therefore as a successful and well-off businessman that I made the trip to Sussex I have been describing.

But I have no 'partner' in the emotional sense of that word. The truth is that in the last fifteen years I have only really loved one person, and that was Jonathan.

CHAPTER THREE

Three days after I had blundered in on Andy's boyfriend sunbathing 'in the nuddy', to use his own expression, I took a stroll through Westhurst in the early evening, after another day spent up on the downs.

I was turning a corner a couple of hundred yards from the house when ahead of me I saw a young man with a dog. Before I had had time to recognise the human, the dog had recognised me; he came bounding up, barking and wagging his tail.

'Hallo, Rex,' I said, laughing. I patted him and walked on with him beside me to his owner: 'We meet again,' I said.

'Yes,' he said, smiling.

He was in a denim jacket and loose-fitting jeans. I looked up at the sky, which had been overcast much of the afternoon: 'No chance of sunbathing tonight,' I said. I was about to add some banal remark about hoping this wasn't a change in the weather, when I was startled by another young man appearing from behind a tree across the road. It was at once apparent what he'd been doing there; he was just zipping up his leather jeans.

He crossed towards us. In those few seconds I had time for two reactions: firstly, that he was one of the handsomest boys I had ever clapped eyes on; and secondly, that I had seen him somewhere before.

He was in his biking leathers again, and his boots, but his jacket was open to reveal a white tee-shirt, and he was, of course, helmetless. His hair grew in thick, nut-brown waves; his eyes, as I have already described, were so dark they seemed almost black, and shining; his skin was smooth and brown, as if he was partly of Mediterranean origin. He was smiling as he joined us; I suspected he was recalling the amusement I had provided for him when we first met, and so I kept my eyes strictly above his neck: 'You must be Andy?' I said, without thinking.

'Yeah. Hi!' – and rather to my surprise he held out his

hand for me to shake. As I took it I looked at his friend: 'I don't think I introduced myself the other day. My name's John. John Paterson.'

'I'm Terry,' the hitherto nameless boy said, and I shook hands with *him*; for a moment we must have looked like a group of Frenchmen.

'You're out walking Rex, I take it?' I said – the sort of idiotically obvious remark you tend to make in these situations.

'Yes,' Terry said, looking down at him. The dog barked and wagged his tail; we all laughed: 'Is he yours?' I asked Terry.

'No, he's Mr Carson's.'

I remembered he had said this before: 'Ah, right.' I felt it would be impolite of me to ask who 'Mr Carson' was, but Andy resolved the mystery: 'Mr Carson's the guy who owns the house we're staying in. We're looking after it while he's away.'

'Oh, I see,' I said.

'He's off on holiday,' Terry added. 'For three weeks. So we're sort of house-sitting for him – you wouldn't believe how many burglaries there are even in a little country place like this.'

'Really?' I exclaimed. This was hardly encouraging information; after all, I myself had charge of a house in the village for a fortnight.

'Oh, yes,' he confirmed.

'And we're taking care of Rex as well,' Andy said. 'Saves him going into kennels. Doesn't it, boy?' – he bent down and patted the dog who, as usual, barked happily at any sign of appreciation.

'Lucky Rex,' I remarked. Even as the words came out I wasn't quite sure if I was referring to his escaping three weeks in kennels, or having three weeks of sharing a house with these two gorgeous boys.

Andy straightened up. It was time for me to round off the conversation with some meaningless pleasantry, and move on.

But I couldn't. Or rather, I didn't want to. During the

few seconds that Andy's attention had been on the dog I had let my eyes run over him. The leather at his crotch was just as stretched as I remembered from our first encounter. The most basic of gay male instincts was beginning to assert itself in me; there could be no acting on it, but at least I could extend our chat for a few minutes longer: 'So you're not from Westhurst, then?' I asked.

'Christ, no!' Andy exclaimed.

I started to smile: 'Is it really that bad?'

'Well, *look* at it,' he said. I burst out laughing: 'You don't like English villages, then?'. I'd intended the question to be slightly mischievous, but Andy's expression suggested he was horrified by the idea: 'God, no. Do you?'

'Well, I've come all the way from Scotland to stay in one.'

'Yeah, but that's different. You're on holiday.'

'And you're not?'

'No, we're still working.'

'Ah! So that's where you go off to on your bike in the morning?'

Andy grinned.

'Not really. I go off *every* morning on the bike – that's my job, I'm a motor-bike courier.'

'Oh, I see.' I nodded: 'So that's why you have such a splendid machine?'

It was instantly obvious he was delighted by the question: 'Do you think so?'

I smiled.

'Oh, yes. A 550 Kawasaki? You must be able to get a ton out of her no bother.'

'Easy as pie! Yeah, she's brilliant on the motorway – you should see me going up and down the M23. Up to London passing everything on the road – leaving everything behind me, the whole way.'

'Oh, don't encourage him!' Terry exclaimed.

Andy turned to him, still grinning: 'Listen to him. Biggest wimp in Sussex, this one.'

Terry smiled. The look they exchanged at that moment totally excluded me. Suddenly I saw they were indeed lovers, and very young lovers at that; as he talked about his bike Andy seemed to become almost the stereotype of a teenager.

But in that look, I briefly thought I detected something about him – some quality about his eyes – which reminded me of the impression I'd had of him when he crossed the road: that I had seen him before, somewhere else.

He turned back to me: 'He won't even let me give him a ride into work, on the pillion. He goes up every day in his *car*' – pronouncing the word as if a car was the grossest form of transport he could imagine. I laughed: 'To London?' I asked.

They seemed surprised: 'No, Brighton,' Terry corrected me.

'Brighton?'

'Yes.'

'You're from Brighton? Both of you?'. They nodded. I explained my reaction: 'I know Brighton well myself. Or at least, I used to. I was a student there.' I smiled. 'Some time ago.'

'A student?'

Andy asked the question with a slight archness which made me smile again: 'Why do you say it like that?'

His own smile became half-private.

'Well, you know. *Students*.'

I stepped back, laughing loudly.

'I see,' I said.

There was another natural pause in the conversation. Once again it was time for me to round off our talk, and move on. But at that moment I caught sight of a building about a hundred yards down the road, on the other side; and in the same instant a lie and a decision came to me.

'I was just on my way to the pub, for a quick pint. I don't suppose you fancy joining me?'

The question, unsurprisingly, visibly surprised both of them. I went on quickly: 'It's just that I'm getting a little tired of drinking on my own.' I affected a self-deprecating laugh. 'It'd be nice to have some company.'

Terry and Andy exchanged glances, the meaning of

which the dimmest of idiots could have discerned though sunglasses on a pitch-black night.

'You're on holiday on your own?' Terry asked, with a hint of emphasis on the last word.

'Yes.' I thought I'd better expand on that: 'I'm using Westhurst as a base, to tour around a bit.' I looked along the road again, oh-so-indifferently: 'I'm planning to drive down to Chichester this evening, so I can't have more than the one pint just now.'

Once again Terry and Andy looked at each other. I saw them reach agreement with the wordless instinct of lovers: 'That's very kind of you,' Andy said. The formality clearly didn't come naturally to him. 'Yeah, we've got time for a pint.'

Terry stooped down to fix a leash to Rex's collar. As he was doing so Andy reflected, or perhaps mimicked, my own air of pretended casualness. Of course they both knew perfectly well that if they had been ugly, or spotty, or dull, I would somehow have managed to find the inner resources to cope with drinking alone.

You mustn't think I am in the habit of inviting virtual strangers I meet in the street to join me for a drink, however handsome they may be or however good they look in denim or leather. In Edinburgh I would never have done any such thing, ever. But I was on holiday. So just this once – what the hell?

CHAPTER FOUR

I had been in the pub, the only one in the village, three or four times during my stay in Westhurst, and I am bound to say that I cannot rate it among the great hostelries of England. The decor was excellent and the beer well-kept; but the landlord – oh dear. The landlord.

In Scotland, even in the allegedly unfriendly city of Edinburgh (which in reality is no such thing), I am used to the idea that if you go into a pub a few times, and see the same barman, that barman will quickly do you the courtesy of recognising you and greeting you; indeed in most Scottish pubs the bar staff will welcome you pleasantly even if you have just arrived from the planet Mars. But the landlord of the Royal Oak was a Sussex landlord. And every single time I had gone into that pub – every single solitary time – he affected never to have seen me before. Or not to be able to remember either my face or my voice, with its distinctive accent, from twenty-four hours previously.

On this occasion, however, he was, for once, all voice as we walked in.

'You can't bring that dog in here!'

Charming. Even I, who am no lover of dogs, felt annoyed on behalf of poor Rex. The landlord was right, of course; since the pub served food the law did not permit a dog inside the lounge. But one couldn't quite suppress the feeling that he might have laboured, for a microsecond or two, to find a slightly more agreeable way of reminding us of this.

Fortunately there was a terrace outside where it would be legal for Rex to spread his diseases, and where in any case, on that grey evening, there were no other drinkers. We chose a table with wooden benches and I took the boys' orders.

'Two pints of lager and a pint of best,' I said to the landlord.

As he began to pull the bitter he asked me: 'Who's the best for?'

I suppressed an instinct to be sarcastic. It was at least the fourth time I had asked for the same beer in that pub.

'Me.'

'Then I'm not sure about the lagers.'

'Why? What's wrong with it?'

He jerked his head to indicate a sign behind the bar: 'I don't serve anyone under twenty-one.'

Oh God, I hadn't thought of that. I hadn't the faintest idea how old Terry and Andy were.

'Hang on a second,' I said, and went back outside.

When I explained the problem Andy sighed. He stood up: 'I get this all the time,' he said. 'Sometimes it's a real drag looking younger than you are. I'll come with you.'

We returned to the bar. From a pocket of his jacket Andy produced a driving licence: 'Here,' he said.

The landlord examined the licence as enthusiastically as he might have read an announcement that his pub was about to be blown up to make way for a six-lane bypass.

'OK,' he conceded after a few moments, and handed the licence back. 'But what about your friend?'

'He's the same age as me.'

The landlord grunted.

Andy pushed the licence into a back pocket of his jeans and went outside again.

As he drew the first pint of lager the landlord ventured yet further on to the sunny uplands of sociability: 'And normally I don't serve motor-cyclists, either.'

Oh, this was too much.

'He's not a motor-cyclist,' I said. The landlord raised his eyes in surprise. I went on sweetly: 'He's just a raving leather fetishist.'

I don't quite know how to describe the look he gave me then. It was a wonder the lager didn't freeze solid as it came out of the tap. If that look could have penetrated bricks and mortar, it would have soured every barrel of beer within a ten mile radius.

The only other words he spoke to me were to tell me how much the order totalled.

I have never mastered the art of carrying three full pint

glasses, so I had to return to the bar for my best. As I approached our ruddy-cheeked host again I realised I was on the verge of doubling up in a fit of giggles. It was extraordinary; I couldn't remember giggling since I was a schoolboy.

Indeed, I felt as if, without having touched a drop of the beer, I was already light-headed. Maybe it was because I hadn't eaten anything since lunch except a bar of chocolate; maybe it was because I was beginning to enjoy the prospect of drinking with two handsome young men; or maybe it was simply an effect of the relaxation produced by being on holiday. After all, just as I would never have invited Terry and Andy to join me if we'd met in Edinburgh, similarly I would never have come out at home with such a sarky riposte to a barman. Sussex seemed to be remoulding my character.

I sat down across the table from the boys. Conversation with young people is rarely difficult; all you have to do is encourage them to talk about themselves. I don't mean this to sound patronising. I enjoy the company of young people for precisely that reason; I love their candour, the lack of contorted lines of self-defence with which almost everyone over twenty-five has learned to surround themselves.

Not that, nowadays, I have much opportunity to speak with young people. Occasionally I make the acquaintance of students who come into the shop and who linger over their purchases; they tend to come in on weekdays when we're otherwise quiet, so there's an opportunity to spend more time with them than would be possible on a Saturday. And if the student who's seeking my advice on a text on Freud, or American history, or the fauna of southern Australia, happens to be male, in jeans, and with a pleasant smile – he's likely to go out feeling that we're a shop where he can be sure of finding friendly and efficient service.

But as I sat with Terry and Andy I realised I couldn't remember the last time I had actually socialised with people who were at least twenty years younger than me. I got Andy on to the subject of biking; and, as I had guessed, it was a lever which released a spate of happy observations from him.

'You know,' I said, when I could get a word in, 'all this is making me terribly nostalgic.'

He was obviously astonished.

'Nostalgic?'

I smiled.

'Yes. I used to ride a motor-bike myself.'

'You?' Immediately he looked shamefaced about the exclamation, but I was only amused. The flipside, of course, of young people's candour about themselves, is their tendency to be equally candid about the person they're talking *to*.

'Why do you say "you" like that?' I asked, smiling.

'Well . . . ' He glanced down at the table. 'You don't seem the type, that's all.'

I felt my smile broadening.

'In what way?'

I could see him trying to back out of an explanation: 'I can't imagine it, that's all.'

I laughed out loud. I knew perfectly well what he couldn't imagine: a younger and more slim-line version of me on a motor-bike.

'When I was a student here in Sussex,' I said, 'back in the Sixties, I had this beaten-up old Triumph I used to splutter around on. It only really got up speed when the wind was behind it. And even then, only if you held up a sheet.' Both of the boys laughed. 'And later – I went abroad after I was a student, but after I came back, I had another bike for six or seven years, mainly for getting to and from work.'

'And what was that?'

'A Honda 400-4.'

'Oh, great! Yeah, they're brilliant bikes, aren't they?'

So we talked about the 400-4 for a while. I waxed so enthusiastic about how it handled, and its power in relation to its modest size, that Andy asked: 'Why did you sell it, then?'

I shrugged.

'I changed jobs, and I could walk to work. Besides, I was buying into a business, and I needed every penny I could get.'

'What do you do?' Terry asked. It was almost the first time he had spoken since I sat down.

'I run a second hand bookshop.'

I saw immediate dismay in the eyes of both boys. I wasn't sure whether it was the word 'shop' which produced this, or the word 'book'.

'In Glasgow?' Andy asked.

'No, in Edinburgh.' Why do all English people nowadays automatically assume that anyone with a Scottish accent comes from Glasgow? Personally, I blame *Taggart*. But as I changed the subject back to Andy – 'you're very lucky to be *paid* to ride a motor-bike, aren't you?' – I pondered something which had just occurred to me: that one of the reasons this conversation was possible in Sussex, as it wouldn't have been in Edinburgh, was because my accent didn't shriek my class at Andy and Terry. Obviously, they could tell I was 'middle-class', but beyond that, neither of them could even identify the city I came from. At home, every time I opened my mouth to working class boys they would have recognised the background of a prosperous upbringing and a fee-paying Edinburgh school. This is one of the great advantages that a Scot, like an American, has in England: in that highly stratified society his accent is almost classless. I remembered that when I lived in Brighton I had noticeably more success at scoring with local girls, in the days when I wanted that, than my English fellow-students.

Andy was talking about his job: he didn't work for a firm of couriers, as I had thought, but for a large firm of solicitors. 'We've got branches all over Sussex, and even a little office in London. So there's loads of other solicitors we deal with, and loads of clients in different places, and that's what my job mostly is – going around them all.'

'And you're out and about every day?'

He nodded: 'Most days. I'm also a kind of general office-boy – doing photocopying and all that, when I'm not needed as a courier. So sometimes it can be a bit dull, when I get stuck indoors.'

'Still, you enjoy the job?'

'Yeah.' But as he said it he glanced sideways to Terry with a wry look which seemed to contradict his answer. His eyes turned to me again. 'While it lasts.'

I saw that for a moment the three words cast a shadow over both the boys. There was no need, of course, to ask why: who nowadays, in any kind of employment, isn't familiar with the thought, 'while it lasts'? I turned to Terry: 'And you work for the same firm?'

'Oh, no. I work for British Telecom.'

'Really?'

'Yes. I'm a trainee engineer – I go round people's houses putting in phone lines, or mending faults – that sort of thing.'

Andy had quickly recovered from his passing melancholy; he was smiling again: 'That means he keeps getting chatted up by all these bored housewives. Don't you?'

Terry jogged him with his elbow: 'Oh, shut up, you.' Andy turned back to me with eyes full of wicked humour: 'He does, honestly. All these housewives wandering around in their negligees, saying, "Oh, Mr Ackroyd, that's a very impressive tool you've got there".'

'Oh, Jesus!' Terry exclaimed. 'Christ, Andy, you can be crude sometimes.' He was genuinely embarrassed; he blushed as he appealed to me: 'Don't pay any attention to him.'

I was laughing; it was years since I'd been party to this kind of youthfulness, ancient as the puns might be. But I was also thinking of something else: in that moment when Andy's face had been full of mischief I had once again had the sensation that I'd met him before – or perhaps, that he reminded me of someone else; there was something about his expression . . . Before I could trace the thought further Terry was talking again: 'Mr Carson – the guy whose house we're looking after – is my boss. He asked me if I would like to house-sit for him while he was away. I thought – fucking brilliant! Three weeks away from the folks, big house all to ourselves' – he turned to Andy and smiled: 'We're just like a married couple, aren't we?'

Andy nodded slowly, and stared straight at me.

'Too right. We've smashed every plate in the place throwing them at each other.'

I started to laugh: 'You're very cynical, for one so young!'

'Me? Nah!'

'Does Mr Carson know about . . . ?' – I looked from one of them to the other.

'Oh God, no,' Terry exclaimed. 'Well, he knows Andy's there – he told me I could have a friend to stay if I wanted, for company – but he's no idea . . . ' As he petered out his expression suggested he was positively startled by the meaning of his own uncompleted sentence.

'You keep it quiet at work, then? Both of you?'

Terry's eyes widened: 'Christ, yes. Nobody at BT has any idea about me – the engineers would make my life hell if they knew.'

'In Brighton? I thought it was supposed to be a very liberal town?'

The boys shook their heads in almost comic unison. 'No way,' Andy said. 'It's worse in Brighton than most places. All the straight guys want everybody to know that they are definitely, definitely, not queer. I think they wish they could have a little badge to wear – a bit like the pink triangle, only different. A black square, maybe.'

'I'm sorry to hear that. I'd like to think that there's *somewhere* where it's easy to be gay.'

Andy shook his head again.

'There's nowhere where it's easy to be queer, John.'

I was taken aback not just by his words, but by the seriousness with which he spoke them. For a moment I considered asking what on earth made him say something so gloomy. But I didn't want the conversation to become solemn; I changed the subject: 'You don't live together usually, then? In Brighton, I mean?'

The question lightened the boys' mood again. They looked at each other and started to laugh: 'Nah,' Andy said. 'We'd have murdered each other by now if we did. I share a place with two guys – straights, do you believe that?'. He laughed again. 'But they're OK. I think they think it's cool to have a gay guy around. I'm not going to go after their girlfriends, you see, even though both their girlfriends fancy me like mad.' He grinned widely as Terry protested: 'So modest, eh? So fucking modest!'

'It's true, I tell you. A couple of weeks ago I'd just come out of the bath – towel round my middle, nothing else – and Jane, that's one of the girlfriends, started getting real fruity. Talking about how much she fancied guys in kilts – I suppose *you* like kilts, do you?'

The frankness of the question slightly embarrassed me: 'Yes, I suppose I do.' Then I was amused by my own embarrassment: 'There's no doubt a kilt looks good on the right man.'

'Yeah. I bet *I'd* suit a kilt.'

'What's that got to do with towels?' Terry asked – I, too, had lost the thread of Andy's meaning. He grinned: 'What Jane was saying about them. How they're a turn-on because you know everything's just – *there*.' He cupped his right hand in the air. 'Dead available. Know what I mean?'

I felt myself smiling: 'I do indeed.'

'And she comes out with all this while I'm standing right next to her in my towel. Cheeky bitch! It was obvious what *she* was wishing was available.'

'Well,' Terry put in, 'if she doesn't know what you've got that's available, she's the only person in Brighton who doesn't.'

'Listen, you!' – and suddenly they fell on each other exchanging mock blows and laughing loudly; I sat opposite them feeling for the moment like an uncle with two rather boisterous nephews.

They separated, and Terry appealed to me: 'He hasn't got one pair of jeans you can call decent – and what about the way he wears his leather?'

I caught Andy's eye. There was a flash of mockery in his grin; I looked down at the table, fearing I was blushing. When I looked up again Andy was still grinning at me: 'Listen to this one! When I first met him, he was in the nuddy too.' He paused as if to make sure both Terry and I had taken in the significance of the 'too'. 'You make quite a habit of it, don't you?' he went on, only turning to Terry at the end of the sentence.

'Oh, be quiet,' Terry said.

'Well, you were.'

'I was in a dressing room, for fuck's sake!' He looked from Andy to me: 'It's normal to be nuddy in a dressing room. I'd just come out of the showers.' He turned back to Andy. 'And what about you and the nudist beach?'

'That's different. That's naturism.'

'My arse!'

I saw Andy open his mouth for what I was sure would be another teasing remark; but, rather to my relief, he changed his mind. I thought it was time he was teased himself: 'If you were in the dressing room as well, I take it' – I hesitated – 'I take it Terry didn't need to ask what would be under *your* kilt?'

Both boys burst out laughing. 'Nah!' Andy said. 'I was just like this – in my leather.'

'In a dressing room?'

'He'd dropped by at the end of the game,' Terry explained. 'A football game, I mean. He came in with a mate.'

'Ah! You're footballers, are you?'

'Christ, no!' Andy exclaimed. 'At least, I'm not. I've got more sense.' He indicated Terry with a jerk of his head: '*He* is. Don't ask me why.'

I shook my head, laughing: 'What's wrong with football?'

'Yes!' Terry said; he seemed genuinely pleased to have my support. 'What *is* wrong with it?'

Andy turned to him.

'Why don't you ask your team-mates?'

Terry's expression changed instantly.

'That was unnecessary, Andy,' he said quietly.

There was an awkward pause. Andy glanced at me; I saw that – for once – he was slightly shamefaced about his teasing of his boyfriend. I asked, as tactfully as I could: 'Is there a problem with them?' – wondering if I already knew the answer.

I did. Terry shrugged: 'It's the usual, John. The same old thing. I don't have a girlfriend, and I'm twenty years old. I don't say anything about it, of course, and Andy keeps away from games, but . . . '. He shook his head. 'The guys aren't stupid, they can put two and two together. So there's beginning to be a bit of an atmosphere – just sometimes, but you can feel it.' He paused, and went on more thoughtfully: 'I can't say I really blame them. After all, they've got to shower with me every week.'

'And what's wrong with that?' Andy exclaimed hotly. 'What do they think you're going to do – rape them?'

'No, Andy,' Terry said coldly. 'They *know* I might be eyeing them up.'

'So? Where's the big deal in that?'

'It gets in the way, Andy.' He looked towards me, as if appealing for more support: 'They just want to be lads together, without having to worry . . . Do you understand?' This time his appeal to me was direct. I understood perfectly.

'Yes,' I said.

'So I'm thinking I might have to quit. I'm going to start the new season again, but after that . . . I don't know.'

Andy wouldn't give in: 'Do you seriously think straight guys don't size each other up in the showers?'

I felt a joke was needed to divert us off this subject: 'There's some truth in that. Look at rugby players – the only reason they play the game is to give them an excuse to grope each other.' It worked; both boys laughed, and I grew more confident: 'That's what's meant by "rugby tackle".' It was humour of their own age-group; they laughed more loudly and I went on: 'And look at a rugby scrum. If you're into feeling men's bums, that's the place to be.' As they laughed yet again I glanced at my nearly-finished pint; was the bitter beginning to stimulate remarks like this from me?

Since I had succeeded in cheering Terry up I decided to encourage him positively: 'Do you want to go on playing football?'

'Yes, sure. I really enjoy it – always have. I've been

playing seriously since I was eleven or twelve.'

'Well, isn't there a gay team somewhere? I was reading about it not long ago – couldn't you join them?'

He seemed astonished by the suggestion.

'Stonewall? But they're in London, John. I couldn't go up and down to London two or three times a week – for training and everything, as well as fixtures.'

I realised I'd been stupid: 'Ah, right. Of course.'

'And even if I could, how would I explain to my folks why I'd left a team in Brighton to join one in London?'

I nodded: 'Yes, of course.' I thought about what he'd just said. 'You live with your parents, then?'

'Yes.'

'And they don't know . . . ?'

He shook his head: 'No, no, no. My old man would do his nut if he knew.'

The triple 'no' almost shocked me. A whole form of gay life lay behind it – a style of living I'd put behind me years ago, and which I had almost forgotten about.

I turned to Andy: 'And what about you? Do your parents know about you?'

Almost to my relief, he nodded.

'My Mum knows, yes. I think my Mum's *always* known, I think she sussed it about me before I did. But my stepfather hated it – that's why I left home, I was just seventeen when I moved out.' He paused. 'My stepfather's gone now, thank the fuck.'

He spoke the last three words with extraordinary bitterness. The whole sentence, with that odd word 'stepfather', seemed like an echo from some grim fairy story; I regretted I'd brought up the subject, blundering into a private area of such sensitivity.

Andy obviously sensed that he had altered the tone of the conversation. 'But my Mum's OK about it. Isn't she, Tel?'. Terry nodded. 'We go round there a lot – not to *do* anything,' he added hastily, as if that idea was indecent. 'Just for tea, and things. My Mum worries about Terry, she thinks he doesn't eat properly. She's always trying to feed him up.' Terry grinned: 'Yeah. Andy's Mum's great.'

I smiled; I was pleased there was at least one older person in Terry's life who treated him properly. 'Good,' I said.

I finished the last of my pint; while we had been talking the boys had reached the end of theirs ahead of me. I wondered what to do now. I would have liked to have lingered with these two, who had proved as entertaining – and educational – as they were good-looking, but my instinct warned me that to prolong the encounter would be to risk its running into bathos, as conversation began to peter out. Besides, I hadn't eaten for some hours, and so I was being perfectly truthful when I looked at my watch and said: 'Well, I don't know about you, but I'm getting really hungry.'

Andy laughed. 'Yeah, same here.' He looked at Terry: 'OK?'. Terry nodded and bent down over Rex, who throughout all our conversation had been lying peacefully on the stone flags of the terrace: 'Come on, boy,' he said. 'Andy's going to burn some dinner for us.'

'Cheeky bastard!'

In order to leave the pub we had to pass through the lounge. I couldn't resist turning to the landlord and raising my hand to him: 'Thanks. See you.' To my huge delight it provoked another beer-freezing scowl.

As we were walking the short distance home Andy asked: 'How much of your holiday have you got left?'

'Just this week – I'm here till Saturday.'

'Yeah, we move out on Saturday too. You going back to Scotland?'

I smiled.

'Yes.'

'I want to go to Scotland some time.'

I turned to him in surprise, less at the words than at his tone: he had spoken with unusual earnestness. He seemed unaware of my reaction: 'I'd like to have a tour around – see places.'

'Well, it's not all *that* far away,' I remarked – rather lamely, I thought even as I came out with it.

'I'd maybe take the bike and go up into the Highlands,

and all that.'

'You'd be better off in a car.' Before he could protest I explained quickly: 'Don't forget what the Scottish climate's like. There's a lot of – mist.' I smiled. '"Mist" is a word the Scottish Tourist Board are very fond of. It means "rain".'

Andy laughed: 'I hear Edinburgh's a nice place?'

I laughed in turn: 'Yes, it is.'

At their front gate – the gate where I had first encountered Andy – we separated.

'Thanks for inviting us for a drink,' Andy said; and then added as if he had just realised something: 'Hey – I really enjoyed that. I really did.'

It was all I could do not to guffaw. I don't know how I managed to keep a straight face; it was perfectly obvious there was a clause missing from his sentence: 'I really enjoyed that, though I never expected to'.

'Well, I'll maybe see you around again,' I said. 'Before the end of the week.'

'Yeah, maybe.'

I took my leave of Terry too, and Rex – who barked – and carried on to my own front gate.

Within five minutes I was out again, and set off for Chichester. When I arrived I realised I was far too hungry to mess around with a restaurant; I went into a fast-food outlet and scoffed – I can't put it any other way – a burger and French fries. I burped my way back to Westhurst.

I ended the evening with an unusually large glass of malt and some rubbishy tv. I was well pleased with the day, with the hour in the pub, and with myself, and in that frame of mind I went to bed and slept the last good night's sleep I would have for many nights.

The following evening, after a long hot day of exploring the west of the county, close to Hampshire, I got back to Westhurst in such dire need of a pint I decided even the prospect of facing the village's answer to Basil Fawlty wouldn't deter me from revisiting his pub.

This time I didn't run into any handsome boys in the street, and so walked into the pub alone. The landlord, as ever, was behind the bar. He looked at me with predictable enthusiasm, but then came out with words I had certainly not expected to hear.

'The usual?'

Well, well, well, I thought. The man's finally acquired a memory.

As he placed the pint in front of me he growled: 'Your friend dropped something last night.'

'Sorry?'

He turned to the counter behind him and handed me a folded piece of paper: a driving licence.

'I found it outside just after you'd gone,' he said. 'Below the bench.'

I glanced at it, and saw the first name 'Andrew': 'Oh, right. Yes, it must have fallen out of his pocket.' I smiled with the first genuine warmth I had felt for the man: 'Thanks. I'll drop it off to him on my way home.' I stuck it into my own pocket, delighted that chance had given me an excuse to call on my neighbours again.

But the house was empty: there was no answer to my knocking, and no music from the garden – which in any case I would have been very hesitant about entering.

In my front hall I took out the licence and put it on the table, to remind me to try next door again after dinner. It was only then that I read the full name on the licence.

And stood astounded, disbelieving – and, suddenly, filled with fear.

I picked up the licence by my finger-tips, as if it might burn me: I re-read it as if I were shortsighted and could have been mistaken about what I'd seen: but nothing, of course, changed. The name read in full: ANDREW LAIRENBROOK BOWMAN.

It was that extraordinary, even ungainly, middle name which held my eyes. For I had come across it before, only once, twenty years previously. It was so rare it was impossible to forget; for six months in my final year as a student I went out with a girl called May Lairenbrook – a local Brighton girl.

Who had a marvellously attractive smile, a way of

smiling which filled her face with mischievousness – I stared at the wallpaper in front of me and saw Andy's face there, saw that look which had caught my attention the night before: which had made me think he reminded me of someone else.

I stared down again at the licence. May's son? Was it possible? I tried to remember if she had any brothers or sisters; I couldn't recall that she did, but equally, I couldn't recall that she didn't. The son of a cousin, perhaps? Family resemblances, I knew, could appear collaterally as well as in direct descendants.

I went into the kitchen and sat at the table, still with the licence in my hand. Was I staying right next door to May Lairenbrook's son?

I don't like coincidences like that. They imply a world-view which disturbs, even threatens: are we players in a game who only occasionally catch glimpses of how we're being moved on the chequerboard? I reviewed similar improbabilities in my life. When I was a student I once walked into the Coleherne in London to see a man who had been in the same class as me at school; neither of us had had the slightest idea the other was gay. Three years later we met by chance again – at the foot of the Great Pyramid. On a boat crossing to Crete a fellow-Scot engaged me in conversation; suddenly he asked, was my name Paterson? It turned out he knew my father, through the New Club in Edinburgh; he had thought he spotted a resemblance – as I was doing now, with Andy. Most perplexing of all: when I first came back to Edinburgh I shared a flat for a few months with some other postgraduates, all of whom were strangers to me when I moved in. One evening I was talking about my time in Greece when one of my flatmates asked if, in the town where I had taught, I knew someone called X. I did. My flatmate had not only been at school with X. in Bath, he had lived in the same street for several years. What was worse, I had got to know X. because he, in turn, had by chance run into an old Oxford friend out there, whose wife was a colleague of a man I was having an affair with – a link so convoluted, so implausible, that just to ponder it was to confront odds beyond calculation.

And now, apparently, something similar was happening. I poured myself a large whisky and sat down again. May had been a bright, attractive young woman; I wasn't surprised she had soon found someone after me – very soon, to judge from Andy's age.

And then, only then, I realised what you, perhaps, being calmer than I was in that hour, have already realised. I remembered two words of Andy's which had sounded odd when he spoke them: 'my stepfather'.

My hands shook as I picked up the licence again. I fumbled with the paper, doing what the landlord had done in the pub: I opened it and read Andy's date of birth.

For long seconds I felt as if all my life of the last twenty-three years was crumbling away into dust.

But then I calculated again, counting back nine months: and sighed out loud with relief.

But it was short-lived relief. For almost immediately another thought came forward: that babies are no respecters of calendars; they can come late, and they can come early.

I don't know how long I sat in turmoil, drinking and refilling my glass, before another terrifying thought occurred to me. Why had Andy spoken so earnestly about wanting to go to Scotland 'to see places'? Did he know – had he been told – that he had a connection with my country?

There was to be no release that evening from turmoil. I went for a long walk, away from the village – the last thing I could bear would be to meet Andy by accident – till it was almost dark when I got back. I ate nothing; I drank and drank. In bed there was no possibility of sleep. I got up and sat in my underpants in the warm Sussex night, watching meaningless tv pictures with the sound turned down, still drinking. When I lay down again it was as if my bed was on a lurching ship. I dozed off; when I woke I had to run to the bathroom in the dark and get my head over the toilet bowl; I vomited and vomited till I was retching up nothing, feeling that I had woken not from a nightmare, but into one.

CHAPTER FIVE

The next day I drove aimlessly around a Sussex still lush and brilliant in the August sunshine. But now the richness of the southern landscape, of the fields standing ready for harvest below the green of the downs, brought anything but heart's ease. I was in the country where Elgar wrote the *Cello Concerto,* and its impact on me was like the impact of that music: its beauty was heavy with melancholy; it stirred a longing for tranquillity which it left unfulfilled.

I got back to Westhurst in the late afternoon and waited for the sound of Andy's Kawasaki. It was twenty past six before the roaring of his faulty silencer came abruptly round the corner from the pub, rose in a crescendo, and stopped. Within thirty seconds I was knocking on his front door.

He was in his biking gear, of course, when he opened the door; the scarf he wore below his helmet hung loose around his shoulders, and his jacket was still buttoned to the neck.

I wished – it was too late – I'd been less impatient, and given him time to change into clothing which was less powerfully sexual: but then realised delay might have created an even worse tension for me; what if he'd come to the door only in shorts, ready to sunbathe?

I explained the purpose of my call. It took just a couple of sentences.

'Hey, thanks!' he said as I handed him the licence. 'I hadn't even noticed I'd lost it!'

'Well, there you are . . . '

'Thanks again,' he repeated.

He looked at me, obviously expecting me to turn and go.

'Andy . . . '

'Yeah?'

'Andy – I couldn't help noticing your name on the licence.'

He was puzzled.

'Yeah?'

'Your middle name – it's very unusual.'

'Lairenbrook, you mean?'. I nodded. He leaned against the doorjamb: 'It's not really my middle name, it's really my real second name.' He started to laugh: 'Christ, that didn't make much sense, did it? I mean, that was my name when I was born. "Bowman"' – he pulled a face – 'that's what I was called after my Mum got married. I keep thinking about dropping it, but it would be a real hassle now.' Suddenly he frowned: 'Why do you ask?'

I stared at the fence between our front gardens.

'I used to know a girl called Lairenbrook. Years ago, when I lived in Brighton.'

'No kidding? What was her first name?'

My eyes went back to him.

'May.'

He stood sharply upright, as if the doorjamb had stung him: '*May* Lairenbrook? That's my Mum! You sure about that?'

'I'm sure about her name. She was about the same age as me – worked as a typist for – a firm of engineers, I think. With three names, I can't remember . . . '

'Preece Cardew and Rider?'

'Yes, that was it.'

He laughed: 'Yeah, that's my Mum, alright! Well, *Jesus*! How did you come to know her?'

I had to look at him straight: I couldn't be evasive or shifty now.

'I went out with her for a while.'

'You . . . ?' Unsurprisingly he was incredulous: 'You went out with my Mum?'

I nodded.

Suddenly his whole expression changed. His happy astonishment vanished: he was alarmed – even suspicious: 'You . . . ?' he said again, and then, almost harshly: 'How long for?'

Whatever he knew about his father, there was no point in my lying to him: 'About six months.'

The words produced the opposite reaction to the one I'd expected. To my surprise he visibly relaxed, as if I'd removed the possibility which had made him frown: 'Oh, right.' For a moment, misled by his tone, I thought he'd said, 'Alright'.

He went on: 'You went out with my Mum for all that time? Really?'

In other circumstances his reaction might have been amusing.

'Yes.'

'But how come . . . ?'

'Sorry?'

'I mean, I thought you were . . . Aren't you?'

'Yes, I am now. I was different then.'

'Really?'

He seemed as if he was genuinely keen to talk about sexuality; I wasn't: 'I'd like . . . I'd like to get in touch with your mother again, if that's possible. Though I very much doubt if she'll remember me after all these years.'

'Yeah – why not? Do you want her phone number?'

'If you don't mind . . . '

'Nah, of course.' He reeled it off. 'I'm sorry,' I said, 'could you write it down? I'm terrible at remembering phone numbers.'

'Sure.'

He disappeared inside and came back a few seconds later with a scrap of paper.

'There you go. Do you want me to ring her first, or anything?' He laughed: 'Warn her you might be calling?'

'No, I'd rather you didn't do that.' I moved off: 'Thanks very much – Andy.'

'No sweat. Listen – I want to know how you get on! And you can tell me all about what my Mum was like when you knew her. What *was* she like?'

I stopped and half-turned back.

'She was very attractive, Andy. A very attractive girl indeed.'

He threw back his head and guffawed: 'Jesus! My old lady!'

As I walked up the path to my own front door I found that I was literally praying: please, if Andy is who I think he is, let me stop thinking about him sexually; take me beyond fancying him; stop me, please, stop me seeing him like that.

I rang May straight away.

The sun lit up May's front room, which faced south; but the light was diffused by full-length net curtains, of perfect whiteness, which screened the bow window. It was two days after I'd spoken with Andy. Flexitime had enabled May to take this afternoon off, to meet me on what should have been the last day of my holiday.

The whole room, in the neat two-storey terraced house, showed how May had become a prosperous and successful woman: she was now Central Services Supervisor, in charge of an army of clerical staff, in one of the town's largest offices. Lightness and sparkle, and – without being sexist – femininity, were the room's keynotes. Crystal glittered on shelves; other shelves were filled with porcelain; framed prints of old Brighton hung on the walls, and above the fireplace an oil painting of the seascape at Seven Sisters. The most obvious gap in the room's decoration was that there were no personal photographs of any kind. But since I had steeled myself to be faced with pictures of Andy as a boy, or with his stepfather, I found I was relieved by this.

The sofa on which I sat was deep and enveloping, facing a similar armchair. But while I had let myself relax backwards, May was sitting upright near the edge of her chair, the straightness of her back suggesting the careful posture she must have had to learn when she spent her working days at a typewriter.

She was not only every bit as attractive as I had told Andy she had been a quarter of a century before, but possibly even more so. Her blonde hair was streaked with grey, but that only enhanced her air of being in the fullness of maturity; she was clearly a woman who had blossomed, not faded, as she passed into middle age. Her figure was, of course, fuller than that of the girl I took back to my bedsit near the railway station; but I have never had any taste for excessively thin women, and as I sat contemplating her in the silence which fell over us as we drank our tea, I realised she was waking in me – no doubt because of the memory of those far-off evenings – my long dormant heterosexuality. The two girlish touches which she retained were her delicate hands – the nails carefully manicured – and eyes of a startlingly light blue. I could imagine them still shining with mischievousness, like those of her son. But just now they were solemn, even anxious. We had exhausted the small talk about our respective histories with which we had been politely avoiding the subject which we both knew had, now, to be broached.

I cleared my throat.

'May – I need to speak to you about Andy.'

Her only reaction was to move her hands so that they lay crossed in her lap. She was staring ahead, to the window.

I sat forward, pulling myself out of the depths of the sofa, and leaned one elbow on my knee.

'May, I know that after all these years it's really none of my business, but I need to ask you' – I stopped. Over the past two days I'd rehearsed the question again and again in my head, but now I had to speak it out loud – the most portentous question I had ever asked in my life.

'Who was Andy's father?'

She turned her head to me. She didn't answer, but simply looked at me in surprise.

I couldn't square up to that look; I spoke down towards the carpet: 'May, I saw Andy's date of birth on his driving licence. He was born on the 27th of September, 1971. That means' – how grotesque that so much should depend on a piece of mental arithmetic! – 'that means he must have been conceived about the 27th of December – at any rate, sometime around the previous Christmas and New Year.' My courage revived; I was able to look at her again as I concluded the argument which was my last chance to stave off the life-changing implication to me of the fact of Andy's existence: 'I was back in Scotland then. I always went home for Christmas and New Year – for two or three weeks, at least . . . '

But May had begun to shake her head. She rubbed the fingers of one hand over the knuckles of the other. She looked down at them; when she spoke she did so with no hint of emotion.

'Andy was five weeks premature.'

'What?'

Her hands continued their nervous movement, but now she looked at me.

'He was five weeks premature,' she said again, with the same flatness of tone. 'He wasn't due till the 2nd of November.'

Her gaze returned to the window, and her hands fell still.

The mental arithmetic closed in on me. May and I had broken up at the end of February.

One final impulse of rebellion made me exclaim: 'Well then, who . . . ?'

Her eyes came back to me; she was briefly frowning, and for the first time her voice showed some feeling: 'There was no-one else, John. I didn't sleep around. I wasn't that type of girl - never. I never was.'

I stared at the carpet as the last line of my self-defence disintegrated.

'It can't be true,' I said. 'It cannot be true.'

I heard her voice again. It was restored to its previous flatness.

'I'm afraid it is, John. Andy is your son.'

I don't know how long it was before I raised my head and next spoke.

'And you tell me this now? You tell me this after twenty-three years?'

She looked at me with alarm. I saw it, but rather than checking the sudden swelling-up of my anger, it provoked me further: 'After twenty-three years, you tell me I have a son? Why didn't you tell me at the time? Why didn't you get in touch with me – it would have been easy enough?'

I had had no idea in advance that I would react like this. When I'd imagined this dialogue, foreseeing that May would confirm my fears, I'd heard myself speaking with dignity and calm; instead I was sounding like a petulant teenager rowing with his girlfriend. May's forbearance - it was she, not I, who was handling the situation with dignity – only made me angrier: 'After all, I didn't leave Brighton for good till early July. By then you must have known for weeks that you were pregnant!'

May looked away, and sighed.

'I had endless rows with my mother. Terrible rows – you can't even begin to imagine.' She turned to me again: 'Of course I'd known for a long time that something was wrong – I'd missed one month, then I missed another. But you always hope – it could be anything, it might be something quite – quite ordinary.' She began to speak with more firmness: 'By the time I knew for a fact, it was May. So I insisted to my mother, I couldn't possibly tell you then – not when you were right in the middle of your exams.'

She stopped, perhaps knowing the effect these words would have on me.

'When I . . . ?'

'When you were in the middle of your Finals. How could I spring it on you then? There you were, swotting away – I knew you were a clever boy, I knew you'd do well if you got the chance - I couldn't give you a shock like that, could I? Tell you just then that – that something had gone wrong with one of your johnnies?'

I sat back: 'That was really why you didn't get in touch?'

She looked away. Her next word was spoken with savage coldness.

'No.'

But at once she seemed to relent: 'Well, partly. But partly, it was because I had to fight to keep the baby at all. I had to fight to keep *my* baby.'

Her change of mood had bewildered me: 'I'm not with you . . . '

'My mother wanted me to have an abortion. She kept on and on at me – that was the main thing we were rowing about, day in, day out.'

'An abortion?'

'Yes.' Once again her head turned - throughout all this conversation she was sitting as still and straight as she had been at the beginning: 'But in those days, abortion wasn't like what it is now. Nowadays they're up at the clinic without turning a hair. But then, it was only a year or two since it had become legal. *You* would remember that?'. I nodded. 'So I was able to hold out. I was determined I was going to have the baby.' There was no mistaking the satisfaction with which she finished. 'And I won.'

I looked across to the window, brilliant with the summer sunshine behind the curtains. I thought of the young man I'd drunk with four days before, so full of energy, so proud of his skills as a biker, so ready to joke as he teased the boyfriend he was clearly very fond of.

'Thank God you did,' I said softly. It was no figure of speech; I meant the words literally.

My tone seemed to surprise May, or perhaps even touched her; she looked at me with a quickly passing expression in which I thought I saw for the first time something of the affection with which she had once looked at me, when we were younger.

When she next spoke her voice was gentler: 'So you see – I felt very possessive about the baby. He was *mine*. Once you were out of your exams, and I didn't have that excuse any more, I told my mother I *had* tried to get in touch with you through the University, but that you'd gone away and they didn't have a forwarding address for you.' She paused. 'I'm not sure if she believed me. But by then she'd pretty well given up, she knew I was going to have my own way, and that was that.'

For some moments I watched her. I was no longer angry with her; I, too, was beginning to recall that there had been more to our relationship than just sex.

'And was it true?' I asked quietly.

She looked down at the floor and shook her head.

'No, I'm afraid not.'

She raised her head again: 'When Andy was born, there was a terrible time – you can imagine my fright, how frightened all of us were – he was in an incubator for three weeks. And he was so *tiny*! It's hard to picture it now, isn't it?' - for the first time all afternoon she laughed. 'He was so – so vulnerable. When I held him, when I got to hold him – I was more possessive than ever. He was my tiny, little Andy. And when he looked up at me . . . '. She tailed off. 'I remember the first time he ever smiled at me, when he came off the breast once – he'd been home for a few weeks by then, of course, and he was growing fast – it was . . . '. Again she tailed off, and gazed down at the floor. 'It was the happiest moment of my life.'

She spoke the words with such simplicity that I couldn't speak; I was afraid my voice would tremble.

She looked up; her own voice was firm as she carried on: 'But then I realised . . . I realised, perhaps you had a right to know that you had a son. And this time I really did try to get in touch with you.'

I was astonished: 'You *did*?'

'Yes. I contacted the University, and of course they *could* give me an address for you.' She hesitated. 'But it was abroad.'

The sentence made me nearly groan.

'Morocco.'

'Yes, that was it.'

There was a long silence. I turned over in my mind the implication of May's words. What I'd always taken as one of the great positives of my life, my escape from Britain into teaching overseas, had deprived me of – of how much?

I didn't want to try to answer, yet, that last question. When I spoke it was to protest gently: 'All the same, you could have written. You could at least' – I stopped; I'd been about to change the verb to 'should', but that seemed carping, after all these years.

When she saw I wasn't going to carry on May asked: 'But what good would it have done?'

'What good?'

'Yes. What difference would it have made?'

'What difference?'. I sat forward, feeling myself becoming indignant again: 'Well, for one thing, I could have *helped*. I could have sent you money' – I saw at once that I'd blundered.

'I didn't *need* your money.' Her blue eyes were fixed on me; she repeated the sentence with a different emphasis: 'I didn't need *your* money. Andy never went short of anything, all his days. He never went without anything he needed, *I* made sure of that.'

I was horrified and embarrassed by my mistake: 'I'm sorry, I didn't mean to suggest - I'm not implying for one moment . . . '. I was reddening, and stumbling over my words: 'I can see you did very well for him. He's turned out very fine – you've every reason to be proud of him.'

May's expression changed. The annoyance went from her eyes, and instead I thought I saw - something like regret; her next words surprised me: 'Well, maybe.'

I insisted quietly: 'There's no "maybe" about it.'

She turned her head away. I realised I was beginning to wish she would relax her posture; that maintained stiffness was making this conversation more awkward than I felt it need have been.

'There's something . . . ' she began. Then she seemed to change her mind: 'There was another reason,' she said, still not looking at me, 'which made me think – that made me think there wouldn't have been much point in me getting in touch with you, after all. I mean, as well as the fact that you'd gone abroad.'

I waited.

'Which was?' I had to ask, a little impatiently.

Now she looked at me, and she was smiling.

'You were always very honest with me, John. That was one of the things I – I really liked about you. And looking back at it now, for your time you were very brave as well.'

I had no idea what she was talking about.

'Sorry?'

Her smile grew broader.

'You told me once that you liked boys a bit, as well. As well as girls, I mean.'

'I did?'

'Oh, yes. At first I was really shocked - and a bit put out too, I can tell you. I wasn't quite sure what it made *me*.'

'I really said that?'

She laughed: 'Don't you remember?'

I shook my head: 'I certainly don't. Was I drunk, or something?'

'As it happens, you were. But I didn't worry about it for long. You soon made it obvious it didn't prevent you ... '. She laughed again, but this time quite differently from before: it was the laugh of a young girl – of the girl I'd bedded for the best part of half a year.

I started to laugh too: 'I get your meaning,' I said, nodding and wondering, as I did so, if I was blushing.

'But by the time we broke up – I was pretty sure you'd been lying to me.'

'Lying?'

'Or at least, not completely honest. I'd begun to suspect you were really – more into boys, altogether. I don't know how I knew, I just did.' She smiled. 'And I was right, wasn't I?'

I nodded again.

'Yes, I'm afraid so.'

'So you can see, there was another reason not to tell you that you'd become a daddy. I suppose I just thought – it would be no good news for you. Not something you'd want to know, at all' - but by now I was shaking my head: 'Oh Heavens, no. No, you're completely wrong there. It *would* have been good news.'

I stopped, to consider what I was about to say. Was it true?

Yes, it was: 'And it's good news now.'

A strange smile slowly changed May's expression: as if these words as much bewildered her as pleased her.

She didn't comment on them. Instead she said quietly: 'I suppose that's the most obvious thing Andy's inherited from you, isn't it?'

Her smile changed again; suddenly I saw in the mature woman the mischievousness I remembered in her twenty-three years before.

'What is?'. And then I understood: 'Good God! I'd never thought of that!'

'Hadn't you? I'm right, though, amn't I?'

'Well, I don't know . . . '

'But they say it's genetic – don't they? They say now they've even identified whatever gene it is. Don't you think?'

I shook my head: 'I haven't the faintest idea.' In all the turmoil of my trying to come to terms with the possibility that Andy might be my son, I had never once considered that the fact we were both gay could be more than coincidence. 'Oh, I don't know,' I repeated. 'And does it matter anyway?'

'Perhaps not.'

I thought about how May had made the point. Her mischievousness began to infect me: 'What *else* do you think Andy's inherited from me?'

Her smile showed she identified my tone, but she looked down as she answered.

'Well, his name, for one thing.'

'His name?'

'Yes. In a way I called him after you' – she looked up – 'that's why I called him "Andrew", because he had a Scottish father.'

I don't know what showed in my face at that moment. Whatever it was, May misread it; she was alarmed: 'I did get the right saint, didn't I?'

I smiled, trying to hide how much that one detail moved me.

'Yes', I said. 'You got the right saint.'

For a while neither of us spoke. I was thinking back to Terry, in the Westhurst garden: 'That's Andy's bike. That was Andy you saw.' How little I'd imagined I was hearing a reference to my own country's patron saint.

Eventually I said: 'Andy knows his father was Scottish, doesn't he?'. May nodded. 'How much else does he know?'

'Not a lot. I'm afraid – I lied to him, John. I thought it was for the best.'

'In what way?'

'I told him I hardly knew his father. He believes he's the result of a one-night stand – a ship that passed in the night. I suppose . . . You know, I think he'll be glad to find out it *wasn't* like that. That I' – she stopped abruptly, as if confused.

'That you . . . ?'

After a moment she made a small sweeping gesture with her right hand: 'That he's not some kind of pure accident. I was never really happy with him thinking that, but there seemed no alternative.'

'Why?'

'Well, it would have been worse, wouldn't it, if I'd told him the truth? That I knew his father well, but didn't try to get in touch with him till it was too late?'

'Ah! Right, I see your point.'

'And of course it was also a very useful lie to tell Bowman. He came on the scene just about the time Andy was starting to ask questions about – about why he didn't have a daddy, like all the other kids at school.'

'Bowman . . .?' I prompted, gently. The use of the surname made much instantly clear.

She shrugged.

'My unlamented husband. In some ways I married him to give Andy a father – though I was fond of him for himself, of course.' She considered for a moment. 'No, that's not fair. At the time I thought I was in love with him.'

I didn't want to pry into this unhappiness. But I could hardly forget how Andy had spoken of his stepfather: 'He and Andy – they didn't get on, did they?'

May surprised me by bursting out laughing.

'What an understatement! No, they didn't.'

'Why not?'

She seemed reluctant to explain.

'Another man's son, you know. I don't suppose that can be easy for any man, John. But what made it much worse was that . . . He couldn't have children, you see. He had tests, and . . . '. I nodded quickly, to spare her: 'Ah - right, right.'

'But don't imagine that Andy was blameless, either. Don't imagine that for one moment!'

'In what way?'

'Well, I suppose I'd spoiled him terribly. And my parents, too – they soon got over the idea I shouldn't have had him, of course, once they had a baby grandson to bounce on their knees. So he was pretty uncontrollable. In fact, he still is.'

This last remark seemed as if it ought to have been humorous: but May said it with some grimness.

'And Bowman was a bit of a disciplinarian,' she went on. 'I mean, I know Andy needed it – but Bowman went over the top. Way over the top.'

'How?'

She simply looked at me, and shrugged.

'You mean he *beat* him?' I exclaimed.

'Beat him up, more like.'

'Beat him up?'

'Andy did provoke him, John. He could be totally impossible – self-willed – you just wouldn't believe it.'

'He beat him up?' I repeated.

'Yes. Knocked him about – slapped him - punched him – till Andy got big enough that he didn't dare.'

'And you *let* him?'

'John, don't start getting at me! It was difficult enough as it was.'

'I'm sorry, I'm not getting at you – but honestly . . . '

'Maybe I'm exaggerating a bit,' May went on quickly. 'I mean, Andy was never black and blue, or anything. But he could try the patience of a saint, and Bowman – did tend to burn on a short fuse.'

I said nothing. I couldn't feel that May wasn't to blame herself, but as she had said, to 'get at' her now would be futile.

Suddenly she stood up.

'Look, I don't know about you, but I am *seriously* in need of a drink.' She smiled down at me. 'I reckon we both deserve one, after the past hour.'

My thoughts were still with 'Bowman': 'Yes. Yes, that would be fine.'

'Gin, whisky . . . ? Brandy?' she added, laughing.

'A gin would be fine. Thanks.'

She went out of the room. I sat staring at the crystal and the painting and thinking about why I'd reacted as I'd just done. Bowman beat up Andy? He beat up *my son*?

'My son.' It was the first time the words had meant anything to me: until that moment they'd just been an intellectual fact, an amazing consequence of my student days. But now the words, as it were, 'became flesh': 'my son' had suffered, had known pain, had lived, lived now, because of me. I had given Andy life.

It was the most banal of all biological events. And it was miraculous; it was the most marvellous thing that had ever happened to me, that this young man breathed and loved because I had once desired a pretty girl. And I had wandered the world for twenty-three years knowing nothing of his existence.

The last time I was in Brighton I might have passed him in the street, a gawky thirteen-year-old; or leaned next to him on the railing above the beach; or stood behind him in a queue – and never knowing who he was.

My reverie was interrupted: May came back with two tumblers, so full of gin that despite the seriousness of my thoughts I laughed: 'May! Remember I've got to drive home in a little while!'

She sat down opposite me again, but now, at last, she relaxed. She leaned back in her chair, crossing her legs. She gulped greedily at her drink – she hadn't been overstating the case when she said she needed it – before she spoke.

'Which of us is going to tell him?'

I looked at her over the brim of my own glass.

'May . . . '

She nodded.

'You're right. It has to be me.' She paused. 'This is going to be the oddest conversation I've ever had with him.' She giggled. 'Or anyone!'

'He's coming back to Brighton tomorrow.'

'Yes. I'll see him on Sunday – and Terry, too. God! I'll have to ask Terry to slip away, somehow.' She looked at me. 'What about your own plans?'

'I have to leave Westhurst tomorrow, too. So I'll get a

room in a hotel here in Brighton, and stay on. Once Andy's ready to see me again, you can call and let me know. Let him choose his own time.'

'What about your work?'

I shrugged.

'I'll ring Sandy tonight and tell him I'm staying on for at least another week. We can manage, we've got an assistant who comes in when we need her. She'll be glad of the extra hours.' I contemplated the explanation I would have to give Sandy. Suddenly I burst out laughing: 'Jesus! I hope he *believes* my story!'

Sandy was, of course, astounded; and then full of questions; and then, as I had known he would be, totally understanding: 'Stay as long as you like,' he said. 'Stay for as long as you need to.' I rang round some gay hotels, and soon found a room in one near the seafront. So the following morning, very early – to make sure I didn't accidentally run into Terry and Andy – I left the 'cottage', deposited the keys back with the lady who looked after the place, and drove out of Westhurst. But when I reached the A23 I didn't turn north, to London and home, but south, to Brighton.

CHAPTER SIX

It was Monday evening when May rang me at the hotel. Our conversation wasn't long: she had told Andy the day before, as she'd intended; afterwards he'd been very quiet and thoughtful; in the morning he asked May to call me – I was neither surprised nor offended that he preferred his mother should do this – to suggest meeting at half-six the following evening, on the forecourt of the Palace Pier.

As the time approached I felt as nervous as a teenager facing his first date. From my hotel to the Pier was barely a ten-minute walk, but I couldn't bear to sit in my room, waiting: I went out about half-past-five and wandered round Brighton, up the Steine to St Peter's Church, across the Level, back down, past the Pavilion, up North Street to the Clock Tower, down West Street to the seafront again – and still I was thirty minutes early, and had to retrace my steps through the windy, sunny evening.

I worried about how I was dressed. I was in a jacket and dark flannels: were they too formal? Should I have worn a jersey or a pullover? Or should I have worn a tie? Had I put on too much aftershave? I was becoming so edgy I wished I had a tranquilliser, and then realised I was longing for a drink. I *had* to have a drink – but how could I turn up to meet my son with the smell of alcohol on my breath?

The question summed up my entire quandary. How was I supposed to behave? How on earth could I learn to be a father, at forty-four years old? How in any case is a father supposed to talk to a grown-up son? When I was Andy's age I'd already been abroad for two years, and away from home for five; my relationship with my own father had long since diminished into little more than a formality.

The churning in my stomach grew so bad I couldn't endure it. With fifteen minutes to go I darted into the next pub I came to and ordered a double whisky. For once I was grateful for the detachment of the southern English; the barman pretended not to notice that a middle-aged man had gulped down a large Scotch in barely a minute.

I had eaten very little all day. The whisky went rapidly to my head, but at least it stopped the turning-over of my stomach.

As I made one last round of the Steine, killing the final minutes before half-six, my thoughts went back to my own father. I found myself interrogating him mentally: well, Dad, how would *you* cope with this? How would *you* handle going to meet your illegitimate son – oh and by the way, he's a homosexual?

The very thought made me smile. I could as easily imagine my father in the predicament I was in now as I could imagine him wearing a clown suit in court.

But then again, was it so implausible? He might not have married till he was thirty-five, but I couldn't believe even he had stayed celibate till that age. He'd been in the War, after all, stationed in England for a long time; and he never exploited the glamour of his uniform? Highly unlikely. And in wartime, of course, people were separated much more abruptly and much more finally than May and I were when I left university. Suppose he *had* knocked up an English girl? Before he got sent out to Italy? But that would mean I might have a half-brother somewhere, wandering around England.

The idea of a pattern repeating itself in two generations took hold of my fancy; and as I turned and finally headed towards the Pier I let it begin to weave itself into a complex plot. Suppose my half-brother also lived in Brighton? Suppose he turned out to be Terry's father? Suppose, then, that Andy and Terry turned out to be cousins – but at that moment I came round the corner of the Royal Albion Hotel and saw, leaning against the railing across the road, Andy.

He straightened up and smiled as I reached him.

'Hi!' he said; and 'Hi!' I echoed; and then, through some kind of shared instinct, we each held out our right hand. We shook hands: it was quite absurd – yet, somehow, it seemed right.

He was dressed completely differently from the last time I'd seen him: in a conventional shirt, with the sleeves rolled up, and loose-fitting fawn trousers. Since it was, to say the least, a breezy evening, I was surprised he wasn't chilly.

But even as I had crossed the road towards him I had recognised the logic behind his choice of clothing. It was, of course, deliberately unsexual; and this fact reminded me, as if I needed any reminding, of the single greatest difficulty we faced now in working out together how we were going to relate as father and son: that he knew, quite unambiguously, that I had first seen him as an object of pure lust.

But it was too late to undo even the short history of our acquaintance. I asked him – he seemed almost tongue-tied: 'Shall we take a stroll along the Pier? Do you fancy that?'

'Yeah – that's fine.'

'You aren't cold?'

'No.'

We walked on to the Pier, our feet clacking on the wooden slats.

'What sort of a day have you had?' I asked.

'Oh, not bad.'

'Been up to London?'

'No, not today. Haven't got further than Lewes today. A bit boring, really.'

'Are you kept busy at work?'

'Could be busier, I suppose. It's a quiet time for us, August – not so many people buying and selling their houses.'

'Ah, right.'

We walked into an amusement arcade. The racket from dozens of noisy games and their juvenile players gave a perfect excuse not to talk again till we came out at the other side. There was a row of seats set against the central partition of the Pier; the westering sun shone across them. They were all empty.

'Shall we sit down?' I suggested.

'Yeah, fine.'

His manner could not have contrasted more sharply with when we met in Westhurst. He clearly wanted, or expected, me to lead the way for us. As we sat down beside each other he looked straight ahead of him, but with a diffident, uneasy air which was almost – childlike.

'Well,' I began. 'Your mother's told you – about everything.'

'Yeah.'

No more.

'Have you had a chance – to take it in?'

He smiled.

'It come as a bit of a surprise.'

'Yes, I imagine it did.'

Again, nothing more from him.

'It was quite a surprise for me, too.'

'Yeah, I guess.'

I looked down at the pier boarding.

'I suppose you'd like to know a bit about me?'

He turned his head: 'Mum's told me something. Like, about you being a student, and then a teacher, and all that.' He hesitated. 'Is it true your family's quite posh?'

'Posh? Oh, I don't know about that.'

'But she said your Dad was a lawyer?'

'Yes, he was an – a barrister.'

Andy's eyes widened.

'A barrister? She didn't tell me that.'

'I'm not sure she knew. Or maybe she just didn't remember.'

'Jeez!'

Oh Dad, I thought: if only you could be here at this moment to see how your profession so impresses your grandson.

Dad's grandson. It was the first time I'd thought of Andy as that.

I began to tell him something about my background, and my – his – our family. I played down the 'poshness', as he called it, but at one detail he interrupted me: 'A judge? Your grandad was a *judge*?'

'Nearly,' I corrected him. 'He didn't actually make it, but I believe he came close. I'm not sure what prevented it.'

Andy surprised me by starting to laugh.

'A *judge*! Jesus!'

I was pleased to see him recovering from his uneasiness – this was more like the Andy I'd first met – though his reaction puzzled me: 'What's so funny?' I asked, smiling.

His new-found confidence seemed to fade away at once.

'Oh – nothing,' he said; and his manner again became closed, cautious.

'I'm afraid I've got no cousins to introduce you to,' I went on. 'No aunts or uncles. You've got some second cousins in Edinburgh, but I don't think you'd want to meet *them*. They're as boring as hell.'

'Has your family always come from Edinburgh?'

'Or thereabouts, yes.'

He gazed out across the sea. I realised what all this information must be doing for him: for the first time in his life he was finding out about a whole side of his own roots.

'Look,' I said. 'I don't know about you, but I could murder a pint.'

He turned to me and smiled.

'Yeah, me too. Actually . . .'

'Yes?'

'I've already had a couple of drinks. On the way here.'

It was my turn to laugh.

'So did I!'

There was a bar on the Pier, but neither of us liked the look of it – it was crowded and noisy; so we turned round and walked through the amusement arcade again. When we were back on the forecourt I asked quietly: 'Do you want to go to a gay pub?'

He didn't look at me; he just shook his head.

'Me neither. There's a nice little pub across the road from my hotel – let's go there.'

It was a typical Brighton pub – scarcely larger than my sitting-room, and almost as dark and cosy as one of the 'brown bars' of Amsterdam. We settled in a quiet corner, with our bitter and lager.

For some time we spoke about our respective work. I told Andy how I'd got tired of teaching – though I didn't, of course, say anything about the incident with Jonathan – and then described the shop and my book-buying trips around southern Scotland and northern England. In turn he gave me a much fuller account than he had done before of his life as a courier and of people he worked alongside in the office. Talking about what was familiar to him seemed to relax him; he began to mimic some of his colleagues, so wittily – he had a real talent for it – I disturbed two or three of the pub's regulars with the noise of my laughter.

Andy insisted on buying the second round, overruling my protests. I knew I was far better off than he was, but I understood his pride; and besides, the last thing I wanted to do that evening was seem to be flashing my wallet.

When Andy sat down again he brought us back to the main subject of our conversation.

'Tell me,' he asked, 'how do you feel about Mum not telling you about – about everything? All those years ago?'

I didn't want to criticise May to him, but I didn't want to be dishonest either.

'Well. . . She had her reasons, of course. And remember that by the time you were born, I'd already gone abroad.'

'Yeah,' he said. I realised he wasn't particularly interested in my answer: 'I'm a bit pissed off with her myself, to be honest with you,' he went on.

'Why so?' I prompted, as gently as I could.

The question obviously surprised him: 'I mean, 'cause she wasn't straight with me, for so long. Like, I had all the wrong idea.'

'What sort of idea?'

'I thought my dad was some sort of – well, sailor, or something like that. She told me she hardly knew him, he was just someone who . . .'. He became embarrassed.

'A one-night stand?' I suggested, using the phrase May herself had used.

'More than that.' Suddenly he grinned, but more with awkwardness than amusement. 'More "a bit of rough".' He was serious again at once; he looked down as he went on: 'That's what I've always thought my dad was like.' He fiddled with a beer-mat on the table. 'I'd no idea he was somebody decent, like you.'

I stared at him. He started to blush.

I could have hugged him – to comfort him as much as anything; I realised just how radical a revaluation of his origins he must be faced with. But I made no move; instead I said quietly: 'You know, in some ways this has been a bigger shock to me than it has to you.'

He looked up as if alarmed.

'How come?'

I smiled.

'Well, at least you've always known you had a father. Until last Friday I had no notion that I had a son.'

He briefly laughed: 'I hadn't thought of that.'

He looked down again. I was distressed to see he was suddenly becoming edgy – nearly as nervous as he had been when we met by the Pier.

Without warning he came out with a question in one breathless rush.

'Look, what do you want me to call you?'

I was taken completely by surprise.

'Call me?' And then: 'Oh, I see what you mean.'

It was a matter I had never given the slightest thought to.

'Oh, just "John", don't you think?'

He raised his eyes. He was obviously relieved: 'You don't mind?'

'Well, it would be a bit – odd, wouldn't it, if you started calling me "Dad".' To ease the situation I half-affected a laugh: 'And it would make me feel very peculiar.'

He looked down again, but now he was smiling. After a few moments I said quietly: 'And besides, I don't deserve it.' I hesitated. 'I'm afraid I wouldn't have been much use to you as a father. Even if I'd known about you, I mean.'

He looked up at once, with a mixture of earnestness and puzzlement.

'How?'

'I'd have kept in touch, of course – always. But your mother and I would never have got together again. For obvious reasons.'

'Yeah, I realise that.'

He obviously hadn't grasped what I was driving at.

'I couldn't have prevented what happened. Your mother getting married, I mean.'

Even then I had to wait before he exclaimed: 'Oh! Right.'

'Your mother told me about how your stepfather treated you.'

'Thumping me, you mean?'

The casualness with which he said it startled me: 'Yes.' I was even more startled when he shrugged. 'Yeah, it's true he was a bit rough with me.'

'Don't you *mind*?'

'I certainly did at the time. But looking back' – he stopped. I saw him seem to close in on himself. 'It was good training, in a way. Toughened me up.'

I couldn't believe what I was hearing.

'Are you *serious*?'

'Oh, yes.'

'Toughened you up for *what*?'

'For life, John.' There wasn't the slightest trace of irony in his voice. 'You got to be tough, to survive in this life.'

I was astounded – and horrified: 'How has life been *that* hard on you?'

He looked away. His manner became almost furtive: 'It's like that, John. Nowadays.'

I opened my mouth. Whatever lay behind this, I wanted to know about right now; but just as I began to speak Andy pre-empted me: 'Tell me, if you don't mind me asking – have you ever been, like, "married"?' The inverted commas were apparent from his tone. 'Is there anyone special in your life?'

I resented the change of subject. I more than resented it: I was alarmed by how obviously he was hiding something. I was about to protest; but then remembered that this was the first time we had spoken as father and son, and there were matters which could be left, if he chose, to another meeting. All the same I was uneasy as I answered, not bothering much about what I said: 'No, I've never had a long-term relationship. A few short affairs, that's all. And no, I don't have anyone right now.'

'Doesn't that bother you?'

'Not particularly.'

'How not?'

I was still only partly paying attention to what we were talking about: 'Why should it?'

I must have replied more sharply than I'd intended. Andy at once looked abashed: 'Oh – no reason, I suppose.'

I regretted how I'd spoken. I carried on more gently: 'I'm used to it, Andy. I've been on my own for years.'

He didn't say anything.

'How about you and Terry?' I asked. 'Is he – "special", for you?'

Immediately Andy grinned.

'Yeah, I guess so. He's the first – the first guy I've been – well, sort of fond of.'

I couldn't help smiling. 'Sort of fond of.'

'Good,' I said. 'I'm glad.'

Andy looked at his watch: 'Actually, I'm due to meet him at eight. I'll need to go soon.'

I was instantly dismayed.

'Soon?'

'Yeah.'

So he'd set a time-limit on this conversation in advance. But, perhaps it was fair enough. The prospect of it had terrified me, a middle-aged man; how much more daunting must it have been to him?

'Does Terry know yet about – all this?'

Andy laughed: 'No. I'm going to tell him tonight. He's got quite a shock coming to him.'

I smiled.

'A pleasant one, I hope?'

'Oh, yes. He really liked you.'

If I'd been fishing for a compliment, I hadn't expected it to be as direct and as spontaneous as this. And a moment later Andy added: 'I mean, we both did.'

I looked away, certain I must be blushing.

'Good,' I said quietly.

'Look,' Andy said, apparently not noticing my confusion.

'Mum says I'm to invite you to dinner tomorrow evening. Is that OK?'

I turned back, delighted: 'Of course it's OK.'

'It'll just be her and me and you.' Suddenly he seemed awkward. 'A sort of – well – a kind of . . . '. He smiled with the same awkwardness: 'A family get-together, I suppose.'

I understood exactly what had made him hesitate. 'A family' – the implications of the word presented me, too, with much to come to terms with.

'Eight o'clock suit you?'

'Yes, fine.'

We finished off our drinks and went out into the evening sun. On the pavement we prepared to part.

I saw him standing in front of me, the wind rustling the thick waves of his hair. He was so full of vitality, so handsome – but the thought wasn't sexual; at that moment I wanted to say to him: 'Andy, I'm really proud of you. I'm really proud I have a son like you.'

Not for the first time in my life I wished I was an American, able to speak with the uninhibitedness of Americans. But it was impossible. The curse of Britishness hung over both of us: I was far too Scottish to say any such thing, and he was far too English to hear it without cringing with embarrassment.

So we just shook hands, and told each other we were looking forward to meeting again the following night.

It was, with the exception of two difficult passages, a successful evening.

The first came early, before we ate. May had several photograph albums ready, full of pictures of Andy. It was thoughtful of her: clearly she believed I would want to see what he had been like as a boy and as a teenager.

But I did no more than glance into the first of them and turn two or three pages; then I had to put it down.

I couldn't bear it. I couldn't bear to see all that I had missed, to think how I might have followed Andy's growth, visiting him from year to year, treating him as I would have had the right to do, as his natural father.

I apologised: 'Some other time . . .'. I couldn't explain my reaction; I felt ridiculous, and shamed. May was diplomatic; I think she understood. Andy merely looked puzzled.

Much later in the evening, by which time all three of us were happily convivial with wine, May said to Andy: 'Show John those photographs of you last year. The ones that were in the exhibition.'

'Exhibition?' I asked; and, 'Oh, *Mum*,' Andy exclaimed. 'John doesn't want to see those.'

May turned to me: 'They're not ordinary photos, John. They were taken by a proper photographer – an artist – she put them in an exhibition she had up in London. She used one of them for a poster as well – go on, Andy,' she urged.

He was obviously very reluctant. And when he came back with them – a portfolio of black-and-white prints – I instantly saw why.

I wouldn't have identified Andy, if I hadn't been told; his face was never seen. But in all of them he was in leather, and in several stripped to the waist. They were very strange: they had been taken in a country churchyard, clearly employing Andy as a model, along with – of all things – a small toddler; moreover in the most disturbing Andy was handcuffed.

They weren't explicitly erotic, in any way; I assumed that some kind of artistic statement was being made – possibly about the responsibilities of parenthood – but I had no inclination to work out what it was. I turned them over quickly and handed them back to Andy: 'Thanks,' I said.

He took them out of the room at once, and for long minutes afterwards he was silent while May and I chatted on. I was astonished she could be so insensitive, or so naive.

Andy was neither. He knew why I had gone through the portfolio with such rapidity; it had stirred awake in me what I wanted killed off for good, the worm of my lust for my own son.

As I was leaving Andy lingered beside me at the open door.

'I'd like to see you again before you go,' he said. I'd

decided I would stay on till after the weekend, and return to Scotland on Monday.

'Of course,' I said – relieved that apparently he wasn't going to let the episode of the photographs re-erect a barrier between us. 'Of course I want to see you again.'

'How about Friday evening?' he asked. 'Early on, before I go out with Terry.' He named a large pub near the Steine.

'Yes, fine,' I said. 'That'll be fine.'

About eight that Friday evening he joined me in the pub, which was already busy and noisy with a weekend crowd. I felt conspicuous; I seemed to be the oldest person in the place by at least twenty years.

Because I'd arrived early I'd been able to grab a couple of seats in a corner, and we took our places there.

PART TWO

ANDY'S STORY

CHAPTER ONE

That night in the King and Queen I told John a bit about myself, things that he had to know. But of course I didn't give him all the detail I'm going into now, I mean if I had, we'd still have been sitting there on Christmas Eve.

If you're from London you maybe saw the poster of me, about the time Caroline's exhibition was on in Neal Street. It was quite a hit, I was told, in the gay places where they stuck it up, like First Out and so on. It was the one which showed the back of me from the waist down, with me in leather and my legs wide apart, pressing my palms flat against my thighs, like Caroline had told me to do. In the distance beyond my left hand you could see a church, and peering between my legs, looking at the camera with a sort of daft grin, so you could tell he hadn't a clue what was going on (and no wonder), was young Tommy.

You've maybe got it on your wall right now – I heard that quite a lot were sold at the show itself, and a lot more were nicked from where they were stuck up. I'm not going to pretend I wasn't *very* flattered, Terry took the piss out of me for weeks, calling me 'Superstar' and all the rest.

A couple of friends of ours, in Brighton, have it up in their spare room, but with the background cut away and also the bit between my legs, so that they're left with just a kind of upside-down 'V'. They say it gives their guests sweet dreams. Well, I don't mind the church going, but cutting out Tommy seems a bit hard on the poor kid. 'Cause he was quite sweet, for a brat.

And all of this happened, like everything else, because Hugo Thomson acted like he had a right hand made of solid metal and I had a magnet in my underpants. It's amazing what one grope can lead you to.

But before all that, it started when I got the job with the solicitors. I'd been working for a couple of years in the print room of a big local office. It wasn't bad, but it wasn't very good either – to be honest, it was pretty boring most of the time. So when I saw the vacancy in the *Argus* for an office assistant/motor bike courier, I was interested straight away.

But there was this one big problem – the fact that it was with a firm of lawyers. 'Cause there was something in my background which you'll need to know about now.

I had a criminal record – one conviction for assault which I picked up when I was seventeen, and another for handling stolen goods, two years later. The first come about because of a disagreement of opinion I had one Bank Holiday Monday with a Londoner who thought he knew everything (but he didn't know how I could use my fists), and the other was so stupid I'd rather not say too much about it. I got mixed up in this stupid racket, I didn't even make much dosh out of it, but three of us ended up in court.

I'd been fined on the assault charge, but I got a suspended sentence for the dealing – which shocked me a lot. I mean, it was only three months, suspended for two years, but even so it seemed heavy for what I'd done. And just the *idea* of me in prison frightened the willies out of me, for a while. My solicitor thought it was heavy too, I think he took it quite personally, but I guess the magistrates reckoned I was a hooligan who was going to end up in jug anyway and they might as well speed things along.

Obviously this wasn't exactly the ideal CV to have if I was going after a job with a solicitor, especially in a little place like Brighton, where most people in the same line of business know each other, and tongues wag. But the first trouble had been three years before, and the second time I'd come up in court in Haywards Heath, which was where our little bit of private enterprise had been based. So I thought maybe I might get away with it, and the job was very tempting. Anyway, I stuck in an application, just to see. And lo and behold, I got called to an interview.

The day of the interview, I wasn't sure what to wear. I mean, it was true they were looking for a courier, but I thought to turn up in a leather jacket and jeans would seem cheeky. In the end I chose smart grey trousers, and of course a decent shirt and tie.

About two seconds after I walked into the Office Manager's room – he was going to interview me – I knew I was in with a real chance for this job. One glance at him suggested one thing to me. And after we'd been sitting opposite each other for a couple of minutes, talking generally, I was certain. He was slim, about forty, and what you could call elegant. Now, my trousers fitted me pretty tight. And this fact was clearly earning me about a dozen bonus points a minute with this guy. I mean, he was spending more time looking at my crotch than at my face.

Oh God, I thought. But I'd been there before, often enough. The truth is, if I can be crude for a moment, any pair of trousers I own have got plenty to be tight about. After a while you get used to it – being eyed up, I mean, when you're not necessarily in the mood for it. So I could cope with this Office Manager and his problem with his eyes, though it was something I could have done without.

But at last he managed to tear his attention away from my kecks and start interviewing me properly, and pretty soon I realised he was OK, he wasn't going to think anything stupid. After a while I even begun to feel we were getting on together pretty well. He cracked an odd joke or two, I risked a joke or two of my own, we relaxed a bit.

He warned me about the job.

'We have clients over a very wide area – anything up to forty or fifty miles away. And that means we have dealings with other solicitors over the same sort of distance. So there's a lot of riding about involved.'

'Suits me fine.'

'In every kind of weather, I'm afraid.'

I nodded: 'I'm used to that.' It was true, I'd been riding bikes of one kind or another since I was fifteen.

'Except snow and ice, of course. We wouldn't expect you to go out in snow and ice.'

'Oh, I can ride on snow alright, if I need to.'

He just looked at me. I realised he thought I was bragging, to try to get the job.

'No – honest,' I added.

All of a sudden he laughed: 'I believe you. But you

won't be going out in dangerous conditions for *us*. In fact, a lot of the work is just ferrying papers up and down from the office here to the Law Courts. Do you know where they are? They're in Edward Street.'

I just nodded. I didn't dare even say 'Yes'. As it was, I was afraid I was going to blush.

'Oh, and by the way, are you familiar with London at all?'

'A little.'

'We have two or three clients in London.' He smiled. 'But I suppose we can always provide you with a map.'

We talked on for a while, and at the end he said: 'I've still got two or three other people I want to see. But I'll be in touch.'

He was. Three days later I opened my front door and nearly jumped out of my skin when I found this huge guy in leathers looming in front of me. It turned out he was my predecessor, delivering a letter offering me the job.

I'd chosen the perfect time of year to become a courier. It was July, and dry, and hot, and everything that makes being out on the road a pleasure. I mean, that first few weeks in the job, it was hardly like working at all.

In those days I had quite a small bike, a 250 Suzuki. But she could do a ton, when you wanted her to. And soon she was, regularly.

If you've never travelled at that speed on two wheels you won't really understand what I'm talking about now. You have to imagine it: the roaring of the air round your helmet – the tar racing past just beneath you – the vibration of the bike – the fact that there's nothing between you and the world you're travelling through so fast, so you feel as if it's *you* who's got the power to move like this – the bike's become part of you, you and it are one unit, screaming along the roads of England – oh, I tell you, the only physical experience in life better than that is sex.

But a lot of the time I was on little backroads, country roads. Then I had to ride dead slow, about forty, 'cause those country roads can be a damn sight more dangerous than most city streets. But now you have a completely different kind of pleasure. When there's long stretches of open road you can ride one-handed. If you want to speed up a bit, you open the throttle through just a few millimetres. If you want to bear left, you lean a little to the left. The slightest movement of your body and the bike responds for you, and so the country rolls past, you're making no effort, you're just sitting there, visor up at that speed, looking around you – master of the road, master of everything you turn your eyes on. Believe me, *that* is perfect freedom.

A lot of our clients, like you'd expect, were people buying and selling their houses, and since we were a kind of upmarket firm they tended to be pretty wealthy people, living in the villages and country towns near Brighton. So a lot of my work involved going to these sleepy places, to other solicitors – all sleepy, of course – and to sleepy estate agents, and sleepy insurance offices, and sometimes to the clients.

But there was nothing sleepy about *them*. I soon realised that not only did they think we were ripping them off right, left and centre, but what was worse, that *I* was getting a straight cut of the profits. When I handed over documents they used to pounce on them with 'Ha!', and snarl at me, and then call to their dogs, which were always about two metres high and foamed at the mouth, and then snarl at me again like they wished they could serve me up for Rover's dinner as a stand-in for my bosses.

You'd be surprised how nasty people can be just because us professionals have to charge a fee that reflects the value of the services we provide.

All of these villages, of course, had pubs, which was a problem for me. I didn't dare go into them for lunch, it just wasn't worth the risk. So I made sandwiches for myself, and come lunchtime I'd roll along to some quiet bit of country, and as often as not up on to a hillside, and have my lunch sitting on the grass. I took to wearing swimming trunks under my jeans so I could strip down and sunbathe. Sometimes I had a midday snooze in the sun. Looking back, I don't know how I managed to handle the stress of it all.

I soon begun to get on well with the Office Manager, who was now my immediate boss. It was him, you might say, who told me where to go.

His name was Gordon. It *would* have to be. I hadn't been there more than a week when I overheard someone having a dig at 'gay Gordon'. What surprised me was that it didn't come, as you might have expected, from another bloke, but from a woman, and what you could call a 'mature' woman at that. If you were in a mood to be polite.

Apart from the fantastic weather for biking, another thing about starting work in July was that the office was quieter than usual, so to begin with I really did have an easy life of it. Like I've said, a lot of our work was conveyancing, and there isn't as much of that in the summer. The court work was down a bit too, and the typists in Litigation (I learned some long words working for a solicitor) told me that people don't even get divorced so much in the summer.

What all this meant to me was that some days I didn't have a lot to do till maybe the middle of the morning, so I used to hang about the office drinking coffee and nattering. I can't pretend that this caused me unbearable suffering, but at the same time it worried me a bit, 'cause naturally, when you start a new job you don't want to look as if you're not really needed.

But it didn't seem to worry Gordon. He often used to come out of his office and join me for coffee and stand around for a while, chatting to me. Yes – chatting 'to', not 'up', though the problem he'd had with his eyes the first time we met still troubled him now and again.

It was quite a long time before we actually said anything to each other about being gay. I don't know how, or when, he sussed out about me. Maybe at the interview – maybe that's why I got the job! But I remember when I found out for certain that he knew. It was just a few weeks after I'd started. We were standing one morning in the little office kitchen, on our own, with mugs in our hands. We'd been talking about the bike, and whether I was needing any more equipment for her, when suddenly he asked: 'Do you own any biker's leathers?'

'Yeah,' I said. 'I've got a pair of leather trousers.'

'Yes?' He looked slightly past me, at a row of mugs beside the sink. 'You don't wear them to work, then?'

He said it so casual, so cool.

'I probably will in the winter. Sometimes they can be too hot in the summer.'

He looked straight at me again – my face, I mean – and nodded.

'Ah, right.'

I sipped my coffee. As I did so I could feel mischief getting the better of me.

'They're good leather. Cost a few bob.'

'I imagine they would.'

Still so cool. It made my mischievousness worse.

'And besides – they're a bit uncomfortable.' I stopped. I'd lost the bottle to go on to say what I'd been about to say. But Gordon smiled very slightly.

'The leather's too stiff, you mean?'

I realised I was having to try not to smile myself.

'No. They're a bit on the small side for me.' I couldn't resist it. 'Too tight.'

He looked away again, to the mugs.

'Yes, well. I suppose there's a limit to the amount of excitement I can stand in the working day.'

He looked me straight in the eyes again.

Suddenly he burst out laughing, and the next thing so did I, and there we were, laughing like idiots, sharing a joke against everyone else in the office, really.

When he recovered he said: 'So, do you think these new signings will do the Albion any good?' I was happy to go along with the change of subject.

That was one odd thing about Gordon, by the way – he was one of those weird gay men who are keen on football. I'd heard people in the office who liked him arguing that he couldn't be queer, could he, since he went to the Goldstone every other Saturday? If only you were right, I used to think.

It was a few weeks after that – we were into October – when he called me into the office one day and told me about the London job.

CHAPTER TWO

'I have something special for you today,' he said. 'It's quite important.' He pointed to a pile of papers on his desk. 'These have to go to London, to our client. He's got to have them before lunch. Then afterwards you'll need to wait around for his answer to come back to us. It might even be an all-day job – don't worry if you're not back here this afternoon, there's nothing we can do again anyway till tomorrow.' He started rifling through a drawer. 'I think you said you didn't know London particularly well?'. I nodded. 'If you come round here then, I'll show you . . . '.

He produced an A-Z and I leaned over him as he pointed out where I was going, and the best way to get there. It was – let's say, somewhere in west London. 'The client's the MD of a record firm,' Gordon said. 'I've never heard of them, but you'll maybe have.' Well, I certainly had, I recognised the name straight off – in the previous year they'd suddenly begun to make it big. I'll call them 'R&R'. 'When you get there,' Gordon went on, 'ask for Hugo Thomson – he's in Press and Publicity.'

'OK.'

So off I went, out of town and on to the A23 and then the motorway, and about forty minutes later I hit the outskirts of London, and about three and a half days after that I finally made it through the traffic to my destination. It turned out to be some terraced houses knocked into one big office, with a very handy little parking lot in front where I stuck the bike between a white Rolls and a Bentley, each of them with personalised number-plates. Then I nearly knocked myself out walking into a front door that was locked – I had to talk into this security thing before they would let me in.

In the reception area they were playing music – their own, I supposed – so loud I had to shout over it to a harassed-looking girl sitting beside a word-processor that seemed to be having a nervous breakdown: 'I'VE CALLED TO DELIVER SOME PAPERS FOR PRESS AND

PUBLICITY,' I said.

At first I couldn't hear the reply, but at the second attempt I made out, 'THIRD FLOOR – STAIRCASE IS THROUGH THERE', and the girl pointed to another door. I was just about to bash right into *that* when I heard a loud buzzing, which turned out to be yet another security lock, and so I stepped through into this narrow corridor.

As I walked along it to the staircase, which was at the far end, I was kind of aware of a guy coming out of a room and following me. He was still behind me as I started climbing the stairs. At the first turning I glanced back and saw him looking up at me.

'Hi,' he said.

'Hi,' I answered, and carried on climbing. At the next turning he asked: 'Who are you looking for?'

I stopped.

'Press and Publicity. I'm told they're on the third floor?'

'That's right. Keep going.'

Oddly enough I was planning to do that anyway, being able to count. He was a handsome bastard, though – maybe in his mid-twenties, very blond, with grey eyes and a neat figure shown off by a blue casual shirt and khaki drill trousers. Still he followed me.

When we got to the top he drew alongside me.

'It's through there,' he said, pointing to a swing door.

'Thanks.'

I was about to fumble with the door – I was carrying my helmet in one hand and a pile of legal papers in the other – when the guy stepped forward and opened it for me.

'Thanks!' I said again.

'No – thank *you,*' he said as I passed him. And a second later my bum was grabbed like it was a lifebelt to a drowning man – grabbed so hard I was damn near lifted off the floor by my buns. Since it was a mild day I was in my jeans, and where I couldn't feel finger-tips I didn't have a lot left where they could get to.

I spun round, too stunned to do more than gawp at the guy. He was grinning from one ear to the other.

'Thanks for the great view on the way up,' he said.

Before I could get a word out he added: 'And the front view's even better, kid.' His hand moved, and for one awful moment I thought he was about to give my balls the same kind of medical check-up he'd just given my arse. Instead he laughed, turned, and headed off in the opposite direction.

I was *very* tempted to throw some choice words after him. The fucking nerve of it! If he thought that just because he was good-looking he could touch up any boy in leather and denim he happened to fancy, then he badly needed to be taught a lesson. It's no joke being treated like that by a total stranger out of the blue, as if you're nothing more than a pair of jeans walking around to give them a quick thrill.

I carried on, into yet another corridor. I had to agree with him about one thing, though – following me up three flights of stairs probably *had* provided him with a great view. All the same, that hardly gave him the right to get his fingers practically jammed in my arsehole.

I found myself at a door marked 'Press', and knocked and went in. There was only one person in the room, a girl, sitting at a desk. She lifted her head and looked at me as if I was the most boring object she had ever clapped eyes on.

'Can I help you?' she asked.

'I'm looking for Hugo Thomson.'

'He's out. He'll be a few minutes.'

And back she went to the work on her desk, leaving me standing there like a prune. Not for long, though. I sat down anyway, I wasn't going to wait for her to be polite.

I'd sat there maybe five minutes when I heard footsteps coming along the corridor. Sure enough, the door swung open, and in walked – Fearless Fingers.

I couldn't believe it. He turned to me and grinned, that same bloody God-I'm-so-handsome-I-can-get-away-with-anything grin he'd had before.

'I see you found us,' he said cheerily.

I wanted to come out with some really sarky answer. But I just said: 'Yes'.

Bored found the energy to raise her head again: 'This guy's looking for you, Hugo.'

'For me? My lucky day!'

Oh, Jesus.

'You'd better come through here,' he said, pointing to another room off the one we were in.

Since he was just at my back I moved sharply, into what was obviously his office. He sat behind a desk: 'What can I do for you, then?' he asked.

Cut your throat and drop dead in front of me, I thought. But I explained my business, as briefly as I could.

'Ah, of course,' he said as he took the papers. He pointed to a chair: 'Have a seat.'

He undid the files, and begun to flick through them. Suddenly he was serious and business-like, you could tell he was a clever man from the way he stopped and read a letter or a memo, and then moved on to the next one that interested him. As he read, the front wave of his hair fell forward over his brow, and occasionally he flicked it back with his hand, without interrupting what he was doing.

He *was* good-looking, I couldn't deny it – a real stud-humpy blond. I could have fancied him easily, very easily, if I didn't have his finger-prints halfway up my bum.

Eventually he looked up: 'It'll take the MD a while to go through these properly, but then we'll need you to take our answer back.'

'Yes, I was told that.'

'It could be quite some time.'

'I was told I might have to wait all afternoon – they're not expecting me in the office again till tomorrow morning.'

He nodded: 'That's fine, then. That's excellent.'

I stood up.

'So, when should I come back?'

He grinned.

'You're welcome to come back any time you like, son.'

Oh, for fuck's sake.

'Will you be serious? I have a job of work to do.'

He went on grinning.

'What on earth's the matter?'

'What do you *think* is the matter?'

Still he grinned.

'Son, if you didn't want to be admired, you wouldn't

show off your exquisite bum in the tightest pair of jeans you can fit into, would you?'

I was speechless.

He nodded in the general direction of my middle: 'And you wouldn't wrap up your *very* impressive assets in a basket like that, either.'

'You are *disgusting*!' I exclaimed.

'Why?'

I couldn't be bothered to answer.

He was still grinning that bloody grin: 'I'm not criticising you, son. If you've got it, flaunt it, I say – and you've certainly got it.'

I glared at him, trying to think of something really crushing to come out with.

He leaned forward.

'So tell me – who *do* you want to admire you? Boys or girls?'

'Someone with better manners than you, at any rate.'

He burst out laughing.

'Oh, I see! I suppose you want me to apologise to you, do you?'

'Yes.'

'What for?'

'You know perfectly well what for!'

'For telling you you're sexy?'

I wondered if Bored could hear this conversation through the partition – maybe right now she wasn't as bored as before.

'I know I'm sexy,' I said as coldly as I could. 'That doesn't mean I'm interested in an arrogant cunt like you.'

'"Arrogant cunt"? That's a bit strong, isn't it?'

He leaned back.

'OK, I'm sorry. I'm sorry if I've offended you.'

I wasn't in a mood to accept the apology gracefully.

'You have.'

'What's your name?'

'Eh?'

'Your name – what's your name?'

I hesitated before I answered.

'Andy.'

'Well, Andy, now you've made your feelings clear, maybe we can move on to better things?'

I wondered what on earth he meant by *that*.

'You still haven't told me when to come back.'

He glanced at his watch.

'Better make it half-four. You can leave your helmet in here, if you like – and your bike'll be perfectly safe where it is. If you don't want to go off on it for the afternoon, that is.'

I thought about it.

'No, I'll go up town. See a bit of London.'

He grinned that grin of his again – God, it was irritating: 'Well, take care of yourself. This is the Big City, you know.'

I'd already opened the door. I turned back, having just thought of the perfect thing to say: 'I don't imagine anything worse will happen to me than running into *you*.' It only made him burst out laughing again.

At least I was right about one thing. Bored had not only woken up, this time she looked at me as if I was a whole gang of Hell's Angels rolled into one.

Isn't London a horrible city? I mean, there's very little to do there if you're not interested in shopping, or photographing the Houses of Parliament, or walking about on top of eight million stiffs in Westminster Abbey. I mooched around for quite a while, and then made the mistake of going into a pub near Trafalgar Square – very packed, very noisy, full of the sort of people who seem to think that everyone within a thousand metres wants to know everything about them. For half-an-hour I had to listen to these types droning on about how the value of their houses was going down, and the value of their second houses was going up, and the value of their cars, and the value of their second cars, and what Fiona said to Gerald last night, and how Perry threw champagne over Julian, and who went after *all* the black studs at Adrian's party, and so on and so on. God, it was enough to turn you Labour, it really was.

I did do some shopping. I went into a jeans store and bought a new pair of jeans – loose-fit. I told the assistant I wanted to wear them out, which didn't faze him in the slightest, and got him to put my other pair in a bag. At least, I thought as I left, it's my jeans that are wrapped up now, and not my exquisite bum or my very impressive assets.

In another shop I bought a couple of pairs of Calvin Klein briefs. The shorts I'd got on weren't dirty or anything – they were clean on that morning – but I'd had them for quite a while, and they were getting a little tatty. I changed in a Gents, making sure the cubicle door was well locked. I don't think there was a single man in there having a slash.

I got back to R&R about half-four, as I'd been told, and went upstairs to Press and Publicity again. Bored nearly jumped out of her skin when I walked in.

'Hugo won't be long,' she said, in a way that suggested I might stab her on the spot because he wasn't there right at that moment. But I still had to sit down uninvited.

When he come back he glanced at me and instantly raised his eyebrows. This time it was me who grinned, I couldn't stop myself.

'Come through,' he said.

He had the files ready for me to take away, and explained quickly about papers I would need to point out the next morning to the partner who was dealing with the case. He wrapped them in a package, pushed it across the desk, leaned back, and looked at me.

'What are you doing now?' he asked.

'Going home,' I said.

'To Brighton?'

Naw, Timbuctoo.

'Yes, Brighton.'

'I can finish off here any minute. I've been in since before eight.'

I just looked at him.

It unsettled him, he had to pretend he was interested in something on the wall behind me. I noticed that now he was getting serious, he wasn't half the cocky little bastard he'd been earlier.

'I live quite a bit away,' he said. 'In Islington. But there's a colleague of mine who has a flat just round the corner. She lets me use it from time to time, when – if I strike lucky here.' He cleared his throat. 'I spoke to her this afternoon. Just in case. She says there's no problem.'

He looked at me again. I didn't say a word. I was beginning to enjoy this.

'Is there?' he had to ask.

'Dunno,' I said.

'It's literally not five minutes walk. You can still leave your bike outside.'

I was getting mischievous: 'You take boys round there regular, then?'

'Sometimes, Andy, sometimes. This is the music business – a lot of very pretty young men pass through this office. And you'd be surprised how many of them are – willing.'

'And I'm another of them, am I? I suppose I'm "willing", too?'

He leaned forward: 'Andy, believe me, it's a long time since I saw as handsome a boy as you in this place.'

Bloody hell! *That* threw me.

He sat back: 'If you go down and sort of hang around beside your bike, just for a couple of minutes, I'll be with you.'

I stood up.

'I'll think about it,' I said as I picked up the files and my helmet.

He was right about it not being five minutes walk – into a side street of terraced houses, very like the street where my Mum lives, except that all these were divided into flats. We went upstairs to a first floor flat and into a big front room, very light and airy.

'Fancy a drink?' he asked.

'Is that OK?'

'Yes, I'll settle up with Caroline afterwards.'

I asked for a beer. While he was getting it I wandered around looking at the pictures on the walls. A lot of them were framed photographs, very odd most of them, and some others were paintings. Sort of – modern. You know the kind of thing. Squiggles and splodges.

'Caroline's an artist,' Hugo said when he come back.

'I'd never have guessed. These her own?'

'I think so. The photos certainly are. She's a professional photographer, she does nearly all our album covers and publicity material.' He laughed. 'I think I can safely say she enjoys her work. Very heterosexual, is Caroline. She gets the shirts off far more hunky men than you or I ever do, Andy.'

We sat down on a cane sofa, with fancy cushions. Hugo had poured himself a whisky and Coke.

He rubbed his free hand on the knee of my jeans.

'You bought these this afternoon, I take it?'

I nodded.

'This is the most interesting example of power dressing I've seen in a long time.'

'Of what?'

He laughed.

'Did I make you self-conscious?'

'No. I just fancied something new.'

'A change of style?'

'Something like that.'

He ran his hand up my thigh and then gently – he was different now – bunched the denim at my crotch: 'But as full of eastern promise as ever.'

'My impressive assets, you mean?'

He laughed again: 'Oh, you're not going to forgive me for that, are you?'. He stroked the base of my balls, and then cupped his hand around me: 'Oh God, Andy,' he said quietly, putting down his drink. 'There is nothing in this world, nothing in the whole wide world, as good as feeling the bulge in the pants of a handsome young man.'

We kissed – a deep, long kiss, till our arms were round each other, and when we broke apart both of us were well on our way: 'Time to draw the curtains,' he said.

I begun to undress, but just as I got down to my briefs he stopped me.

'Hold on,' he said, and sat on the sofa again in front of me. His shirt was off and his trousers unzipped. He drew me to him and buried his face in my crotch with a sigh of pleasure – and then sat back, looking surprised.

'These are brand-new,' he said.

Hell, I'd never thought he might find that out.

He grinned.

'You bought these this afternoon as well, didn't you?'

'Yeah.'

His grin grew wider and wider.

'And this is the guy who was "going to think about it"! "Dunno", he said!'

I grinned too.

'I might have changed my mind.'

'You liar!' He ran his hands up and down over my buns. 'I ought to put you over my knee and tan your backside till you could fry an egg on it.'

'No,' I said at once. 'That's not my scene.'

'Pity.' He slid his hands inside my briefs: 'An arse as gorgeous as this was just made to be spanked.'

He moved his hands to the waist of the briefs and with one tug pulled them down.

'Are you *sure* you don't fancy the idea of being whacked?' he asked cheekily. Then he buried his face in me again, squeezing my hard-on up against his forehead: 'Anyway there isn't time,' I made out from the region of my pubes.

When everything was over we lay together on the floor. We didn't have any condoms, so we'd ended by jerking each other off. Now Hugo ran his fingers through the cum on my chest and rubbed it into my pubes. Then he did the same thing with the cum on his own chest.

'What was that for?' I asked.

'So that when you ride home tonight you'll have the spunk of both of us inside your pants. I like the idea. Don't you?'

'Well . . . I don't know.'

He rubbed more cum into me: 'It'll turn me on again tonight, thinking of your pubes inside your clean white briefs all stiff with dried spunk.'

I didn't know what to say to that. This was a new kink to

me altogether.

He propped himself up on one elbow and grinned.

'But next time I'll send you home with an uncomfortable bum.'

'Look, I told you, I'm not into that at all.'

He laughed.

'That's not what I meant. Next time I'll make sure I'm prepared.'

I sat up: 'What makes you so certain there'll be a next time?'

'Won't there?'. He stroked my cheek. 'I hope there will, Andy.'

The truth was, so did I, but I wasn't going to admit it right away.

'You know, Andy,' he went on, 'this case of ours is going to run and run. You could be up and down to us a lot.'

'I see.'

'And even if you're not, you don't *have* to come up to London just on business, do you?'

'What else would I want to come up here for?'

It only made him laugh: 'We'd better get dressed,' he said. 'Caroline'll be home soon.'

As I was pulling on my jeans he asked: 'Why don't you wear leather?'

'I will be doing, once it gets colder.'

'Ah!'

Oh, God. I realised at once I should have thought before I said that.

'Look – don't get any wrong ideas.'

'What sort of wrong ideas?'

'About me in leather. I like leather, but that's as far as it goes.'

He nodded slowly.

'I see. OK, Andy, I understand.'

For once he was serious. I was relieved: 'I've had problems with that before. And I never, ever, wear leather on the scene.'

'Because people think . . .?'

'Yeah. Either they want to belt the arse off you, or they

want you to belt the arse off them. I don't know which is worse.'

'And you've never been tempted?'

'No,' I said simply. Actually I have gone along with it a little, once or twice, to keep people happy, but I've never much enjoyed it. The truth is, I got enough S&M off my stepfather to last me a lifetime.

Just as we were getting ready to leave – Caroline still hadn't come back – Hugo asked me another question.

'What do you wear *under* your leather?'

'Eh? Underpants, of course.'

'What sort of underpants?'

'Short ones, with an opening at the front.'

'I mean, you idiot, do you wear boxer shorts or briefs?'

'Both. Not usually at the same time, though.'

He laughed: 'God, you're a cheeky little runt, you really are. Will you promise me one thing?'

'What?'

'Don't ever wear shorts when you come to see me. Always wear briefs.'

I was astonished: 'Why?'

'Because I'm a total underwear fetishist. Those Calvin Kleins you've bought today are perfect – always wear something like those.'

'What difference does it make?'

'What *difference*?'. He sounded positively shocked. 'It's the difference between having your finest points held tight and obvious, and having them invisible behind drooping cotton. Don't you feel the same way about guys when they get their trousers off?'

I grinned.

'No. All that interests me about their underpants is how quickly *they're* coming off as well.'

'Oh, God! You're a real romantic, aren't you?'

'Anyway, how am I supposed to know when I'm going to be coming up here? Do you expect me to carry a pair of briefs around with me all the time, just in case?'

'Why not? Or maybe swimming trunks.' He grabbed my crotch: 'I'd love to see this splendid equipment packing out a pair of swimmies.'

I backed away, laughing too: 'You've got a one-track mind, do you know that?'

He didn't deny it: 'Isn't there some way you could find out in advance if you're going to be sent to London?'

'Not really.'

'Couldn't you ask your boss about it – diplomatically? And try to arrange to be here in the afternoon if you can, so that we can come back to this flat after work, like we've done today.'

I shook my head: 'I really don't think . . .'

'Tell him you're seeing a girl in London. He'll understand.'

'He certainly won't buy that! He knows I'm gay.'

Hugo was surprised: 'Really? Well, tell him the truth then.'

That hardly seemed possible either, but I didn't want to argue about it.

We went outside and Hugo locked the door behind us. He had to go one way along the street to the Underground, and me the other, back to the bike, so we separated by the front gate. He patted my arm: 'Hey, kid,' he said. 'I really enjoyed that. I hope we *can* do it again.'

'Yeah, me too. I'm sure I'll be back soon.'

I couldn't have gone on being mean to him. Though he could be a crude bastard at times, with all his talk of 'finest points' and 'splendid equipment', and the hand actions to match, I reckoned he was basically OK.

And besides – I wasn't the only one of us who could pack out a pair of swimmies. Though it isn't always my scene, he had a dick on him I knew I wouldn't at all mind getting a chance to feel well up my bum.

Not that there's anything crude about *me*, of course.

CHAPTER THREE

Well, I got my way with Hugo – not that he wasn't happy to oblige – though as it happened I didn't see him very often through that winter. It wasn't till the spring that I started going up regular to London, to and from his office, when the case they were involved in begun getting more and more complicated.

It was about then that Hugo started pressing me – I nearly wrote 'pestering me' – to fix it up with Gordon that he should warn me about these trips, if he could, the day before, and that I should always try to be in London in the afternoon. I was very reluctant about this. I mean, it's hardly easy, is it, to ask your boss, whoever he is, to sort out your working day so you can fit in a really good shag at the end of it.

Anyway, what I did eventually was, I kind of made out to Gordon that something quite romantic was happening in London between me and this guy – I didn't tell him, of course, that it was our own client – and that I liked to see him up there after work . . . Maybe I come across all bashful about this, which wouldn't have been difficult, considering that in fact I was dead embarrassed, and maybe that made the whole thing sound really plausible. But Gordon amazed me by being incredibly helpful – of course he'd do what he could, though naturally it wouldn't always be possible, since he didn't always know in advance what the partner concerned would be wanting . . . I felt dead guilty about it, 'cause he was so kind, and almost touched by what I'd told him. Maybe he was just a sucker for a sob story about young gay lovers. And the truth was that Hugo and me couldn't have been less romantic if we'd tried.

The next time I saw Hugo I told him all this, and he hooted with laughter.

'Well done, kid!' he said. 'I didn't think any queer would be able to resist you if you flashed your basket at him – I mean, your soulful eyes' – and he hooted with laughter again. I was furious, and I said so, with a few good choice words thrown in. He could really get on my wick sometimes, Hugo.

It was about then that I met Caroline for the first time. All through the winter she'd never been around when I was in their office – Hugo told me she spent most of her time out and about, on shoots. But one evening, it would have been into May, Hugo and me were sitting around her flat after – after the usual – like we always did, him drinking a large gin and me a glass of lager. It had been a warm day, and we were both still in the buff.

Suddenly, as we were talking, I heard the front door open.

'Who's that?' I exclaimed.

'That? Oh, it'll be Caroline – she said she might be back early today.'

Well, I tell you, I never moved so fast off a sofa in my life. The room door opened barely a second after I got my jeans up round my waist. Hugo, of course, thought it was all one huge joke: 'Caroline, this is Andy,' he said, in between his laughs. 'Andy, Caroline.'

She had a heavy photographer's bag over one shoulder. She put it down and come across to me, smiling: 'Hi!' she said. We shook hands as normally as if I wasn't stripped to the waist and we weren't standing right next to a ballock-naked man sprawling on cushions.

'I'm pleased to meet you at last,' she went on. 'Hugo's told me a lot about you.' She stepped back slightly and looked at me. She smiled again: 'You're every bit as handsome as he said you were.'

Dear Christ, I thought. These Londoners really don't beat about the bush, do they? I think I was blushing as I sat down again beside Hugo.

Caroline was a short woman, rather thin, with very bright eyes and dark, tightly-curled hair. She was in a calf-length skirt, high boots, and a bright red bodice. I thought she was a year or two older than Hugo, maybe in her late twenties – in fact, I know now she was thirty-five.

She went to the sideboard and picked up the gin bottle.

'Hugo, love,' she said. 'You owe me a new bottle.'

'No problem.' She poured herself what was left, and turned with her glass in her hand. She smiled to him and said, more softly than she'd spoken before: 'If you're not careful, I'll have to think about increasing your rent.' I saw him grin to her as she went off to get some ice.

'Will you put some clothes on?' I hissed to Hugo as soon as she was out of the room.

'Why? Really, Andy, you didn't need to go through that amazing acrobatic performance when Caroline arrived.'

'Are you fucking stupid? Do you think I want to meet a total stranger without a stitch on?'

'Oh honestly, Andy. Don't be so *provincial*.'

'Look – I don't care about how *you* feel, but you're embarrassing me to death sitting around like that.'

'For Heaven's sake, Andy! Caroline's not seeing anything she hasn't seen before – believe me.'

I thought for a moment.

'You don't mean . . . ?'

He burst out laughing: 'Now you're letting your imagination run away with you!'

At that moment Caroline come back into the room with her gin. She sat down in a big armchair opposite us and lit a fag.

'Andy's worried you might be shocked,' Hugo said. 'He thinks I should make myself decent.'

Jesus, he could be patronising when he wanted to be. Caroline smiled and blew smoke away: 'It's OK, Andy,' she said. 'I'm a photographer, as you know. I've done a lot of studies of the male nude.'

Oh.

'Not just any male nude, either,' Hugo said, grinning.

'You?'

'Sometimes.'

'I was in an exhibition a couple of years ago,' Caroline explained. '"Women Look at Men", it was called – there were five of us showing. Hugo was one of my models.'

'It got a government grant, I might tell you,' Hugo put in. He patted himself: 'My dick has been supported by the

Arts Council of Great Britain.'

Caroline smiled again. She smiled a lot, I noticed, but in a slightly odd way, as if she was amused by some idea of her own, rather than by what anyone else had said. She blew out more smoke: 'All the same, Hugo, Andy has a point. You *could* put on some clothes.'

That took the smarmy grin off his face.

'OK,' he said, apparently surprised. Our clothes were lying around the floor, so he just stood up and got dressed. That left me, of course, as the undressed one, but since I couldn't quite think of a way of putting on my briefs without taking off my jeans first, I stayed as I was, waiting for a chance later.

'Maybe *you* should pose for Caroline,' Hugo said as he was zipping himself up.

I saw Caroline quickly smile to me – Hugo had his back to her – and shake her head.

'It's all serious stuff,' he carried on. 'Proper art.' He picked up his tee-shirt and from behind it he added: 'That means she gets to show hard-ons.'

'Oh, do shut up, Hugo,' Caroline said – taking the words out of my mouth.

He turned to her: 'Time of the month, love, is it?'

'No, just time you grew up a bit.'

Hugo didn't reply, he simply looked at me and raised one eyebrow, as if to say, 'Women!'. But I was wondering more and more about these two – if they weren't lovers now, then I was sure they must have been some time in the past, for them to talk to each other like this.

Hugo sat down, and he and Caroline begun talking about work – all shop-talk, which wasn't of much interest to me except when they dropped the names of singers and groups on their label, some of whom were very well known indeed. Eventually I realised this could go on all evening, so I took a chance to say: 'You're going to have to excuse me. I need to be getting home.'

'Of course,' Caroline exclaimed. She stubbed out her fag – it was about the fourth or fifth she'd smoked since she'd come into the room – and stood up. 'I'll leave you two boys together,' she said with that strange smile of hers, and in the same way added: 'Hugo, are you staying on?'. He nodded.

Once I was dressed Hugo hugged and kissed me, and ruffled my hair: 'Christ, you're beautiful, Andy,' he murmured. 'Don't make it too long before I see you again, eh? Don't make me wait too long again?'. So, of course, as usual, I forgave him for all the patronising and the irritating ways he had, and reminded him it was up to him when I'd next be in London: 'All you have to do is say you need some new legal papers . . . '.

Maybe I was wrong a few pages back when I said there was nothing romantic about me and Hugo. Maybe, in his own weird way, he was quite fond of me. Either that, or he was an even better liar than I think he was.

It was the next time I saw him that he put his little scheme to me.

For reasons which you'll quickly see for yourself I have to be vague about details here. Basically, what he suggested to me that evening was that I should carry some stuff down to Brighton for him, to pass on to a pal of his. Stuff that would fit easily into my panniers. Like, CDs. For sale. With a share of the profits for myself.

Hugo had to work on me before I'd agree. I didn't tell him why I was hanging back – I was afraid that would only make him worse – but I was thinking, naturally, of that damned record of mine. In fact, at that time I was still in the two-year suspension period for my three months.

But it seemed such an easy way to earn a few extra quid. And it was. Ridiculously easy. Hugo had recently bought himself a car, and on the evenings when I was going to do a collection he would fetch the stuff from what he just called 'the lock-up'. I'd no idea where this lock-up was, and I didn't ask, but it was obviously not far from his office, 'cause he took the stuff to Caroline's flat, and I picked it up there.

Caroline, of course, didn't know anything about this. As far as she was concerned we were using her place for – for the same reason as before. Which, needless to say, we were doing as well, usually. Then I would load my panniers, ride off into the sunset, and ninety minutes later unload the panniers at Hugo's pal's place in the North Laine in Brighton. Child's play.

Soon I was going up to London on purpose for this, and we didn't even always have sex before I turned home again. Within a few weeks I'd sold the Suzuki and bought a much better bike, a 550 Kawasaki, with a fairing and all the works. I'd been thinking about this for some time, but the extra dosh from the ferrying meant I could go ahead without any worries.

And it was an investment too, the Kawasaki. 'Cause the panniers on it were much larger than on the Suzuki. Which meant I could carry more, and I could fit in videos as well. And since I got paid on a fixed rate for each item I carried ...

Sometimes I wondered if I wasn't being a total bloody fool. I mean, I would be in a hundred kinds of shit if the scam got busted. But then I reckoned I was safe enough. After all, I only had the stuff for less than two hours, on the road to Brighton. Where it all come from, I didn't ask – it wasn't just R&R stuff, Hugo could lay his hands on anything anyone wanted. And where it all went to, I was never entirely sure – I couldn't believe *all* of it got sold in Brighton. But none of that concerned me. I never kept any of it, not one bit of it, though I was often offered. But I had enough sense to realise that wasn't too bright an idea. I collected it, I left it, I put the cash in my pocket, and I went home clean as a whistle. Your Honour.

CHAPTER FOUR

About a couple of months after I started the ferrying I went up to London one day straight from work, to pick up a new load of CDs. But I was in a mood for more than just business. Or if you like, for more than one kind of trade. I'd had two bad weekends on the trot in Brighton – nothing doing at the Revenge or anywhere – which I wasn't used to, and I was getting in a bad way. I mean, you can't control a bike properly if your right wrist is aching.

It was a fine sunny evening, but despite the warmth I was in my leather. This was Hugo's wildest turn-on. The first time I wore black leather to R&R he nearly went doolally, and seriously – quite seriously – wanted me to come into the office bog with him, he reckoned he couldn't wait till the evening. So of course I made him wait. And this evening I knew that even if he wasn't feeling particularly randy before I arrived, he soon would be once I did.

But when the flat door opened, it was Caroline there.

'Oh, Andy,' she said, 'do come in. Hugo told me he was expecting you. But he had to go home from work, he wasn't feeling well at all. Come in, though.'

'Oh. I'm sorry to hear that.'

I certainly was. I had to hope my disappointment when I saw Caroline hadn't shown in my face.

'And I'm sorry you've had a wasted journey.' Suddenly she smiled wickedly. 'But come through and at least have a drink, or something. Are you hungry?'. I shook my head. 'Well, make yourself comfortable. What can I get you?'

I asked for a lager and went into her front room, which was getting to be as familiar to me as my own. There were papers strewn over half the sofa, and a large gin beside it and an ashtray with a smoking fag, so I sat down in the big armchair opposite. The window was closed, and the room was stuffy – and smoky – so I took off my jacket, feeling a bit of a prat. There I was in my tight white tee-shirt, that you could see my nipples through, and my leather jeans, and my boots – all dressed up and nowhere to go.

Caroline come back with the can, and sat down and picked up her fag – I wondered if she was *ever* without a fag – and we fell into conversation, chatting about all sorts of things to do with her work and mine. It was only the second time I'd met her, but I soon found I was beginning to like her a lot, and get on really well with her, till – till, with a second large gin in her hand, she begun to comment on how often I was at her flat.

'I think you see more of it than *I* do,' she said with a laugh.

I sort of moved in my seat.

'Well . . . Hugo says it's OK. He says you don't mind.'

'Oh, I don't,' she said at once. But then she smiled in a way that made me shift in my seat again. 'But I do like to get some rent in exchange.'

'Rent?' I exclaimed.

'Yes. A sort of – favour. In exchange for my hospitality.'

'What kind of favour?'

She smiled that worrying smile again.

'Well, in your case I know exactly what I would *like* it to be.' And she raised her eyebrows and looked at me. Closely.

And when I say closely, I mean closely. Bloody hell! It was practically a piece of quantity surveying. She might as well have produced a ruler on the spot and measured me up in both inches and centimetres. I swear that, mentally, that was exactly what she *was* doing.

I couldn't believe what I was seeing. I'd never been looked at that way by a woman, ever. By men, yes, often enough, but then, you expect it from men. But a woman!

At last she took her eyes off my middle and burst out laughing.

'Don't worry!' she said. 'You're going to tell me it's strictly men only in that department, right?'

Strictly, it hadn't been, not always. But no way was I going to admit that right now. God knows what she might have done next if I had.

I didn't have to answer. She laughed again: 'Yes, I've no illusions on that score. But a gay guy can provide a bit of fun for a woman as well, you know.'

'Sorry?'

'You can provide a bit of fun just the same. Like I said, by way of – rent. Or you can think of it as a fee. For the use of my flat for your assignations with Hugo.'

I didn't say a word. I didn't want to give the impression I was too thick to understand what she was on about. Especially since I was.

'You know I have a boyfriend – Johnny?'. I nodded, Hugo had mentioned him to me once or twice. 'You know what I like watching Johnny doing? Press-ups.'

'Press-ups?'

'Yes. I love watching Johnny doing his press-ups - best way there is of admiring a man's buns. Don't you agree?'

'Yeah, I suppose' – what was I saying?

'I'm glad you agree. Because Johnny's got a great pair of buns.' She laughed. 'And so have you.'

Oh, dear God.

'So that's your – fee. That can be your payment for use of this flat. You can do me some press-ups, here and now.' She paused. 'I think we'll have thirty. Can you manage thirty? You certainly look as if you can.'

'Thirty – ?'

'Can you or can't you?'

'Yes, but – '

'Good. Get on with it then.'

'But – '

'What are you hanging around for?'

'You want me to do thirty press-ups?'

'Yes! How often do I have to repeat myself?'

'Whatever for?'

'I've already told you! Because I want to sit here and admire your buns.'

I stared at her.

'You're seriously weird, do you know that?'

She laughed so much she choked on her cigarette smoke: 'Oh, get on with it,' she said in between coughs.

It *was* weird, I was certain of that. But on the other hand, if that was what she wanted, there didn't really seem much harm in it. I stood up, and looked down at myself.

Caroline said what I was thinking: 'You won't find it easy to do press-ups dressed like that, will you?'

'No.' I wanted to make some sarky remark, but I couldn't think of one.

'Well then, get your kit off.'

'*What?*'

'What's wrong with you now? You can't possibly do press-ups in leather and boots, can you?'

'No, but – '

'How many more times are you going to say "but"?' She laughed again. 'It's not your "buts" I'm interested in, Andy, it's your butt – B-U-T-T.'

'Look – '

'That's exactly what I intend to do. Get peeled.'

'Listen – '

'What *is* the matter with you? Will you get stripped off?'

I didn't make a move. It only seemed to amuse her: 'Oh, Andy, if you're wearing ladies' knickers, I really won't be shocked. Surprised, possibly, but not shocked.'

'I am *not* wearing women's knickers.' God, what a thing to find yourself saying.

'So what's the problem then? If your shorts have a rude slogan on them, I promise not to read it.'

I relaxed slightly, one arm on my hip.

'Look, Caroline, I don't mind a joke, but don't you think you're going too far?'

'No, I don't. You've had a lot of fun in this flat, haven't you?' I nodded, I couldn't deny it. 'Right. So now you're going to give *me* some fun. It won't take two minutes, and it's perfectly innocent. So for the last time, get on with it and get your kit off. But you'd better draw the curtains first.'

Oh, God. I decided, if it would keep her happy, I might as well get it over and done with.

I closed the curtains – since the sun was on them the room was still light – and stripped. By the time I was down to my briefs I was cursing Hugo. If it hadn't been for him and his damned fuss about underwear – bloody fetishist – I'd have been wearing a pair of shorts which would at least have been halfway decent. As it was, when I turned round from undressing I was just a little self-conscious. No more than, like, totally.

'Well,' Caroline said. 'This reminds me of the days when I used to take photos for mail-order catalogues.'

'Does it really?'

'Yes. Photographing guys in knickers all day long, and having to keep watching them change – they've no shame, male models, you know. Out of one pair and into the next right there in front of me, and me just a slip of a girl from the country.'

'Look – can we get on with this?'

She ignored the question: 'They used to say that if I was going to photograph them all morning in their underpants, modesty was a waste of time.' She laughed and nodded towards my middle: 'You can see what they meant, though, can't you? They nicknamed briefs like those "no hiding place".'

God, if Hugo had been there right then I'd have strangled him on the spot, I swear I would.

'Not that it matters,' Caroline went on, 'since you're about to take them off anyway.'

'I'm *what*?'

'I asked you to do press-ups, didn't I? I didn't say anything about modelling underwear.'

I just stared at her. Then I turned round and picked up my jeans again.

'Wait a moment,' she protested. 'What are you doing?'

'Getting dressed,' I said, putting my left foot into my jeans.

'Why?'

I stood balancing on one leg.

'Why do you think?'

She jumped up: 'Hang on, hang on. Don't fly off the handle.'

'Who's flying?'

'You are. Drop those trousers again and wait a moment.'

I was reluctant, but I couldn't 'wait a moment' on one leg. I put down the jeans and looked round. She found something on the sideboard, and come across with it.

It was a one pound coin. For a moment I thought she was going to try to bribe me into getting my pants off. I had a crack ready about the sight of my crown jewels costing more than one lousy quid, when she said: 'We'll toss for it. Double or quits.'

'Eh?'

'We'll toss for it. If you win, you can get dressed, and we'll say no more about it. But if *I* win' – she smiled that terrible worrying smile of hers – 'off come those briefs.'

I stared at her.

'You're evil, do you know that?'

'Flattery will get you nowhere. Now, do you accept the bet or don't you?'

I didn't know what to say. A fifty-fifty chance of finding myself putting on the best show in the West End? Dodgy odds, in the circumstances.

'Hurry up!'

'OK, OK. I accept the bet.'

That terrifying smile again.

'If you lose, I'll hold you to it.'

I nodded.

'Fair enough,' I said, trying not to sound as nervous as I was beginning to feel. I looked at the coin in her hand and positively *willed* it – good little coin, nice little coin – not to land me and my buns right in it.

Caroline tossed the coin and caught it on the back of her right hand. Then, to my astonishment, she took her covering hand away.

She didn't look at the coin, she looked straight at me.

'Call,' she said.

'Eh?'

'Call,' she repeated. 'It's your call.'

'You what?'

'Your call, I said.'

Still she looked at me, not at her hand. She wasn't smiling now, in fact she was quite serious.

I shifted my weight from one foot to another. I could clearly see that the coin had come up tails.

And then I understood what she was doing. And I couldn't help laughing.

Christ, but it was a clever move. A real stroke of genius. 'Cause what guy, gay or straight, faced with this, could call out 'tails'? What guy, if he was half a man, would take the chance and wimp out? Shit, she'd got me so that there was only one thing I could say.

I gave in to her. 'Heads,' I called.

She looked at the coin for the first time. She didn't give away what she thought, she just said, very calmly: 'You lose.'

She cleared the papers off the sofa and sat down, drew up her legs under her, lit yet another fag, blew out the smoke, and looked at me.

'OK,' she said. 'Pay up.'

Now that it had come to it, I wasn't all that horribly embarrassed as I tugged down my briefs and chucked them on top of the rest of my clothes. I mean, I'd stripped off often enough on the Brighton nudist beach, and as Caroline had reminded me, she was well used to seeing blokes undressed.

Even so, I didn't want to hang about – if you'll pardon the expression – and I dropped to the floor straight away.

'Over here,' she said. 'Come over here.'

I had to wriggle sideways, like a crab.

'No, closer,' she said. 'I want you right below me.'

Bloody hell, she wasn't going to make it easy for me. I got myself to within a few centimetres of the sofa. Still she wasn't satisfied: 'Move up a bit,' she said.

'Is there anything more you'd like?' I asked, with the tiniest hint of sarcasm, as I scrabbled forward on my elbows.

'No,' she said simply. 'Now I've got a grandstand view of your neat little arse.'

And immediately I thought: oh, oh. What *have* I got myself into?

'Cause you couldn't make any mistake about the way she'd come out with that last sentence. And nobody talks to you about your 'arse' unless they've got a definite interest in it, one way or another. This wasn't a joke any more, this wasn't any piece of 'innocent fun'. She was beginning to seriously enjoy herself.

And the next thing she said left no doubt about that at all: 'OK, I'm going to sit here and watch your bare buns going up and down thirty times. Get going, and count each one out loud.'

Oh dear God, I thought. This is way-out kinky. I've been hooked into an S&M scene. I spend half my life avoiding S&M with blokes, and then I end up flat on my face ballock-naked being ordered to do press-ups by a woman. Bloody brilliant.

For a moment I wondered if I should stand up and say, 'Stop there – no way.' But then I realised that standing up might not be such a bright idea either, considering how I was dressed. Oh, what the hell. I hadn't wimped out of the bet, and there wasn't much point in wimping out now. Best just to get it done as quickly as possible.

'One'- look on the bright side, I thought – 'Two' – at least she hasn't got a cane – 'Three' – and if she does produce one – 'Four' – you'll just have to grab your clothes – 'Five' – and run like hell into the street – 'Six' – and hope the Metropolitan Police – 'Seven' – will believe you when you tell them – 'Eight' – that you were running away from – 'Nine' – a woman who conned you – 'Ten' – into doing thirty press-ups – 'Eleven' – in the sweet altogether – 'Twelve' – at the age of twenty-one – 'Thirteen' – which is really going to make you look – 'Fourteen' – streetwise dude of the month – 'Fifteen' – isn't it? – 'Sixteen' – so you may as well just relax – 'Seventeen' – easy when you're doing press-ups – 'Eighteen' – and enjoy it – 'Nineteen' – and try and not think – 'Twenty' – what kind of spectacle – 'Twenty-one' – Caroline's seeing right now – 'Twenty-two' – with her grandstand view – 'Twenty-three' – charming way of putting it – 'Twenty-four' – of your neat little arse – 'Twenty-five' – she's right enough there at least – 'Twenty-six' – 'cause if you do – 'Twenty-seven' – you'll be so embarrassed – 'Twenty-eight' – even your buns – 'Twenty-nine' – will start to blush – 'Thirty'.

I lay flat on my stomach, just a little breathless. I'd never done thirty press-ups so fast in my life.

Caroline didn't say anything. After a few moments I looked round and up at her.

'Well? Are you happy now?'

She nodded.

'I think that was fair payment for the fun you've had here in the past.' She paused. 'But what about the future?'

'Eh?'

'Are you and Hugo planning to go on using this flat – if I let you?'

Ah. Tricky.

'Well . . . '

'I take it you are?'

'But that – that depends on you, doesn't it?'

'I don't mind.' She laughed. 'If I get my fee first.'

Oh, God. I hesitated to ask the obvious question. It's not often you find yourself negotiating a deal from such an awkward position.

But it had to be asked: 'What – what "fee" have you got in mind this time?'

'Well, I'm enjoying the view I've got in front of me right now so much' – oh, Jesus – 'I think I want to go on seeing it for a while. So you can just stay there, as you are. That's the fee.'

'How long for?' I exclaimed.

'Oh . . . ' She pointed across the room. 'See that clock over there?'

I twisted the other way.

'Yeah?'

'Five minutes by that clock. Then you can get dressed.'

This was kinkier than ever. But I knew we – Hugo and me – had to keep in with Caroline, if we were going to carry on using her flat as the pick-up point for my deliveries.

'OK. But not a second more.'

She laughed.

'Relax and enjoy yourself!'

Oh yeah, no problem.

'And shift over to the middle of the room. I want to stand up.'

I had to scrabble sideways like a crab again – talk about undignified – while she slid off the sofa and went across to the sideboard. I watched her pour herself another gin and tonic. Then she come back and sort of strolled around me, slowly.

'You believe in getting your money's worth, don't you?' I said. Either she didn't notice I was meaning to be sarky or, more like, she pretended she didn't: 'Yes,' she said from somewhere behind me, as cool as anything. She went on: 'Remember you're paying me rent for the good times you're hoping to have in this flat. And all you have to do is lie there and think about how your bare rump's being looked at. Which is something I can see you're perfectly used to.'

I twisted my head round: 'What do you mean?'

She laughed again: 'Andy, it's obvious you don't always sunbathe with swimming trunks on. I had plenty of time to notice that while I was enjoying the sight of your buns going up and down in front of me a few minutes ago.' She paused. 'Well? Am I right?'

'Yeah.'

'On the nudist beach?'

'Yeah.'

I practically grunted the word. Caroline stepped forward: 'So, like I said, you're quite used to lying about with a bare butt.'

'Oh, give over! I don't get people at the nudist beach walking all round me.'

She wasn't fazed: 'No, but I bet they'd like to. And what about when you're sunbathing on your back? I bet they'd certainly enjoy themselves then.'

Was there any end to this woman's cheek? Before I could think of a thing to say she went on: 'Anyway, you're not going to tell me that at the nudist beach you don't get people wandering past you looking you over out of the corner of their eye?' Suddenly she went into a ridiculous little mimic of them, with rolling eyes. Annoyed as I was, I couldn't help laughing. 'Aren't I right?' she asked. 'And I bet half of them are creepy old men with pot bellies.'

'It's a bit like that sometimes, yeah.'

She smiled.

'Anyway, the point I'm making is, you're hardly a shy lad, are you?'

It's true, not many people have called me that.

'I suppose not.'

'No. Because if you were, you'd have taken the chance to get out of all this when I gave it you, wouldn't you?'

I lay looking up at her.

Then I said: 'You think I'm a little tart, don't you? You think I just enjoy flashing my bum?'

Her reaction wasn't a bit like what I'd expected. She seemed positively startled: 'Oh, Andy, no!' she exclaimed. 'I didn't mean that at all. I just meant' – she stopped and crouched down beside me. 'I just meant, I think you're very sporting. A real sport. You've gone along . . .'. She stopped again.

Then she ran her hand lightly through my hair. 'You've gone along very good-naturedly with my jokes. I didn't mean anything more than that.'

I didn't know what to say. Her mood had changed so sudden I was thrown.

She sat down on the floor beside me, so that for the first time in what felt like ages I could look her straight in the eye.

She ran her hand through my hair again, but much more slowly than before.

'You know, Andy, you are just so bloody handsome it isn't true.'

Oh, oh.

'You know what I like most about you?'

I didn't answer. Somehow I guessed I was going to be told anyway.

'It's your smile. I bet you've broken a thousand hearts with that smile of yours.'

Oh, God. Not exactly an original chat-up line, but it was the first time I'd heard it when I was lying stark naked next to a woman. I could imagine a straight guy would think he'd died and gone to Heaven if he'd been in my position, but he wasn't, I was, and as far as I was concerned things were getting out of control here.

'Caroline – '

She put a finger to my mouth: 'Don't say it, Andy.'

She ran her hand slowly down my back. It felt cool against me, I was still sweating a bit from the press-ups. It reached the base of my spine and for a moment I wondered how far, in more ways than one, she was meaning to go. But she stopped with her hand resting just above my behind. Then she kissed my shoulder.

I couldn't believe how sexy it was, that light touch of her lips on my skin.

She straightened up slightly. After a moment she begun to rub her fingertips, very softly, across my lower back – across, and towards her again, and away again. She stopped, and for the second time she kissed my shoulder, very gently, like you kiss a child to 'make it better'. And for the second time I realised it was incredibly sexy.

She took her hand back to my neck and begun stroking me again, across my shoulders at first, and then slowly down my spine and back up, and down my spine again, and up. She watched her own hand as she did this, not looking me in the face. I wondered if she was afraid of what she would see. But as I felt her hand going softly down my back again I realised that this time I did want her to go further, I wanted her to carry on and run her hand over my arse, and then down between my legs, I'd open them so that her fingertips could brush against the back of my balls – and at the thought of it I started to harden.

Now she looked at me, and I saw that she understood. She took her hand away from my back, rested it amongst my hair, and kissed me on the forehead.

It was stupid, really. Something as simple as that, and I was hooked. I couldn't turn to face her, because I was shy about my hardening prick. I lifted the arm beside her, twisting uncomfortably, drew her down to me, and we kissed – awkwardly at first, because of the difficult positions we were in, and then properly, fully.

She slid away from me and with one movement pulled off her top. It was strange when we kissed again, so strange, to feel her breasts against me, when for years I'd been used to the muscles of men. And it was good too – different, beautiful.

The next time we separated she said: 'Andy, would you be offended if I asked you – have you ever been with a woman?'

I wasn't offended, I thought it was the most natural thing in the world for her to want to ask right then.

'Yes, I have. But not since I was a schoolboy.' And not very often then, I might have added. I had a short period when I experimented with girls. 'I'm afraid . . .'

She smiled.

'What about?'

'I'm probably not very good' – she stopped me by putting a finger against my lips again: 'Oh, hush. Nonsense.' She sat up: 'We have to do the usual boring thing. Hang on.'

She padded out of the room – she'd kicked off her shoes while we kissed – and come back a minute later with a condom.

Well, I still don't know if I was any good or not. I know how to give a bloke pleasure, and of course, with a bloke you're never in any doubt that you've succeeded – but a woman is so different. I was so unused to it all Caroline even had to guide me into her with her hand, which really embarrassed me, I felt as green as a kid years younger than me. And I wasn't sure I didn't come too soon, I doubted if I'd been able to give her any real pleasure. But the truth was, it was so good for me I couldn't hold back as long as I wanted, I shot my load with a cry of satisfaction – something I don't usually do, I usually hold my breath as I come.

Afterwards, as we lay together, I realised I was wondering why we all make such a fuss about being gay or being straight. Where's the big deal, if you seriously think about it? Making love to a woman, making love to a man – where's the huge, amazing difference, that we have to have such a song and dance about it?

It was when we were dressed, and I was back sitting in the armchair opposite Caroline – she'd filled half the sofa with her papers again – drinking an erotic post-coital mug of tea (the bike, you see), that she asked me: 'Andy, did Hugo tell you I have another show coming up in November?'

'No, he didn't.' I grinned. 'Not the same thing as last time, is it?'

'Well, it's men again, yes.'

'What a surprise!'

She laughed: 'But with their clothes on this time.'

'Really? Now, *that* is a surprise.'

She drew on her fag – I wondered if she only ever stopped smoking to have sex – and looked at me sort of sideways.

'Hugo warned me you had a bit of a sarcastic tongue in your head.'

'Christ! *He* should talk.'

'Ah.' For once she put down her fag. 'I think we should maybe – talk a moment about Hugo.'

I nodded.

'You mean . . . ?'

'Yes. I don't think there's any need . . . Do you?'

'No, no way.' I got my own back on him: 'He'd only be sarcastic.'

'Yes, he would.' She smiled. 'I mean, love him as I'm sure we both do, we both know what he's like.'

I wasn't sure about the 'love' bit, but I let it pass: 'Yeah. Mum's the word, is it?'

'Definitely.'

She picked up her fag again. As she was reaching for her lighter I took the chance to get in: 'Caroline . . . '

'Yes?'

'You and Hugo – do you ever . . .? I mean, does he . . . ?'

She laughed. 'Pay me rent, you mean?'

'Yeah.' Then I remembered she'd mentioned something to him about rent the first time I saw them together.

'Hugo's done me many favours,' she said. 'For example, posing for me for my last exhibition. And other things.' She hesitated. 'But – well, I suppose there's no harm in you knowing. He and I have never' – suddenly she was embarrassed. 'Oh, I see,' I said quickly. So he *had* told me the truth about them. She laughed, obviously to try to hide her embarrassment: 'Hugo really is totally gay. And when he has young men around him as handsome as you, I can't say I blame him.'

'Oh, give over.'

Now she laughed with real amusement: 'Anyway, what were we talking about? Oh yes – my new exhibition. I'm wondering if you would like to be a model for it.'

'*Me*?'

'Don't panic! Remember what I said – this time I'm photographing guys with their clothes *on*. In fact, that's the whole point. It's all about dress and context. I'm photographing men in very different styles of dress, in ways that underline the social meaning we give to what people wear. The way we read expectations into people we meet, from their clothes. I'm doing that by photographing my models in situations where their dress is completely out of place – so that the viewer's expectations of the model are completely confused, or undermined you might say, by the setting I've put them in.'

Don't ask me what any of this meant. I'm just passing on what she said.

'And one thing I would love to do, is photograph you in your biker's leathers.'

I was instantly suspicious.

'Oh?'

'Don't get the wrong idea! I'm not doing a portfolio for *Leather Fetishists Anonymous*, or whatever. I'd like to photograph you straight up – dressed as you are right now – maybe even with your helmet on. Have you got a black helmet?'

I just shook my head.

'And what about a jacket with studs? Anything like that?'

I shook my head again. I was totally lost.

'Well, never mind, maybe I can borrow one. What size are you? You see, my idea is . . . '

CHAPTER FIVE

Well, you know what her idea was. About a month later – the shoot had to be postponed for a week because of rain – we met up one Saturday morning in Sussex, a few miles north of Brighton. I rode out all dressed up as I'd been told to be, in full leather, and wondering, as I rolled along, whether I really was doing the right thing. I'd complained to Hugo that Caroline had more or less bullied me into it. He just thought it was a hoot, of course.

'That woman,' he said, 'has a knack you wouldn't credit for getting people to do things they'd much rather not.'

You don't know the half of it, I thought. But I kept my mouth shut, as Caroline and me had agreed.

What was making me even more nervous was that the evening before she had rung me to tell me she'd had another concept for the portfolio (that was how she put it), which was, a friend of hers was also going to come along, with her toddler son. And the boy would be in some of the photos with me.

'What difference will that make?' I asked, not expecting to understand a word of the answer.

'It'll add another dimension – put another question-mark into the mind of the viewer. Is the boy meant to be your son? Is he a young brother? Does he represent innocence, against the experience of the leather-clad biker? Is his presence an ironic comment on the church in the background – or a straightforward comment on the imposition of a masculine role-model?'

I hadn't been wrong.

Anyway, from three different directions we gathered at this country church Caroline had selected, which was in the middle of nowhere, about a mile from the village it was supposed to belong to, up a road that ended in a dirt track. God knows (no joke intended) what use it was to anyone stuck out there, but the advantage of it from our point of view was that on a Saturday morning there wasn't a soul around to embarrass me to death by watching me being photographed in black leather next to a two-year-old.

When I arrived there were two cars already there. As I parked the bike and got off Caroline come towards me, followed by her friend and her little boy: 'Hi, Andy! Let me introduce you to Jane and Tommy.'

Tommy was hanging back, holding his mother's hand. He took one look at me and promptly burst into tears.

Oh, a brilliant start.

'He's frightened of the bike!' Jane said brightly.

'No, he's not,' I said. 'He's frightened of my helmet' – and I took it off. Sure enough, as soon as he saw I had not just an ordinary head but a face as well Tommy stopped crying, and let himself be led up to me. I crouched down to say hallo to him, so I wasn't looming over him, but he was much more interested in my helmet. He tapped it two or three times.

'Hat!' he said.

You're getting there, kid, I thought.

'What I'll do,' Caroline said, 'is take a few general shots of you and Tommy, till Tommy gets used to the idea and is more relaxed.'

And so off we went.

About a thousand photographs later Caroline decided Tommy was relaxed enough – she never asked whether *I* was – and she begun trying to get him to pose with me, which was, to put it mildly, easier said than done. But gradually – flash, flash, flash, flash, flash – she got the shots she wanted, including the one that later become the poster I told you about, where Tommy was peering at her from between my legs. By now I suspected he was thinking the same thing I was – this woman's clearly off her rocker, but I'll play along with her if it keeps her happy.

'It's looking really good,' she said.

Flash, flash, flash, flash, flash.

'Are you nearly done?'

'Just a few more and then I think we can let Tommy and Jane get off.'

Flash, flash, flash, flash, flash. She was obviously having a whale of a time.

At last she put her camera down.

'That's enough for the time being,' she said.

For the time being!

As a reward for his trouble we sat little Tommy on my bike. Immediately he stretched forward to try to reach the handlebars, but of course he couldn't. So Caroline photographed him perched on the saddle. The photo never appeared in the exhibition, which I thought was a shame, 'cause, to tell you the truth, he looked rather sweet sitting there with a big soppy grin on his face. And Caroline could have said it was all to do with masculine role models.

Anyway, Jane and Tommy drove off. Then to my horror Caroline said: 'Now, I just need to finish off with a few more shots.'

'*A few more shots*? How many more?'

'These will be different,' she said. 'Hang on' – she disappeared into her car and reappeared with something metal. After a moment I saw it was a pair of handcuffs.

'What the hell . . . ?'

'I need some darker shots, Andy. That is, darker in meaning. It won't take long. Come on, put these on.'

'Is this another of your games?'

'No, it isn't.' She sounded quite annoyed. 'This is an integral part of the concept.'

'But what's it supposed to prove?'

'It adds another layer of ambiguity to the pictures. You being handcuffed could be taken as an ironic comment – '

'I'll do it, I'll do it.'

For this set of shots Caroline chose completely different angles. She photographed me from much closer in, sometimes kneeling down and sometimes, by standing on the low wall round the churchyard, from above. But it was always from the side, and every time she told me to turn my face away.

'Why?' I asked. 'Am I really that ugly?'

'Don't be silly! In fact, Andy, your face won't be seen in *any* of the pictures I select for the exhibition. The same goes for all my other models, too.'

'What on earth's the point of that?'

'It means they all remain anonymous figures. It'll make the exhibition more enigmatic – more mysterious.'

The only thing that was mysterious to me was how I'd once again managed to get myself into an S&M situation with a woman – and this time in broad daylight. But after she'd taken, like she said, a few more shots, no more than five or six hundred, she released me from the cuffs.

'Now, for the last set . . . '

Oh, for heaven's sake. I was beginning to wonder if Kodak kept a whole factory in business just to provide this woman with film.

'I want you stripped to the waist . . . '

'Oh, yes? I thought this was all about clothes?'

'It is. I'm not asking you to take your trousers off.'

'That makes a change, doesn't it?'

But I did as I was told, and pulled off my jacket and tee-shirt. Caroline took these shots the same way as the last lot, photographing me from close in, but this time straight on, either to the rippling muscles of my manly torso or to my back. I could feel the heat of the sun on my skin, and to tell you the truth, at last I was beginning to enjoy all this. A little.

'That's fine!' she said eventually. 'That's great! You can get dressed now.'

'Well, thank you.'

'I'm very pleased with this morning's work, Andy – you've been terrific.'

I had the decency to be embarrassed: 'Oh, don't mention it.' I pulled my shirt over my head but hung my jacket off my shoulder, I was warm enough without it. Meanwhile Caroline went across to her car and begun putting away all her gear.

As I watched her I felt a little mischievousness coming over me.

'Can I ask a question?'

'Of course.'

'Where did you get the handcuffs from?'

She turned round – she was half-kneeling on the front seat – and laughed: 'Where do you think?'

'You mean . . . ?'

She laughed again: 'Yes, I do mean. Out of my own – toy cupboard. Sometimes I like to keep Johnny firmly in his place.'

I don't know what my look was then, but whatever it was, it sent her into a complete fit of laughter: 'Oh, Andy, don't pretend you're shocked! Or do you think only gays should get all the fun in life?'. Before I could think of anything to say to that she went on: 'And are you telling me you've never handcuffed a man to a bed?'

'Not recently, no.'

She slammed the car door shut and locked it, and turned round with that wicked smile I'd seen on her before: 'Well, it certainly produces an effect on Johnny, I can tell you. Gets it up like a bloody flagpole.'

'Christ, you can be crude at times!'

'Oh, I do hope so. Anyway, let's go and have a look inside the church. I could do with a seat after all my work.'

I wasn't keen on going into the church – I wanted to get away and get some lunch, I was starving – but I followed her. Inside it was dark and smelled of damp, and so chilly I had to put my jacket on again. But to my amazement Caroline exclaimed: 'I should have thought to bring the camera in here. This is lovely.'

'"Lovely"?'

She didn't answer, instead she picked up a hymn-book: 'And look, it's named after you! What a coincedence!'

Sure enough, the hymn-book was stamped 'St Andrew's Church'.

'I don't know about the "saint" bit.'

'No, neither do I, now I come to think about it. But they've even got your flag!'. I looked where she was pointing, and saw a banner like the St Andrew's flag of Scotland, with a white 'X' on a blue background.

'So they have,' I said quietly.

'And the hassocks, too.'

'The what?'

'These cushions for kneeling on.' She was right, they were embroidered with the same white cross. Caroline crouched down: 'Reminds me of Johnny when I've got him tied to the bed' – and she put her hand on one of the kneelers and wiggled a finger at the middle of the 'X', looking up with that terrible smile of hers.

'Christ!' I exclaimed – before I remembered where we were. 'Don't you know how to behave in a church?'

She stood up: 'Oh, don't be ridiculous. I'm a vicar's daughter' – and she swept off up the aisle.

'You're *what*?' I exclaimed after her.

'A vicar's daughter. Didn't Hugo tell you?'

'No.' I thought for a moment. 'And neither did you.'

She shrugged.

'Well, it's no big secret. My father's a vicar in Lincolnshire.'

I sat down on a pew. A vicar's daughter who got young men doing press-ups in the buff, photographed them in black leather, and then went home to relax by handcuffing her boyfriend to the bed? It was like something out of Jackie Collins.

But suddenly I wasn't so sure I saw the funny side of it. As Caroline interested herself in the other end of the church I sat looking up at the blue-and-white banner. She hadn't thought to ask how I knew straight away what she meant by calling it 'my' flag, and I had no intention of telling her that I was, in fact, named after St Andrew of Scotland, and still less, why.

I didn't often think of my father, but now I couldn't prevent myself, and my thoughts weren't pleasant ones. You've become just like him, I thought. You've grown up to be a bit of rough yourself – nothing else. A bit of rough to give a girl a good time – but no, I knew that whatever my Mum had been like as a girl, she hadn't been like Caroline.

No, I was worse than my father – I was a bit of rough who let himself be used by a woman of a different class. 'Cause what else, really, did Caroline make of me? What was the point – suddenly I saw it clearly – of everything we'd been playing at all morning? That was the meaning of the whole thing – I was your typical working-class yob, all black leather and boots and motor-bike, being photographed in this dinky little, pretty little country setting where my sort wasn't supposed to be. That was what she'd meant by saying the setting would 'confuse the viewer'. What a load of crap! Why hadn't I realised what she was up to from the start?

She come back along the aisle and stood at the end of the pew.

'What's wrong? You look really pissed off.'

I didn't want to get into explanations, I just stood up: 'It's time I was getting home.'

'Are you hungry?'

'Yeah.'

'Good. Because I'm going to stand you lunch.'

'You what?'

'It's the least I can do for you after this morning! You've certainly earned it. A really good, slap-up lunch – there's a restaurant I know in Hurstpierpoint which is simply *fabulous*.'

I just stood looking at her.

'But I've got the bike . . . '

'There's no problem about that. You can follow me in the car. It's only about a quarter of an hour's drive.'

At last I remembered my manners: 'Well, that's very kind of you.'

'Oh, rubbish. You deserve it.'

So we went out into the sun again. But as I stood by the bike I exclaimed: 'Caroline! I can't go into a restaurant dressed like *this*!'

She turned round.

'Whyever not? You're perfectly decent.' She laughed: 'Listen, if anyone says anything, I'll have something to say to *them*. Don't worry!'

I was still hesitating. But then I thought: oh, what the hell. At least I'll be a bit of rough that got fed.

Well, the people in the restaurant *did* stare when I walked in in full leather and boots, and who could blame them? But they were far too polite to say anything, and once I'd taken my jacket off and sat down, and got my leather jeans hidden under the table, I didn't feel quite so conspicuous. Though I still wondered what they made of my accent, when they overheard it. 'Cause Hurstpierpoint isn't the kind of place where you find a lot of people who talk like I do.

I wasn't happy at all, for a long time, till I got stuck into this chicken and pasta dish which Caroline had recommended, and by Christ, it was good. That got us talking about how I lived by myself in a flat-share, and so on. Caroline seemed astonished I did all my own cooking, but – as I didn't say to her, I didn't want to be sarky over the meal she was paying for – if I hadn't learned to cook a bit, by now I'd be a lot thinner than would be entirely healthy. And I do try to make an effort – maybe it goes with being gay, I don't know. That, of course, got us on to why I'd left home in the first place, and my dearly loved stepfather. I didn't go into detail, and certainly not about how he used to use his fists on me, but I gave her the general picture.

'He might be moving out himself soon,' I told her, and as I said it I thought the words made my meal taste even better. But at once I realised it wasn't too pleasant from Mum's point of view. 'They're going through a really bad patch,' I went on. 'Though God knows why she married him in the first place.'

'Who was your real Dad?' Caroline asked. 'Do you know him, at all?'

I shook my head: 'Nah, he vanished before I was born.' I told her, briefly, what Mum had told me about him. 'He doesn't even know I exist.'

I hadn't meant this to come out sounding sad, but just as I finished I realised it had done, and I saw Caroline's eyes widen in sympathy. For several moments she didn't speak. Then she said, almost solemnly: 'Well, in that case he's a very unfortunate man.'

'How do you make that out?'

'Not knowing that he has a son like you. You're a son any man could be proud of.'

'Oh, give over!' I exclaimed. I tried to pretend I was amused: 'I'm sure he'd be delighted if he walked in here right now and found he'd got a motor-cyclist in black leather for a son.'

'What's wrong with that? Why shouldn't he be?'

I didn't want to go on with this. I said, quietly enough to make sure I couldn't be overheard: 'And what about a son who poses for photographs in handcuffs?'

Caroline laughed: 'That's art!'

'Well, we'd just have to hope he believed you.'

She wouldn't give up: 'You shouldn't run yourself down, you know. I tell you, you *are* a son a father could be proud of.'

Now I really did want to end the conversation.

'Oh, yeah? And what do you think he'd make of a son who's a poofter?'

Her whole expression changed.

'Oh, but surely . . . ?'. She looked down at the table: 'Surely . . . ?' she tried again, and then I saw that this last thrust had worked.

She dropped the subject, and we moved on to other things. But as we talked I thought how little Caroline knew about me, really – and in particular, that she was having lunch with a man with a prison sentence hanging over him, who all the same was once again dealing in stolen goods. No, I thought, if you were wise to all that, you might not be so sure what my father would think of his son.

By the end of the meal – we lingered a long time over our coffees – I had the feeling she was talking to me different from before. As if, now, she wasn't just seeing me as Hugo's well-hung young number in leather, with an arse and a packet on him she'd had more fun from than any other grown woman. No, I got the feeling she'd suddenly noticed I was a grown-up myself, with a bit of history behind me.

But then I wondered if I wasn't being unfair to her. Maybe I'd become a bit paranoiac about her being a vicar's daughter, and the rest of it. Maybe she'd always been interested in me for myself.

When we went out into the street we paused beside her car and my bike. She put her hand on my arm: 'Well, Andy.

Thanks for all your co-operation. It's been brilliant.'

'And thank you for lunch.'

She leaned forward and kissed me on the cheek, ever so lightly – almost like a sister. Then she smiled.

'See you in London again before too long, I hope?'

'I hope so.'

She spoke very quietly.

'I enjoyed the last time, Andy. I hope you did, too.'

I couldn't prevent myself grinning.

'Well, I enjoyed the ending of it, at least.'

She smiled a huge smile of pleasure.

'Good.'

We looked at each other. Then the same idea seemed to come to both of us at the same moment, and the next moment we had our arms round each other, and we were kissing properly, tongues in each other's mouths, right there in the middle of Hurstpierpoint.

When we broke apart I caught sight of some very disapproving passers-by.

Oh, I couldn't stop myself. I said very loudly: 'Anyway, Caroline. Don't forget to keep those handcuffs properly oiled.'

Her screech of laughter must have been heard from one end of the village to the other. And suddenly those passers-by were passing by at a speed you wouldn't believe.

CHAPTER SIX

It was such a fine afternoon I rode around the country for a couple of hours for the sheer fun of it, watching the villages and the farms go rolling past, and then the downs speeding towards me as I headed for home. By the time I reached the outskirts of Brighton I was dying for a slash, so I stopped at a playing fields where I knew there was a Gents, and made a very quick dash for it.

I was walking back towards the bike, more slowly this time, past a football field where there was a match going on, when I heard a voice shout: 'Andy! Andy!'

It was a guy called Phil, who I'd been at school with. I hadn't seen him for months, so of course I wandered across to him, and soon we were chatting away and catching up about each other.

'How's your love-life?' he asked. 'Still no steady bird?'

As you can gather, he wasn't *that* close a friend.

'Nothing steady,' I said, with a shrug. Then – well, it wasn't a lie, was it?: 'I've been having a bit of a fling up in London lately. Bit of a classy girl. Artist, and all that.'

'Artist, eh? You going up in the world?'

'That's one way of putting it, I suppose.'

He roared with laughter – Phil was always easily amused – and then the whistle blew for the end of the match. He shouted encouragement to the guys as they trooped off – 'that was fucking *rubbish*, do you hear?' – and then turned back to me: 'Hey, you got time for a pint? Me and these fucking useless knobheads will be going over to the Cornwall Arms – fancy joining us?'

'Are you their manager, or something?'

He looked astonished.

'No – usually I play for them, but I've got a calf strain at the moment.'

I thought about it: 'Yeah, one pint wouldn't do any harm. I'm on the bike – that's her over there, see?'

He looked across to it politely, but I could tell he was as much interested in bikes as I was in football.

'Cool,' he said. 'Listen – let's go into the dressing room, there's no point in hanging around here while we're waiting for those wankers to wash the mud off themselves.'

Well, I thought. Sometimes it's very useful not being out to some people. And sure enough, when we walked into the 'dressing room', as Phil called it – this dead scruffy, tiny, smelly changing room – there I was surrounded by a dozen guys either in the showers or coming out of the showers, and of course not a stitch on any of them. I mean, I didn't know where to look. First.

There were only three of us in there with clothes on – me, Phil, and an ugly tubby little man who I assumed must be the manager, to judge from the cheerful way he was talking: 'Fucking useless fucking wanking fucking poofy fucking girly fucking fuckers fucking . . .', and so on, and so on. I won't repeat every 'fucking' he used, or this chapter would be several pages longer, and besides, I'm trying to tell a story here, not win the Booker Prize.

Anyway, I'm hanging around at the edge of all this, sweating a bit inside my leather, when I notice one young guy about a couple of metres away – on the other side of the room, in other words – and immediately I think, well, *you're* a pretty little numberette, and no mistake. He's short, and quite skinny, but not so as he's bony, with dark curly hair, and (I'm ashamed to admit this now, but this was what went through my head at the time) with a knob on him that isn't half bad at all.

And then I notice this guy is noticing me, very quickly – I mean, with quick little glances as he's drying his shoulders, looking over to me and away again at once, but then back to me, and away again, and back again, and away again.

And I think: oh, yes?

You see, that's one of the great advantages of wearing black leather. You can suss out any gay guy you come across, 'cause I swear no gay guy on this planet can keep his eyes off a pair of leather trousers.

Then I notice the number is looking more and more

pissed off, and he's giving the manager some very dirty glances indeed. Tubby's still being the same little ray of sunshine, but he seems to be running out of ideas: 'Fucking poofy fucking nancy-boy fucking shirt-lifting fucking brown-hat fucking . . . '. For a moment the number's eyes meet mine, and very slightly – 'cause I can't forget he's got his naff mates all around him – I just nod, a tiny little nod.

Immediately he goes so red he has to hide his face pretending he's drying his hair, and I wonder his face doesn't burn a hole in the towel.

Oh, he's sweet, this kid. I like him a lot. What the fuck – God, Tubby's got me at it now – what the fuck's he doing mixed up with this shower?

Anyway, I keep my eyes off him after that, in case I make him blush again, but once everyone's dressed, and Tubby's finally run out of 'fucking's, or maybe just breath, I say to Phil, quite loudly: 'Phil! Before we go to the pub I'll just have to go across to the bike – I want to pick up my helmet.'

'OK,' he says, not in the least bit interested. So out I go, into the fresh air – and believe me, after that changing room I need fresh air – and over to the bike, which, by sheer chance, I've parked where everyone will have to pass it on the way to the pub.

I'm hanging around it, pretending to check the petrol, when I look up – and to my delight the number has come out of the changing room ahead of the others, and he's strolling across towards me.

He stops beside the bike. Already the naffs are following him.

'Hi,' I say.

'Hi.'

'You interested in bikes?'

'No.'

Well, *that* briefly takes my breath away. No wasting time with this kid.

'I'm going to the pub with Phil and your mates,' I say.

'Right.'

The naffs are closing in towards us.

'But I'm only staying for one pint, and then I'm going

home – I've got a place of my own, in Hove. It's at' – and I give him my address.

He just nods, and then he's nearly knocked off his feet by a hearty back-slap from one of his team-mates: 'Come on, my son. Beer calls.'

In the pub I chat away to Phil, and one or two of the more intelligent players – some of them can almost speak English – and pay no attention at all to the number, who's at the other end of the bar. Then, after two pints – I had to buy my round – I pick up my helmet with a clatter and tell Phil I've got to get home.

'See you again before too long,' he says, and I say: 'Yeah. See you soon' – and hope my voice carries along the bar.

Back at the flat I rushed around trying to get my room tidied up a bit, and dusting and hoovering it – the carpet changed colour – and then quickly washed all the relevant bits of me and splashed body lotion on the well-made torso and after-shave on the manly jaw-line, and was about to change into denims when I thought, no, hang on a moment here. That might be a wrong move. So I put the leather back on, with nothing underneath, and a clean tee-shirt, and then poured myself a lager, and sat down and begun waiting. I realised I was dying for a fag. Which was a bit odd, 'cause I don't smoke.

I didn't know why I was so excited about this guy. You'd have thought I hadn't had sex in months.

But when the doorbell rung I jumped up out of my one moth-eaten armchair – neither of my flatmates was in – and was at the door like greased lightning. And sure enough, it was the number, his hair still a bit dishevelled from the shower, and a sports bag over his shoulder, and a very shy look on his face – very serious, too, he didn't even smile.

'Hi.'

'Hi.'

He was so pretty I stood there for a moment like a complete idiot, just staring at him.

Then I snapped out of it: 'Come in,' I said. 'You remembered the address, then?'

God, what a bloody stupid thing to say. As if he'd have got there by trying every front door in Hove.

'Yes,' he said, still very serious.

I showed him into my room.

'Nice,' he said.

'Do you want to put your bag down?'

'Thanks.'

He put it down and we stood and looked at each other.

'Would you like a drink?'

For the first time he smiled.

'Yes, but I need a slash first.'

'Oh – right. It's just across the corridor. What can I get you?'

'A can'll do fine, thanks. Whatever's handy.'

So while he was in the bog – I was wishing I'd checked it was clean – I fetched a can from the fridge, and then thought, a glass you fool, and dashed back to the kitchen for one, and on my way back to my room nearly knocked him over as he come out of the loo.

Inside my room we stood and looked at each other again.

'Would you like to sit down?'

'Thanks.'

He chose the armchair and I sat on my bed, a single bed, against the wall. I took a swig from my can as I watched him pour his drink, carefully, holding the glass at an angle. Then I saw him wriggle a bit.

'I'm afraid that chair isn't very comfortable.'

'No, it's fine, thanks.' He put the can down and said, 'Thanks,' again.

For the second time he smiled.

'You haven't told me your name.'

'Oh! I'm Andy.'

'Hi. I'm Terry.'

And for some idiotic reason – everything I was doing seemed to be idiotic – we leaned across the scruffy carpet between us and shook hands.

'Tell me a bit about yourself,' I said, and then thought: Shit! Why haven't I put on some music?; and then: For

God's sake, calm down.

So he begun telling me what you already know about him, from what John said about that evening when we had a drink together in Westhurst, and while he's chatting away I'm watching him and thinking how nice he looks in his green cord jerkin, and dark blue shirt, and rather baggy black jeans. And how much nicer he'd look in the yellow shorts I knew he was wearing. And how much nicer yet once I'd got him back to where we started.

He asked me a bit about myself, of course, so I filled him in about being a courier, and so on, and he nodded, and asked a few questions.

Then there was a sort of gap in the conversation.

'Tell me,' I begun – I was so curious I had to ask this – 'why do you play football?'

He burst out laughing.

'Because I like it! In fact, I love it.'

'You *like* football?'

'Yes! Why not?'

'Well . . . That manager of yours – he's not exactly Mr Happy, is he?'

'Walter? Oh, he's OK. He was in a really foul mood today, though.'

'Yeah, I noticed that, somehow.'

Terry laughed again.

'The trouble was, we were total crap this afternoon. Really bad. We lost 5-1, you know.'

'Yeah, but all the same . . . All that "poof" and "nancy-boy" stuff – I could see it was getting on your wick.'

He shrugged.

'Yes, that kind of thing does. But it doesn't mean anything, it's just a way of speaking.'

'Really? Well, it's a very unpleasant way of speaking.'

Terry laughed yet again – he was starting to lighten up: 'You're right there. But I don't let it spoil the game for me.'

Well, I thought, I'll never understand this, so there's no point in going on about it.

I saw Terry wriggle again slightly.

'I did warn you about that chair,' I said.

He just smiled.

'You know,' I added, 'this is a lot more comfortable.' And I touched the bed.

He looked me in the eyes, and I looked him in the eyes. Then without a word he put his glass down and crossed the two or three feet to sit beside me.

I put my arm round him and drew him in towards me. He leaned forward, and we begun to kiss – very gently, very softly.

After maybe a minute we broke apart. I lightly stroked the nape of his neck, he had some stray hairs there, below his dark curls. Then I kissed him again, but this time not on the mouth, I let my lips wander down his cheek, feeling the stubble on his jaw-line where he hadn't completely shaved. I begun slowly unbuttoning his shirt, down to his waist, and when we separated I could see the strands of hair on his chest. I wanted to kiss him there as well, I wanted to feel that hair against my lips.

'Would you like to take your jerkin off?' I suggested.

So he pulled it off, and I drew his shirt further open. He put his hand on my thigh and ran it up and down over the leather.

'This is really nice,' he said.

'You're into leather, then?'

'No, not usually.'

'Oh?'

He smiled. 'But it's terrific on you. You really suit it.' I hugged him. 'No, I mean it,' he insisted. 'The moment you walked into the dressing room I thought how sexy you looked.'

'And I thought *you* looked very sexy, too.'

To my surprise this seemed to embarrass him.

'You know . . .' he begun. 'I've never done it before with anyone who – who first saw me when I was starkers. It feels a bit – odd.' He smiled. 'I mean, you've already seen everything I've got.'

I squeezed his knee: 'Well, why worry about that? Anyway – don't you ever go to the saunas?'

'Oh God, no. I haven't the guts.'

'"Guts"? Why would you need "guts"?'

He smiled and rubbed my chest.

'It's alright for you. You've got a great body. You obviously work out a lot.'

'No, not really. I go up the gym once a week – that's all.'

'Then it's all you have to. Why don't you take your shirt off?'

'OK.' I laughed. 'And you.'

Within seconds we were both stripped to the waist.

'There's nothing wrong with your body,' I told him as I put my arm round his shoulders.

'I'm too skinny.'

'Rubbish!'

We started kissing again. His hand went up and down my thigh, and mine up and down his, but never any higher. I thought how different he was from Hugo, grabbing my crotch and wittering on about 'eastern promise'. But I begun to wish he *would* carry on, he wouldn't keep drawing back every time he come close to my balls. It inhibited me, I didn't want to move at a faster speed than he was happy with, though by now I was dying to close my hand round his middle.

Suddenly he whispered in my ear: 'You can go further, you know.' He moved his legs wider apart. 'After all, you've seen it all already. Have yourself a good feel of it as well.'

For a moment I was startled. Then I realised that, though he'd been waiting for me to take the lead, he wasn't quite as shy a youngster as he'd been making out.

I didn't need any second invitation. I felt his hard-on squeezed inside his shorts and denim, and his hand at last exploring between my own legs.

He spoke in my ear again: 'Tell you one bad thing about leather, Andy – it's too stiff to let you get a decent handful of what's inside.'

I laughed, and whispered to him: 'You can be a crude little bastard when you get going, can't you?'

He leaned away from me slightly.

'Am I being crude?'

'Yes. But carry on!'

He come in close again.

'OK,' he said. 'Though once you're out of this leather I'll want more than a handful of you, Andy – I'll want a mouthful of good hard cock.'

'You'll have it,' I murmured.

'And what about you? You want your mouth outside what you saw in the dressing room?'

'Too right!'

'And your spunk running down my chest?'

'Yes!'

'And I've got a load of spunk waiting to shoot over you, Andy.'

'Oh, stop it!' I exclaimed, and broke away from him. 'Get your pants off *now*!'

CHAPTER SEVEN

So that was how Terry and me got started. As you can gather, below that shy surface he's as randy a sod as you ever met. I don't want to suggest sex is all we're about, like Hugo and me were – far from it – but all the same, how many johnnies we've got through by now, I wouldn't care to guess. He just has to start whispering in my ear – he does a line in dirty patter you wouldn't believe – and I'm tearing open yet another packet.

When we decided we wanted to stay together as an item, which we did about the third or fourth time we met, we also decided we'd be faithful to each other. I can't pretend it's been easy, but apart from once or twice – no more than that – I've stuck to it.

When I next went up to London I wasn't at all sure what Hugo would say when I told him this.

Well, it turned out he didn't *say* much at all. But if he'd raised his eyebrows any more they'd have been on the back of his head.

He rubbed his hand over my crotch – I was in denim that evening: 'So – no more of this for poor Hugo, eh?'

'No, Hugo.'

'You're just going to flaunt your splendid basket at me and tell me to leave it alone?'

'Oh, give over, will you?'

He squeezed me, lightly: 'Well, I shall miss our fun, Andy. I really will.'

I was embarrassed, though I might have been a lot more embarrassed if I didn't know how many other boys he had 'fun' with. But to get his mind off my basket, and anything else it might suggest to him, I asked: 'Look – what about the ferrying? Do you want me to give that up now?'

He took his hand away.

'Do *you* want to give it up?'

'Well – the money does come in very handy.'

'So you'd like to carry on?'

I nodded. He thought for a moment.

'I can't see any problem. We'll just go on as we've been doing. You can come here' – he laughed – 'I mean, come to the flat, and pick up the gear, just like before.'

I was relieved: 'Great. That's OK by me.' I added: 'If it's OK by you.'

He laughed again.

'I suppose it is. Though it means I'll have to have a cold shower every time before I see you.'

'Oh, will you stop it?'

'But give me one last grope, Andy. One last proper grope. For old times' sake.'

'No, Hugo.'

'Come on! One last feel of that dick of yours – nothing more. Think of it as a favour in exchange for me keeping you on as a courier.'

Oh God, I thought. But at least he isn't asking me to do press-ups with a bare arse.

'Alright, then.'

It was a mistake, of course. By the time he'd finished stroking my balls he had more dick to feel than when he started, and I had the sight of his trousers looking even better at the crotch than usual. As my jeans come off I thought – am I really such a hopeless little tart? Will I never learn how to say no to a good-looking guy with a bulge in his pants?

But afterwards I felt so guilty I knew I had to start learning right then. I said quietly: 'Hugo, please don't get any wrong ideas about the future, when I'm here next. This really *was* the last time.'

He smiled, and ruffled my hair.

'OK, kid.'

And give him his due, he never tried it on again. In fact, about a month later he said to me: 'You know, Andy, I've been thinking. There's not much point in you coming to this flat now to pick up the stuff, is there?'

I grinned.

'You mean, 'cause you're not getting your oats off me any more?'

'Cheeky sod! But yes, that's the gist of it. You've no idea how cold my shower was this afternoon.'

'Oh, stop it.' He had made a standing joke of this: 'I tell you, today it was minus ten. Ice-cubes hitting me all over!'

'Will you be serious? What are you getting at?'

He laughed: 'I'm getting at – you might as well come straight to the lock-up in future. I can't see any harm in it. I've talked to Gibb about it, and he's happy as well.'

'That's certainly fine by me. Where is it?'

So he told me, and like I'd thought all along, it was less than a mile from the flat, in an arch under a railway line.

'From now on you'll just go there, then?' he asked.

'OK!'

One day in October an invite come through the post to the opening of Caroline's exhibition, in this gallery in Covent Garden. It was a postcard, and at first I read the printed side of it. I hadn't been in touch with Caroline since the day of the shoot, so I was surprised, but very pleased, that the invite was addressed to 'Andy and Terry'.

It was the first time I'd ever seen that. I stood for a while looking at it, at our names joined together. Then I turned it over, and I nearly died. On the other side was a photo – the same photo that was on the poster, though of course I didn't know about that yet. There was Tommy grinning between my legs, and the church, but most obvious of all, my arse in leather.

Oh my *God,* I thought. How many of these has she sent through the post? And what's Terry going to say when he sees it?

To make things worse, the title of the exhibition was *Cool Cheek/Chic Culs,* which totally mystified me till a couple of days later, when I met Hugo again, at the lock-up. He'd got an invite as well, of course, and the grin on the man when he told me nearly split his face in two.

'Sexiest piece of paper I've seen in years!' he said.

'Oh, shut up.'

'Do you know what the exhibition title means?'

I looked at him with a horrible suspicion I was about to

find out something else I'd have trouble explaining to Terry.

'What?'

'Well, it's a pun, of course. *Chic culs* is French. It means, roughly, "nice arses".'

'*What?*'

He literally doubled up with laughter. 'And I must say she couldn't have chosen a better illustration for it!' He grabbed my behind, which as it happened was in leather again that evening: '*Culs* don't come much more *chic* than yours, kid!'

I wriggled away: 'Do you mean to tell me this exhibition is all . . . ?'

'Men's bums? I wouldn't be surprised. They're one of Caroline's main interests in life.'

Oh, my God.

Terry didn't know anything about my trips to London. We didn't meet up regularly during the week, in fact sometimes we went from one weekend to the next without seeing each other, so me being out of Brighton of an evening didn't cause any problems. And no way, no way at all, was I going to tell him about my source of extra income.

But he knew about Caroline, of course, and that I'd come on from a shoot the afternoon we met. I said I'd got to know her at the R&R office, when my firm was handling their law case. And I felt I had to tell him something about what had happened between us. I said I'd gone to her flat once, to collect papers from her, and that we had ended up – in more than a business relationship. But I didn't tell him *how* she'd seduced me. I couldn't think of any plausible explanation of why I'd ended up face down on her living room carpet giving her a chance to make comments about the sun-tan on my *chic cul*.

He wasn't offended, or hurt – it had happened, after all, before he come on the scene. In fact he seemed amused more than anything, and even begun to sound like Hugo: 'If you must insist on wearing leather that leaves nobody in any doubt about what sex you are, what do you expect?'

'That's a bit rich, coming from you. I don't remember hearing any complaints about how tight my leather was when I walked into that changing room.'

I warned him what some of the photographs Caroline had taken were like: 'I had my shirt off for some of them.'

'Well, I suppose we should be thankful you managed to keep your trousers on for a change.'

'Oh, ha, ha. But that's not all – for some of them she put me in a pair of handcuffs.'

'Oh, really? You never told me you were into bondage.'

'I am *not* into bondage. They were purely for – artistic reasons.'

He hooted with laughter: 'Oh, yes! What an excuse!'

But I'd no idea that my arse was going to be used to advertise a whole exhibition of arses. Which is not the easiest thing to tell a boyfriend you've only being going out with for a couple of months.

I showed Terry the invite when he come round to the flat that Friday evening. At first he was just the same as when I'd told him about Caroline: 'Well, you've found fame at last. Or maybe I should say, *in the end*.'

'Oh, very funny.'

And he begun singing: 'Andy Bowman, Superstar, who are you . . .?'

'Will you shut up? What we have to talk about is – are we going to the opening, or not?'

He looked at the photo in his hand.

'Do you want to go?'

I'd made my mind up about that several days earlier.

'No.'

He put the invite back up on my mantelpiece.

'Why not?' he asked.

'Well, can you imagine it? A room full of strangers looking at photos of my bum? And checking out to see if it's as good in real life as it looks on the wall?'

He laughed: 'Come on, you're not the only guy in the exhibition. Why should they pick on you?'

'But, Tel – think what sort of people they'll be.' I hesitated. 'They'll be arty types, Tel. London arty types.'

He nodded slowly.

'Ah. Right.'

'I mean, we'd stick out – well, I would, anyway – like a sore thumb. The moment I opened my mouth.'

He nodded again.

'You think they'll be saying to themselves, "Oh, that must be the bit of rough in the leather"?'

'That's exactly what I think.'

'Well, you could be right.'

'I know I'm right.'

He grinned: 'Let's talk about it later, when we get back.'

So we set off, heading first to the Marlborough and planning to land up at Club Revenge. That night we were going to be able to stay together till morning, which of course we couldn't do very often. But sometimes Terry spun a yarn to his people about how he was meeting mates up in Haywards Heath – he made out he knew them through the football – and that he'd be too much over the limit to drive home the same night. Except when he did this he had to leave me about two or three, which meant we didn't often go on to the disco after the pub.

As we walked along Western Road I was hoping Terry would agree with me about the opening. Everything I'd said to him was true, and it would have been enough reason to stay away just by itself. But I had another reason – we were bound to meet Caroline and Hugo, who was sure to be there, and I was terrified that one or other of them would blurt out something about my London trips.

When we reached the Pavilion Terry said: 'Andy, let's not bother with the Marlborough. Let's go to the Black Horse instead.'

I was astonished. The Black Horse wasn't really our kind of pub. It's the sort of place where you meet people who are doing Lesbian and Gay Studies at the University, and the barman writes for *Gay Times*, and things like that. But I agreed, and we turned off towards it.

We'd only had a couple of pints when Terry surprised

me even more: 'I don't fancy the idea of the Revenge after all. Let's go back to the flat.'

'Already?' I exclaimed. It was hardly half-past-ten.

'Yes. I'd prefer that.'

'Well, if you're that keen, I'm certainly not going to object' – I was making a joke of it, but I could see that something funny had come over him, he was in a much more serious mood than earlier.

Once we were home – by now my flatmates and their girlfriends were all out, so we had the place to ourselves – we sat in the kitchen with a couple of cans. And suddenly Terry come out with what was on his mind.

'Andy, you know how we're trying to be faithful to each other . . .'

Oh, God.

'Yeah?'

He looked me straight in the eye.

'Have you been?'

I'd have liked to lie, but I couldn't. I shook my head: 'But only once, Tel. Just the once – with an old flame. He kind of got the better of me.'

He didn't say anything.

I had to ask it: 'What about you?'

He nodded, and said quite casually: 'Oh, yes. I have been.'

I felt about two centimetres high.

'I'm sorry about that time, Tel. Since then I've stuck to it, I really have.'

He smiled.

'I understand.'

But then his voice changed completely. He burst out: 'Andy, I think I'm incredibly lucky to have you at all. I really do.'

I was so stunned, at first I was speechless. He looked as if he might be about to cry.

I leaned across the kitchen table and took his hand: 'What makes you say that, Tel? Why shouldn't you have me?'

'Because it won't last. You're so sexy, Andy – you're too

sexy, loads of people will always be after you. You'll always be able to have more than me.'

And then I realised what was behind all this – that blasted invite sitting on my mantelpiece. At that moment I wished I'd never heard of Caroline, let alone posed for her fucking photographs and allowed her to turn me into some kind of public property. I held his hand more tightly: 'Tel, that's nonsense! Don't you know *you're* incredibly sexy, too? Don't you know I thought that the moment I saw you?'

He half smiled: 'When I hadn't a stitch on?'

'Yeah. And I thought straight away how beautiful you were – and don't you think I couldn't believe my luck when you turned up here? Do you imagine I just took it for granted?'

'But Andy, sometimes I feel there's nothing of you that's really mine. Just *mine*.'

'I'm sorry – I don't understand . . . '

'There's nothing we do you haven't done before. Nothing that's special to *us*.'

I realised I had to be very tactful here: 'But, Tel, you had done everything as well . . . '

'I know, I know.'

'And we're special just being ourselves. What we are. I've never had a relationship like this before – no-one's ever meant as much to me as you do.'

I hadn't known I was going to say that till it come out. For a moment I wished I hadn't. And then I was ashamed. 'Cause it was true.

He was smiling again, a bit more convincingly now: 'And I've never had a relationship like this either. I just wish – I wish we could do something *special*. Something neither of us has ever done with anyone else in the world.'

I wondered what he was driving at: 'Have you got something in mind?'

He shrugged.

'I don't know.' He hesitated. 'Have you ever had sex on the beach?'

I wished I could have answered differently.

'Yes – I'm afraid I have.'

He laughed – I was glad to see he was recovering: 'I might have guessed. What about up on the downs?'

'On the downs?'

'Yes.'

'Well – no, I haven't.'

He was immediately eager: 'Well, let's do that. Let's do that tonight – let's drive up to the downs, and have it there.'

'Tonight?'

'Why not?'

'But Tel – it's the middle of October.'

'So? It's a very mild night. And I've got a rug in the car – we can put it on the ground, and we'll have no bother at all.'

I was amazed by what had come over him.

'Are you sure about this?'

'Yes!' He picked up his can and drained it: 'Come on!'

He was so keen I couldn't see any way to object: 'OK. Let me finish my beer.'

He stood up: 'While you're doing that I'll get the necessary.'

So a minute or two later we went back outside, and into Terry's car, and it wasn't long before we were on the road to Falmer. At a high point up there Terry turned off on to a farm track, and we bumped along it for maybe a quarter of a mile. Then Terry stopped, and switched off the head-lamps. To one side the ground fell away steeply into a dip, where there was some mist gathering, and across the hollow you could see the lights of Falmer clearly. But here on the ridge we had the downs completely to ourselves.

For a minute or two we sat quiet, looking into the darkness. Then Terry said: 'Maybe this wasn't such a great idea, Andy.'

I was tactful: 'Well – perhaps not . . .'

He turned to me: 'I just wanted . . .'

'Never mind. It's nice being up here, just the two of us. Why don't we go for a little walk?'

'OK.'

We got out, and stood side-by-side looking at the lights of Falmer and the roads and other villages, further away, towards the Weald.

'I'm dying for a slash,' I said after a while. 'Watch out.' I hadn't been kidding, it seemed to last for ages.

When I'd finished Terry asked: 'Tell me – would you have done that with any other guy?'

'Done what?'

'Just unzipped yourself where you were and got on with it like that?'

'You didn't mind, did you?'

He laughed: 'No, of course not. That's not what I meant.'

And I understood what he was getting at. I tried to imagine Hugo there beside me – and I knew I'd certainly have been a lot more self-conscious, 'cause he'd have been sure to come out with some crude remark about it.

'No,' I said. 'I don't suppose I would.'

'That's what I thought,' Terry said. But he seemed pleased that I'd confirmed it.

'Let's walk on,' I suggested.

So we did, along the track. There was enough light for us to see where we were going, though once or twice we stumbled on chunks of flint. We stopped when we reached a point where the track turned at a sharp angle, heading up the slope of the ridge.

We leaned on a fence there, looking along the downs. A dog was barking somewhere, and you could still hear the traffic from behind us and below us, but otherwise there was quiet, and a few stars, and us.

We didn't speak, we didn't touch each other, we just leaned side-by-side for a long time. Then Terry turned round: 'This is nice, Andy. This is really nice.'

'Yeah,' I said.

'This is something to remember,' he added quietly.

I wondered *when* he was imagining he'd remember this. But I didn't want to ask.

'Still,' he said, straightening up and speaking more quickly, 'it's turning a bit chilly now. Shall we go back?'

'OK.'

We were soon in the car again. Terry reversed it carefully to the road, and within just a couple of minutes we were coming over the crest of the ridge. All the lights of Brighton were spread out below us, and beyond them the dark of the sea, and above the sea the sky full of stars. And I thought I had never seen my native town looking half so beautiful.

Once we were home we didn't speak about the outing, we made ourselves coffee to warm us, and when my flatmates and their girlfriends come back we sat joking with them and drinking vodka for a long time.

But when we were alone in my room again we had more than good sex – we had great sex, the greatest sex we'd had yet.

We went up to London to have a look at Caroline's exhibition the Saturday after it opened.

The first thing we saw when we arrived outside the gallery was that poster.

'Oh, my God,' I said as we stood in front of it. 'She might have warned me about this.'

It didn't upset Terry, like the same photo on the invite had done. Rather the opposite – it set him off singing 'Superstar' again.

'Will you be quiet?' I whispered to him as we went upstairs to the gallery, which was on the first floor. 'And keep your trap well and truly shut about who's on that poster.'

'OK, Superbowman.'

'Oh, *God* . . . '

The first strange thing about the exhibition was that all the photos, every single one of them, were in black and white. The second was that despite what it was called it wasn't just *culs* at all, though there were quite a few in it as well as mine. It was, like Caroline had said at the beginning, all guys dressed in very odd ways, considering where they were – such as the man in rugby kit (very muddy, too) shopping in what looked like Harrods. Or the guy in the queue to get into the Brighton Pavilion, in a complete skiing outfit – including skis. (Since the photo had obviously been taken on a summer's day he must have been boiling.) A lot of the photos made you laugh, though I suppose the funniest were of a poor man in swimming trunks, who she'd got to pose in all sorts of odd places, and always with a little dog beside him – watching the Changing of the Guard at Buckingham Palace, for example, or doing press-ups on a London tube. The best thing about *that* was the way all the other travellers were trying to pretend they hadn't noticed there was a half-naked man exercising at their feet. It would have been nice to think Caroline had had to ask them to look like that, but I'd an awful feeling she didn't. On the other hand, the man in a clown suit outside the Houses of Parliament had gathered quite a little crowd of amused onlookers.

And in the middle of all this, half-a-dozen photos of yours truly, with my shirt off, and in handcuffs, and with little Tommy. I couldn't judge how well they went with the others, but Terry got chatting with the man in charge, who was looking after a bookstall, and when he come back to me he said: 'Guess what? All but one of those photos of you have been bought.'

'Will you keep your voice down?'

He didn't: 'Not only that, but you can buy the poster as well. And he says they're selling like hot cakes.'

'Oh, Jesus . . . '

But I was flattered, of course, I'd be lying if I said I wasn't. Even though the thought of what some people might get up to in front of the poster made me squirm a bit at first – till I got used to the idea. After all, if looking at a picture of my arse has given a few guys a really good wank, why should I mind? At least I've brought some pleasure into the world.

There was never any chance, though, of me letting all this go to my head. For the rest of the day, and off and on for weeks afterwards, I had to put up with Terry calling me 'Superbowman'.

But that was nothing compared to what I had to put up with

from Hugo when I met him ten days later, at the lock-up.

'I've got the poster up on my office wall!' he told me. 'So now I can sit and contemplate your delicious behind all through the working day. Even Monday mornings are a pleasure now!'

'It's amazing how you can go off people,' I said. It didn't stop him: 'And I've ordered a copy of the full portfolio, to brighten the dullest wet weekend. Which reminds me – Caroline asked me to tell you she'll soon be sending on a set of prints to you as well.' He paused. 'Have you written to congratulate her on the exhibition?'

'Well – no, I haven't.'

'Then don't you think you should? After all, she's made you into one of the sex symbols of contemporary gay London.'

'Oh, *will* you give over?' – I was quite relieved that at that moment we were interrupted by Gibb, the owner of the lock-up, and one of the main partners in our little business enterprise.

I did write to Caroline, of course, a day or two afterwards, to tell her that Terry and me had seen the exhibition and enjoyed it. I sat for a long time with my pen wondering what to say next. In the end I just finished off: 'PS. Terry asks me to tell you he liked the poster.'

A couple of weeks later I got a parcel which turned out to be a large folder with nearly two dozen prints in it from Caroline's shoot – a whole load more than the ones she'd chosen for the exhibition.

Enclosed was a Christmas card, on which she'd written:

To Andy – a great sport
a terrific model
and a fantastic pair of buns
and to Terry – a very lucky guy

'That's nice of her,' Terry said when I showed it to him. 'But she's a bit blunt, isn't she?'

'In what way?'

'Making that remark about your "buns". Don't you mind?'

'Oh, it takes all sorts,' I said casually.

And so we went on, through that winter and spring, without much happening at all, really. Terry and me turned into more and more of a couple – complete with some terrible rows sometimes – and Hugo and me carried on in business together, though my ferrying runs were getting fewer and fewer, down to about one a month by the late spring. I never saw Caroline at all, though I heard her exhibition had gone on tour, to York and Glasgow.

Everything seemed just fine and hunky-dory, till one evening in May when I was at the lock-up with Hugo and Gibb, as usual. My panniers were full, and I was getting ready to set off back to Brighton, when a police car suddenly appeared at the end of the lane, come along to where we were, and stopped. Four coppers got out, all in uniform, put on their caps, and walked up towards us.

Now, if this had been tv or a film, at this point we would have run off as fast as possible in the opposite direction, and the coppers would have come chasing after us, leaping over a couple of fences on the way, and cornered us next to a set of dustbins – the villains always get cornered next to a set of dustbins – and we would all have been panting and sweating as the coppers grabbed us and twisted our arms up our backs.

But the fact was, there was nowhere we *could* run, since twenty metres further on the lane come to a dead end against the railway embankment. And in any case we were too gob-smacked to move, never mind run. So the coppers didn't have to leap over fences, or break into a sweat, or produce cuffs on the spot, or anything. They just calmly approached us and ever so politely told us we were under arrest.

CHAPTER EIGHT

This last part of my story I'm going to pass over quickly, 'cause a lot of it is too painful for me to want to write about in detail. And besides, I can't say too much about the ins-and-outs of the case, because of the other people involved.

The gist of things was, the police had had an eye on us for ages, and not just in London – the Sussex police had been watching the place in Brighton where I did my deliveries, and my bike had been noticed there, of course. It really was a total mess – not a hope in hell of a defence, because of how we'd been caught red-handed. Nothing to do but plead guilty to a set of specimen charges, and hire a solicitor, which of course I did quickly, to think up some kind of mitigation.

Unbelievably, though all this happened in May, the hearing of the case in the Magistrates Court was set for September. We were told this was because a couple of others who were involved, but who I'd never even heard of till then, were pleading not guilty to some more serious charges which were also being laid against them.

Hugo and me didn't get away from court till nearly lunchtime on the day after we were arrested. He was in a hell of a state, poor guy – he'd found it all much more of a shock than me because, of course, he'd never been inside a cell before. As we stood in the street he turned to me.

'Andy, I don't know what to say. If it wasn't for me you wouldn't be in this mess. I've told the police that in my statement – I've told them it was all my fault you got involved.'

Scruffy and tired as I was, I had to smile.

'Hugo, that's very decent of you, but there's something you don't know. This isn't the first time I've been in trouble with the law.' I told him about my previous conviction for dealing. 'So you don't have to go blaming yourself. I'd have got mixed up again in something, sooner or later. I'm just that kind of guy, I guess. A jerk who never learns.'

He was dead concerned then, he started to wonder what might happen to me, but I shut him up quickly. I didn't want to think about that right the very moment we'd stepped out of custody.

The next news I had of Hugo was that he'd lost his job overnight. My only hope – and it was a pretty slim one – was that I could keep things quiet in Brighton because the case was being heard in London. But that would only be possible if I got off with a fine, or another suspended sentence. But as it was, I was lucky I was out of the two-year suspension period for my last conviction. So things didn't look at all good for me in that respect. My solicitor confirmed to me, what I'd known straight away, that this time I was almost certainly looking at an actual spell inside.

And this was what I had to tell first my Mum, and then Terry.

I can't say anything about how I told Mum, and how she reacted – you'll just have to imagine that for yourself. It's too awful for me even to think about, let alone write about. In all the business, nothing, absolutely nothing, hurt me like that did. I coped with all the rest of it, but I very nearly couldn't cope with Mum's tears – she cried, but what was worse, she didn't call me any of the names she could have done and should have done. I even think she blamed herself, somehow – maybe for the fact that I didn't have a father when I was young, or maybe for how Bowman had treated me when he was around.

And the irony of it is, if my stepfather had still been on the scene – he and Mum had separated by this time – and if he'd taken a belt to me and thrashed the living daylights out of me for how I'd hurt her, I wouldn't have raised a murmur of protest. After all the times he hit me and punched me when I didn't deserve it, on that occasion I'd have deserved everything he might have given me.

I told Terry on a Friday evening, when he come round the flat. I had to sit him down and break it to him as gently as I could, that for near enough nine months he'd been going out with a crook who already had two convictions and now seemed to be heading for a prison sentence.

He went horribly, unbearably, quiet. I already knew him in that mood, and what it meant. When he got angry he didn't show it at first like ordinary people, he just seemed to go right into himself, and brood. Usually this made me furious, and I would provoke him till he burst out and we could have a proper, open quarrel. But this time, of course, I wasn't angry with him.

I'd already thought about the possibility – I wondered if it was even more than that – that he'd break it off with me at once. After all, in a sense I'd been lying to him ever since we met. The Andy Bowman he'd thought he was having an affair with wasn't the real Andy, or at least not the whole one.

After a long, long terrible time when he hardly spoke, and I was trying to reassure him I'd be OK, he suddenly stood up.

I looked up at him, convinced he was about to tell me he was going home. But instead he said: 'We'll talk about it more later. Meanwhile let's go to the Marlborough.'

It was a pretty dismal evening, as you can imagine. Even the alcohol didn't seem to have much effect, though both of us were drinking much faster than usual.

Then about half-ten or so Terry excused himself, and went over to the payphone. I wondered who on earth he could be calling at that time – I even wondered if he was ringing up an ex-boyfriend to say, 'Hey, fancy joining me in the Revenge tonight? I'm on my own again.'

But when he come back he said: 'I've just been ringing my folks. I've told them I've met some guys from the team and we're going on to a party, and I'll be staying over at one of their flats.' He said it so deadpan, as if it meant nothing particular. 'They're quite happy about it.'

I wanted to hug him right then, and I suppose in the Marlborough I could have done, but I knew it would be wrong, he didn't need to be rushed.

When we got back to the flat we didn't talk about the business, we just drunk the remains of a bottle of wine. Then Terry said – I was letting him decide everything: 'Can we have an early night and go to bed, Andy? I'm too tired for anything tonight. I've had a very busy day at work.'

Of course I agreed. But it was the first time he'd ever been 'too tired' for sex at the end of the day.

I begun to wonder, though, if he hadn't been partly telling the truth, since he fell asleep very quickly. God knows how long I lay awake – it felt like hours – before I too fell into a kind of doze, troubled by dreams in which I couldn't forget I was in a terrible mess, though in my dreams it was for stupid, bizarre reasons.

I was woken by a strange noise behind me. I realised Terry was making weird sounds, and still being mostly asleep I couldn't work out what they were.

Then I felt a wetness on the back of my neck, and at the same moment it dawned on me what was happening. I twisted round and stared at Terry's face, just inches from my own.

'Tel,' I said. 'Oh, Tel – don't cry, Tel. Please don't cry. It'll be alright, Tel – I'll be alright. Please, Tel, don't cry.'

We said many things then, whispering to each other in the dark. He told me he'd stay by me, however things worked out. He said he couldn't bear to think of me in prison, but he couldn't bear to lose me. He said I was the best thing that had ever happened to him. I told him I didn't deserve him, that he deserved better for a boyfriend than a crook and an ex-con. He told me it didn't matter, that he'd help me sort out my life when I got out again, and that he just wanted us to stay together. And I told him there was nothing else, nothing in the world, I wanted more than that, whatever I did with my life once I'd put all this trouble behind me.

We decided we wouldn't let the thought of what might be coming in the autumn spoil the summer for us – we were going to enjoy it, and worry about the future when the future arrived.

That summer started with terrible weather, cold and miserable right up to the end of June. Then, suddenly, it changed, into the hottest and driest summer for years.

And we had this fantastic break – out of the blue one of Terry's bosses, a Mr Carson, told him he was looking for someone to house-sit his place in the country and look after his dog while he was away on holiday. With the result that at the end of July we moved for three weeks to a huge, luxury house in Westhurst, complete with a garden which was so private we could sunbathe in the nuddy there no trouble at all.

Next door to us was a very similar house, which we'd been told was sub-let in the summer as a holiday place. The first week we were in Westhurst it was taken by a family with horrible screaming kids, but much to our relief they went off on the Saturday.

Things were so quiet then we thought the house was standing empty, till we spotted a guy coming and going who seemed to be staying there on his own. He was middle-aged, a little plump, but a very dapper figure, and one evening I remarked to Terry, after we'd seen him passing the front window, that I was willing to bet a penny to a pound he was one of us. I just couldn't imagine a straight guy of his age going on holiday alone, and besides, he had that air of looking after his appearance which no middle-aged straight man ever seems to have.

My job was taking me up to London more than ever, to a new office we'd opened there. To be honest I could have done without this – London wasn't exactly a city of happy memories for me. One evening I'd just got back, wearing my leather despite the heat in case I had a spill at speed, when I bumped into our neighbour right by the front gate. Much to my amusement his eyes popped down to my trousers – that old test that never fails. Then he looked very embarrassed about what he'd just done.

'Told you so,' I said to Terry when I went indoors.

The next day when I come home I was surprised to find Terry in the garden in his football shorts, since, like I said, we sunbathed in the buff there. He told me how the guy had walked in on him earlier holding a parcel, which sent me into fits of laughter: 'I bet that's the best thrill he's had in years!'

'Oh, don't be mean, Andy – he was only being neighbourly. He's a nice guy – took an interest in Rex, and everything. Oh, and by the way, he told me to tell you he reckons that's a fantastic bike you've got.' He grinned. 'You'd think a man of his age would have more sense than to be interested in motor-bikes.'

Two or three days later I got home to find Terry all ready to take Rex out for his evening walk, and I went with them without bothering to change out of my bike gear. By the time we were on our way back to the house I was gasping for a slash so badly I had to pop behind a handy tree.

I was at my business there when I heard Rex barking, and then Terry talking to someone. I zipped myself up, and come out to see that it was our friendly neighbour again, stopping for a chat. As I walked across to them I noticed, and I couldn't quite keep a straight face, that this time he was very obviously *not* looking at my jeans.

We introduced ourselves to each other, and shook hands.

And you, of course, already know what that handshake meant. It was the most amazing thing that has ever happened to me, perhaps the most amazing thing that ever will happen. At the age of twenty-two, I had met my father.

PART THREE

JOHN AND ANDY'S STORY

CHAPTER ONE

I had never regretted not having children. Indeed, as I grew older I even began to think of my childlessness as a positive aspect of my life. I imagined my children reaching their late teens and being faced with unemployment statistics which my generation thought had been banished into history; I imagined them as students living with a financial hardship which I had never so much as contemplated as an undergraduate. Each remorseless, savage undoing of the work of the Attlee government during the Thatcher years made me more and more glad I had brought up no youngster to reach maturity in such a society, where nothing was of more importance than making money, and the principle of lowering taxation had been granted the status of a divine commandment. Even my father, who had been a Conservative all his life, refused to vote Tory in 1979 and 1983, but instead – to my amazement – voted Nationalist.

Because our shop is close to the Grassmarket, where many down-and-outs congregate, I was particularly aware of the growth in homelessness. Every winter I saw more and more lost, drunken, drugged wanderers in the Edinburgh streets which literally lie below the tourist city.

But there was also, of course, a straightforwardly selfish side to my feelings about my childlessness. As I watched my heterosexual contemporaries being ground down by parenthood – and ageing much faster than I was – I knew I remained free to do easily what they could do only with difficulty: to travel, to live in comfort, to read in peace, to continue intellectual exploration with undistracted energies. On winter evenings when I sat by my fireside with a good book in my hands, a glass of malt beside me, and Mozart playing on the stereo, I did not consider myself an unlucky or an unhappy man.

As Andy told me his story that night in the King and Queen he became visibly nervous. I realised he was afraid of my reaction – perhaps imagining I would immediately turn against him, or that at the very least he would lose the place in my affections he had gained in just one week. His fears were groundless. I can truthfully say that as I absorbed the significance of what he was saying there wasn't for one moment the slightest qualification in what I felt for him. I saw at once that he'd been stupid, of course – very stupid. But even while we were discussing the implications of what had happened, and I was questioning him about the details of his legal situation, the thought went through my mind that in that respect he was recognisably the son of the man who once groped a seventeen-year-old boy in a school changing room.

We concentrated on practicalities; I think that made the conversation easier for both of us. I was certain he was being too pessimistic about the likelihood of his going to prison: 'You've got yourself a good lawyer?' I asked.

'Yeah,' he said, and suddenly, briefly, smiled. I realised he was thinking about his newly-discovered grandfather, and smiled too: 'Well, in that case, he should be able to make out a very good case that you were talked into it – conned into it, even. He could say it was all because of Hugo's influence, and that you – '

'Oh, I don't want that,' Andy interrupted me.

'Why not?'

'Well, it would make me look a right dork, wouldn't it? As if I was so soft-headed any idiot could talk me into anything.'

I was firm – I could hear, to my astonishment, my schoolteacher's manner coming back to me after all these years: 'Listen, if it makes the difference between a hefty fine and a prison sentence, it doesn't matter if your solicitor has to pretend you were a complete innocent abroad.'

'With *my* record?'

'Well, that's certainly the most difficult problem we face. But there's ways even round that – you've told him, I suppose, that you and Hugo were having an affair?'

Andy was positively shocked: 'Christ, no! I don't want that coming out in court at all. That would make things a hundred times *worse*.'

I saw at once that he was right: 'Yes . . . Yes, I imagine it would.'

'Too right it would. Remember that Hugo and me got together before the age of consent was changed – that was against the law too, when we started. So were Terry and me, till a few months ago.'

I nodded: 'Of course, of course. Yes, on second thoughts it would be best to say nothing in court about you being gay.'

He looked at me as if it was me, not him, who was in need of advice.

'Yeah, I'd worked that out.'

Grim as our topic of conversation was, I couldn't help smiling. He had worldly wisdom, of course, where I had none.

'Well, listen, we've still got time to think about this . . .'. I sat back and looked round the packed, noisy pub. 'I'll put off going back to Edinburgh again, for a few more days. There shouldn't be any problem about that. If I can't stay on in the hotel I'm in at the moment, I'll easily find a room somewhere else.'

Andy was surprised: 'What good will that do?'

'I might be able to think of some way I can help.' I shrugged. 'I don't know. Apart from all else, I need to talk to your mother.'

Andy laughed: 'Oh, God! My parents getting together to talk about me!'

It took me a few moments to understand what had amused him; then I realised I still hadn't fully adjusted, mentally, to the fact that I was now one of a pair of 'parents'. Heavens, but it was an odd, odd sensation to hear Andy describe me like that.

'If you carry on like this,' he added, 'you'll never get back to Edinburgh.' We both laughed.

He looked at his watch: 'Listen, I've got to be going soon. I'm due to meet Tel at half-nine.'

'Certainly.' I finished the last of my pint. 'Be sure to give him my regards. Since I'll be here for a few more days, maybe I'll have a chance to take the two of you out for dinner one evening?'

Andy's smile suggested he saw an irony in this invitation. A moment later I saw it myself. Obviously he was thinking of the last time I had invited them to join me, in Westhurst.

Outside, he headed off towards one of the town's gay bars, and I went for a long, slow walk along the Palace Pier. I needed the refreshment of the sea air, after the shock of yet another conversation containing yet another revelation.

At the end of the Pier I leaned against the railing, with all the racket of the funfair around me, and pondered the bizarre timetable of this holiday which had begun so placidly. Two weeks ago, I thought, I knew no more about Andy than his name. It's only one week since I learned he's my son. Now I learn he might soon be going to prison. This, as Glaswegians would say, is nae real. Just nae real.

What next? I thought. All we need now is for Caroline to announce she's pregnant by Andy and I'm about to become a grandfather. What a selling-point for this town: come to sunny Brighton and get yourself a horde of descendants.

I saw a couple of people a few yards along the railing look at me very oddly. I realised I had begun laughing to myself, and turned away quickly, red with embarrassment.

As I walked back towards the land I wondered why I had been laughing. What, after all, was so funny? It certainly wouldn't be funny for Andy if he did go down and had to serve time – and him gay, too – in one of Her Majesty's disgusting prisons.

And as for me – as my steps clattered along the wooden pier slats I realised I was at last beginning to realise that I was, indeed, a father, with a son to care about and worry about.

I saw May on Sunday afternoon. We sat in her front room again – Andy was out somewhere.

'Now you know what I meant when I told you he was "uncontrollable",' she said, so wryly that I burst out laughing. Through those days I frequently found myself laughing unpredictably – no doubt, as a release of tension.

'I nearly told you about all this when you came round here that first time,' May went on. 'It was on the tip of my tongue, but then I thought – poor John, he's got enough to cope with as it is.'

'You were certainly right there. I've decided to ration myself to one shock a week.'

Now May laughed: 'I hope there's no more to come!'

'Well, you never know' – and I told her my theory that Caroline might be the next person to surprise us. But May was surprised for a different reason: 'Caroline – pregnant by – ? Are you saying that Andy and Caroline . . . ?'

Oh, God. It simply hadn't occurred to me – I was so inexperienced in this role of being 'a parent' – that Andy would hardly be likely to discuss the details of his sex life with his mother.

'Apparently, yes – but just the once,' I said quickly. 'At her flat, once.' (This was all I knew myself at the time. Andy hadn't described the rather baroque nature of the incident to me, but even if he had, I can safely say I would have shared his reticence about discussing that with May.)

'Well, I never!' she exclaimed. 'What will he get up to next?'

I couldn't help grinning.

'May,' I said quietly. 'He's not the first predominantly gay young man to have a fling with a pretty girl – now, is he?'

She went into a peal of laughter: 'Oh, John! You haven't changed a bit!'

I sat back in astonishment: 'What? I don't think that's entirely true.'

'Oh yes it is. You were a sweet-talking rogue twenty years ago, and you're no better now.'

'Me?' I exclaimed. 'Was I ever "sweet-talking"?'

She nodded.

'Oh yes, John. You were.'

I just sat and stared at her. Then I shifted forward again: 'Well, anyway – to get back to Andy . . . '

May laughed: 'To get back to Andy . . .?'

'I don't think we should be too pessimistic about what's going to happen to him. There's no reason at this stage to assume he's necessarily bound to be sent down.'

'But he's told you about that earlier trouble, hasn't he? And what his solicitor said?'

'Yes, but I think his solicitor might just be warning him – to be ready in case the worst happens. I'm going to stay on here for a few more days yet, to see if there's anything I can do to help.'

'Such as what?'

I shrugged.

'To be honest, right now I haven't a clue. But I want to at least try.'

May shook her head and smiled.

'Oh, John. You're a good man, you really are.'

I had to very quickly make a joke of this: 'Are you determined to embarrass me this afternoon? One moment I'm a seducer, and the next moment I'm a saint!'

She laughed: 'But it *is* good of you to be so concerned about him. You only met him ten days ago.'

My jokiness was gone as soon as it had come.

'What difference does that make?' I said quietly. 'He's my son – that's all that matters to me.'

Now May's expression was almost solemn.

'Are you still angry with me?' she asked.

'About what?'. Then I understood, and shook my head: 'No, no,' I went on quickly. 'That's history now.'

We looked at each other. I wanted to say more; I wanted to go on: 'The important thing is I've found you both again at last'. But my reserve – that Scottish curse that lies over my whole character – made it impossible for me, as it had done so many times in the past, to express my deepest feelings.

May broke the silence: 'What worries me most, John, is what'll happen if he does go down. I mean, it's not just that he'll lose his job – how on earth will he ever find another one, with a prison record?'

'Oh, come on, May. Things won't be as black as that, whatever happens.'

'Won't they? Do you think it's likely he'd find another job in Brighton?'

I didn't want to try to imagine that far ahead: 'Well, May,

we'll cross that bridge when we come to it.'

To my surprise May started to laugh: 'Good Heavens, John! You really are your son's father!'

'Sorry?'

She was still laughing: 'That's exactly what Andy said when I asked him the same question. "We'll cross that bridge when we come to it."'

Once again I fell back on humour: 'I see. So you're telling me that me and my son both talk in clichés?'

'I don't know about that. Maybe you're just as feckless as he is!'

In the end it turned out there was, indeed, very little I could do to help. I satisfied myself that Andy had found himself a competent solicitor, and beyond that, I was powerless to alter the course of events.

There was just one other thing I could do; I told the solicitor that when the case was over his bill was to be sent to me. At first May protested about this. She had been preparing to meet all the legal costs herself, and felt that at most we should split them fifty-fifty. But I was insistent. It wasn't that I wanted to flash the fact that I was, relatively speaking, a wealthy man; it was simply that, to quote Dickens, 'a great many back-payments were included'.

Before I left Brighton I took Andy and Terry out to dinner, as I had promised. It was a pleasant evening, with a steady flow of conversation and jokes. We never once touched, of course, on the subject of what was now approaching rapidly; the hearing of Andy's case was just three weeks away. Nonetheless there was an undernote, faint but discernible, of awkwardness about us, and I was in little doubt as to its nature.

I had, as I had so strongly wished, ceased to see Andy in sexual terms. I admired his handsomeness, and was glad to be in his company as one is always glad to be in the company of a good-looking young man; but the incest taboo had already exercised its massive psychological power on me. As soon as I had really begun to think of him as my son, and the idea wasn't an improbable, ludicrous joke, I could no longer lust after him. It was as if a sluice gate had closed in me against an entire current of feeling: and had closed never to reopen again.

But the same wasn't true of Terry. He too was, as Andy has described him to you, an extraordinarily attractive boy. And neither of us could possibly forget – though, naturally, it was never spoken of – how I had discovered him in their Westhurst garden sunbathing in the nude. When he walked into the hotel reception beside Andy, when we strolled through the Lanes towards the restaurant, when he went to the bar in the pub afterwards, I couldn't not notice his slim figure, what a fine, tight arse he had, the creases at the crotch of his jeans.

I need hardly say that though we drank heavily – I treated the boys to their first-ever taste of champagne – I maintained an iron discipline over my eyes. I never let them rest where they often wanted to rest; but Terry, as you already know, was no fool. I guessed that he guessed how much I was having to resist a recurrent temptation.

It was only afterwards I realised the dilemma I was faced with that evening couldn't have been in any way exceptional. How many fathers have had to come to terms with an identical problem about their sons' *girlfriends* – or even their wives? This must be one of – another of – the great unspoken facts about heterosexual life; for any middle-aged straight man is just as vulnerable to the beauty of young women as I am to the beauty of young men.

I finally left for home almost a fortnight later than I had originally planned. In Edinburgh my flat lay exactly as it had been when I had left, except for the pile of mail on the mat and thin dust everywhere.

I turned on the fire – in Edinburgh, even in August an unoccupied flat becomes damp – and put some Schubert on the stereo. I went quickly through my post; there was nothing in it but bills and catalogues and magazines of the book trade.

Then I poured a huge tumbler of whisky and sat in my leather chair, that was once my father's. I looked round at the shelves and piles of books, and my antiques, and my paintings, and the furniture which I had partly inherited and partly bought through the years of my prosperity.

Nothing had changed; nothing, except me. I had changed, and I knew I would never again, could never again, be the same John Paterson who had locked up that flat just four weeks previously.

I drank long and deep from my whisky.

CHAPTER TWO

I knew the first time I come up in court for the hearing of my case nothing definite would be decided. They never do anything straightforward like that, to make things easy for you. No, the most that would happen would be a three-week remand for a social work report, before sentencing.

It turned out even that nearly didn't happen. There was a terrible mix-up about the case against Hugo and me and the case against the others who were involved, who were still pleading not guilty. Our lawyers and their lawyers and the prosecution lawyers all got together in a huddle, the magistrates looked crosser and crosser – I couldn't say I blamed them – and after two adjournments it was finally decided, would you believe, that Hugo and me should have been dealt with separately from the very beginning. (But afterwards my solicitor told me he thought the prosecution had been hanging on in the hope they could pin some extra charges on us as well.)

So Hugo and me pleaded guilty, again, and like I said, we were remanded for three weeks.

Poor Hugo! He was very different from the guy who'd grabbed my arse at the top of the stairs in R&R, two years before. I tell you, my stomach turned over when I saw him that morning in the court lobby. He'd lost weight, he was pale, he was clearly terrified of what might be going to happen. Of course, the thought of going to prison must have been far worse for him than it was for me. I mean, I wasn't exactly thrilled by the idea, but at least I'd be among more or less my own class, and I reckoned that somehow or other I'd cope.

But Hugo was totally middle-class, he had a posh accent, he'd never had a rough time of anything, and to cap it all he was gay – Christ, but it would be hard for him inside, unless he was sent on quickly to an open prison. I tried to joke with him about it, but sort of seriously: 'I don't know what *you're* worried about – *you* haven't got any previous! You'll just be told you've been a naughty boy, and get a fine.' But it didn't work, I don't think he believed me.

All the same, I suppose you shouldn't feel *too* sorry for him. Old lags have a saying: 'If you can't take the time, don't do the crime'.

Anyway, we come out of the court together, into a lovely sunny day, and said cheerio to each other, for three weeks.

Christ, but three weeks pass quick when there's a prison gate waiting for you at the end of them.

A few days days later it was my birthday. I stayed at my Mum's the night before, and when I come downstairs in the morning there was a card from her, of course, and one postmarked 'Edinburgh'.

'Hey!' I exclaimed. 'John's remembered my birthday!'

'I've a feeling,' she said, 'it's a date he'll find quite easy to remember.'

It was a classy card, too, with a nice picture of some Scottish mountains and a loch. While I was looking at it Mum pushed a little brown parcel towards me: 'This is from your Dad and me.'

For a moment I was astounded – why had Bowman suddenly come back on the scene?

And then I realised who she meant.

It was a watch, a flash new watch, which I'd been badly needing.

'Fantastic!' I said. 'Hey – thanks!'

'Well, you can thank your Dad that it's a bit more expensive than you might have got otherwise. He rang me up to ask if I had any ideas about a present for you, and I said I was going to buy you a watch, which I knew you wanted, and we decided to go halves on it.'

I put it on and admired it – it had real style.

'Thanks!' I said again.

'Well, don't forget to write to your Dad, or give him a phone.'

It was the third time she'd spoken about my 'Dad'. Yet he'd signed his card 'John', I always thought of him as 'John', and I always called him 'John'. I wondered if Mum was trying to drop some kind of a hint.

'I will,' I said.

I looked at the watch again, and put John's card up on the mantelpiece. And then I thought – well, it *is* bloody decent of him to remember my birthday, and pay towards a present, considering that it's not much more than a month since we first met. Maybe – maybe this business of us turning out to be father and son had really meant a lot to him?

I intended to ring him, honest I did. What made me keep putting it off was thinking how the conversation was bound to move on to other things I didn't want to talk about. So in the end I dropped him a little line. I'm afraid it was like when I had to write Caroline to congratulate her on her exhibition – it was, you could say, brief and to the point. I'm hopeless at writing letters like that, I never know what to say.

As for Terry – he bought me a very sexy pair of silk boxers, and that night he sucked me off when I was still in them. He said this was a birthday treat as the second half of my present, but I think I can definitely say it was a shared treat.

A Probation Officer come round to see me, for the social report. I had a pretty fair idea what to expect, 'cause I'd been through all this before, the last time I'd been done for dealing. In fact, the Officer had a copy of that report with her.

She was a cheerful, good-looking woman, called Pat, maybe in her early forties or so. She couldn't have been friendlier in her manner. She was dead taken with the fact that I'd looked after myself for several years, and when she found out I could cook I thought she was going to go into ecstasies. In fact, she was so friendly I soon begun to suspect it had to do with something more than my amazingly attractive personality. And I knew for a fact when we got on to the subject of my 'home circumstances'.

'Have you got a steady girlfriend?' she asked.

'No, I haven't.'

She laughed: 'Still playing the field, are you?'

'Well, not that either.' Oh, God. 'I've got a steady boyfriend.'

Well, I tell you, her face fell a mile, and I didn't think it had anything to do with homophobia – a Probation Officer, in Brighton of all places, wouldn't get very far in their job with that kind of attitude.

'Oh, I see.'

I noticed she didn't write that down.

'I don't want anything coming out about that, though,' I said quickly. 'I don't think it would help at all.'

'No, you're right. It wouldn't.' She chewed the end of her pen, and then begun scribbling again: 'We'll just say you haven't got a regular girlfriend at the moment.'

But later on we come to a much more ticklish point. She started asking me all sorts of questions about Bowman – he was mentioned in my previous social report – and the whole business of me growing up without a Dad, and then how Bowman had treated me. I got more and more uneasy, till eventually I said: 'Listen, I don't want all this coming out in court. My Mum's planning to be there, and I can't have her sitting listening to all this. It's bad enough as it is, the way she blames herself.'

'Oh, the details won't come out in court,' Pat said at once. 'And you must be realistic, Andy – this could make a crucial difference to how the magistrates look at you. A history of child abuse is something that's given a lot of weight nowadays when a court's considering an offender's background.'

'I wasn't abused!' I exclaimed. 'Bowman wasn't *that* bad – he never laid a finger on me.'

'That's not the only kind of abuse, Andy. What you've been telling me about would still be regarded as child abuse.'

'But I wasn't a child either! I was eight when my Mum got married.'

Pat just smiled. I was getting really annoyed, I didn't want her making out I was a pathetic victim of tragic circumstances, or any of that kind of crap. But she was absolutely stubborn: 'Andy, believe me, this could mean the difference between you going to prison and you staying out of prison.'

Well, since she put it like that, I had to think again. So though I was still reluctant, I gave her more details about my stepfather, and she wrote them all down.

'What about your real father?' she asked. 'Are you in touch with him?'

'Yes, I am.' Suddenly, I don't know why, I felt dead proud I could say that. 'He's a businessman in Edinburgh – he has his own shop.'

'Good,' she said, and duly wrote it down. Fortunately she went on to something else. If she'd wanted to know *how* I was in touch with John we'd have been there till midnight.

Towards the end of the interview I asked her, quietly, what she thought I'd get. Straight away she looked glum.

'It depends on who you come up in front of – which magistrates are sitting that particular morning. It's very much a lottery, I'm afraid.'

I knew that, of course. But I had to have it confirmed. Pat cheered up: 'But let's not look on the dark side! We can only do our best for you.'

Then, for a moment, I thought I caught her looking at me with something like pity. And that annoyed me again.

I had to start preparing for the worst. My flatmates were brilliant, they promised to look after my things and help sort out about my rent being paid by the Social Security, and so on. And one of them had a mate who was willing to put up the bike in his garage, so I arranged to take her round there the night before I was due in court again.

God, though, but it was a strange feeling leaving the bike with him not knowing if I'd be picking her up again the very next evening – or not for months. Fortunately he knew about bikes, he'd had one himself once, so I could rely on him to look after her properly if she was standing unused for some time.

Then there was the question of how I'd keep in touch with Terry. It wouldn't be possible, of course, for me to write him at home – his folks might have some questions to ask if letters started arriving with 'HM Prison' stamped all over them. But once again my flatmates come to the rescue. It was agreed I'd write to him care of my own flat, and they'd ring him at work when they had a letter for him.

The worst of all was knowing what the hell to do about my own work. I arranged to take another day's leave for the second hearing, there was no difficulty about that. It was what was going to happen afterwards that caused the headache. I was still hoping, of course, I'd get away with all this, and be able to breeze in again the following morning with a yarn about how I'd had a nice day out up in London.

But suppose I couldn't? Suppose instead I was breezing into a prison dining hall?

Mum and me talked round and round the problem for hours before we finally decided there only seemed to be one possible solution, and it brought back all the guilt I'd felt at the very beginning of my trouble. If it become necessary, Mum would have to write to the office and tell them what had happened.

Imagine having to ask your mother to do something like that. If you can, you'll understand exactly how I felt when I realised I had no choice.

And once again you'll have to imagine a lot of the details of those final few days, because I can't write about them, it's too sad for me to think about. Terry and me spent an evening together not knowing if it was going to be the last time we'd see each other for weeks, or just for forty-eight hours. He was being incredibly brave, but – oh, shit. Shit, shit, shit. At the end of the evening he blubbed a bit, he couldn't help himself, and I have to own up – he wasn't the only one.

I spent the night before the hearing at Mum's place. She was absolutely determined to come to court, nothing on God's earth was going to stop her, though, to be honest, it was the last thing I wanted.

And that wasn't all. John insisted he was going to be there too – he was going to come back down from Edinburgh for the hearing. I couldn't believe my ears when

Mum told me he'd been on the phone. I was amazed he would travel all that way just because of me.

At first I didn't know what to make of it. Part of me didn't want yet another person sitting in court listening to whatever garbage the lawyers and the magistrates spouted, and then maybe having to see me being taken down from the dock.

But it was obvious that in the short time since we'd met John must have become very fond of me, even though he still really didn't know much about me, and the bit he did know couldn't have been all that encouraging. And for the first time I realised that the fact I was his son was important to him, so important that he'd make a round journey of eight hundred miles just to be near me when I was facing the worst trouble I'd ever been in in my life.

CHAPTER THREE

I hadn't thought twice about going to London for Andy's hearing; even before I left Brighton I planned to be there. When I rang May to find out the details she was surprised, but I told her: 'May, it would be intolerable sitting up here wondering what was going on – I wouldn't be able to concentrate on anything else.'

'But, John . . . It's such a long way to come, for something that might not last ten minutes.'

'That's not the point. Besides, it isn't far for me – you forget I'm used to travelling up and down the country on business.'

This was, I have to admit, stretching the truth; my work very rarely takes me south of Yorkshire. But May was satisfied: 'If you really insist . . .'.

'I do. Anyway, I *ought* to be there – don't you think?'

There was quite a silence on the line before she replied.

'Well, John, I wouldn't have blamed you if you weren't. But I'm sure Andy'll appreciate it. And I know I will – I might need some moral support, if . . . If things don't go well.'

I had already thought of that; it was perhaps the main reason I was determined to be present. There was nothing practical I would be able to do for Andy, other than show him I cared about him, but I had a mental picture of May having to leave that court on her own and go back to Brighton by herself, and I couldn't bear it. I didn't tell her on the phone, but I was ready, if need be, to travel down to Brighton with her, to spare her the dreadful loneliness of that journey.

I had to prevail yet again on Sandy's good nature to look after the business for the couple of days I would be away. I was perfectly frank with him about the reason for my trip, and, as ever, he was kindness itself, though by now my private life must have begun to seem quite surreal to him.

I arranged with May to meet her and Andy at Victoria on

the morning of the hearing.

In the best of circumstances London is not my favourite city, and these, of course, were hardly the best of circumstances. I had come down the previous afternoon by train, and checked into an hotel in Bloomsbury. But after I had eaten I had no idea how to fill my time; neither the theatre nor the cinema had any appeal, since I knew I would never be able to get my mind off Andy. In the end I drank in a couple of pubs, retired to my room early with a book, and then found that between the traffic noise and my anxiety it was nearly impossible for me to sleep. I was awake by six.

Andy had to be in court for half past ten. To make sure there was no chance of their being late May had decided to take a train which arrived in Victoria a few minutes before nine. It drew in on time, but disgorged such a colossal mass of commuters – I had forgotten just how strange the lifestyle of the south-east of England is – I had difficulty spotting May and Andy amongst them.

Then, suddenly, there they were, right in front of me, smiling. And I was pierced with a tenderness for both of them I had never anticipated, a tenderness so sharp I could hardly speak.

They were in their smartest clothes. Andy looked astoundingly handsome in grey flannels, dark jacket, and tie; he stood some six inches taller than his mother, who, in a turquoise business suit, had the air beside him of being squired by a young gallant. The purpose of their journey seemed beyond belief – beyond belief the possibility that before the end of the day Andy might be wearing prison denims and May travelling home alone.

I had to work hard to hide my reaction. I made myself smile too, and speak conventional words of greeting: 'How was the train? Did you manage to get a seat?'. I suggested, as we were hurried past by the commuters for whom we were no more than an irritating obstacle, that since we had plenty of time we should go for coffee nearby. They agreed; and we strolled in the middle of that frenetic throng as if we were up in London for a long slow day of leisure.

It was only then I noticed that Andy was carrying a small bag. Instantly my stomach churned; I realised it must contain the few personal possessions he would be allowed inside.

Over coffee we did the best we could to be cheerful, talking about anything and everything except what was foremost in our minds. A tube took us quickly to west London, and within five minutes we had joined that morning's collection of the puzzled and the lost in the entrance hall of the Magistrates Court.

I recognised, with a cold sickness, an all too familiar atmosphere. More than once I have had to be a witness in our local Sheriff Court in a case of shoplifting, and have stood in just such a crowd with the same dismay. The legal system might be different, the accents might be different, but the social complexion is exactly the same: a wave of sad humanity pushed up against the entrance door to the court, and moving amongst them, dark and detached, the lawyers for whom they are merely another day's work.

My father, I recalled, always told me he hated criminal cases, and once he was established at the Bar avoided them completely. I have never had any difficulty understanding why.

We found a hard bench to sit on. We had been there maybe five minutes when Andy exclaimed: 'Ah! There's Hugo.' He jumped up: 'I'd better have a word with him.'

He pushed his way across the lobby and greeted a short, blond man who turned and recognised him with one of the sickliest smiles I have ever seen on any human being.

'He looks absolutely terrified,' I remarked to May.

'So he bloody should be,' she said, with startling venom.

'You blame him, then?' I asked.

'Don't you?'

I shrugged.

'I don't know. Andy's old enough to make his own mistakes.'

I wasn't sure how she would take that. She didn't say anything for a few moments, and then remarked: 'It looks as if he's by himself.'

'Seems like it,' I agreed. 'Maybe he doesn't get on with his family.'

'Still, you'd think' – she cut herself short.

We fell silent again. I was watching Hugo, of course, with a double curiosity, and I wondered if May shared it. I could see why Andy had found him attractive, though his looks were too conventional for my own taste; he had the dull handsomeness of a male model, which always leaves me cold. He and Andy were talking with an air of forced cheerfulness which, again, I recognised from my visits to the Sheriff Court, till they were joined by two men who were obviously lawyers, and the conversation at once turned serious. It was some minutes before Andy came back across to us.

'Hugo's shitting bricks,' he said.

'Andy!' May exclaimed.

'Sorry, Mum.'

In the middle of all that dismalness, I had to laugh.

'I think, May,' I said, 'this is hardly the time to worry about Andy's language.' They both smiled.

We were stuck on that bench for the best part of an hour, while the magistrates dealt with what I imagine must be the everyday fodder of a court in that part of London – a succession of 'notorious and public prostitutes', as I think English common law describes them. Then, about half past eleven, they reached the first substantial case of the day. It was ours.

* * *

The moment Hugo and me stepped into the dock I knew we were sunk. 'It's very much a lottery who you come up in front of', Pat had warned me, and I saw straight away our luck was out.

There were only two magistrates sitting, instead of three – I don't know why. The Chairman was a large, grey-haired man, who never gave over frowning. It turned out this was due to the fact he was slightly deaf, so he had to strain all the time to hear what was being said. The solicitors and everyone spoke up, but even so, every so often he'd turn his head to one side and frown more than ever, to let them know he was losing them again. Like a lot of deaf people he spoke louder than he needed to, and what with that, and the solicitors raising their voices for *him*, the whole case went on as if they were standing at opposite ends of the Albert Hall or something.

But what really chilled me was the little man sitting beside the Chairman. If there's a sourer-faced human being walking this earth, I hope I never run into him on a dark night. His mouth turned down hard at each end, and his frown looked as if it was chiselled into his face – he seemed to be trying to frown even more than Big Brother next to him, like they were in a competition with each other or something. He had a bent pair of specs which were sitting skew-whiff on his nose, and behind them his eyes were tiny and dark.

From one glance at the man you could tell he'd come into this world to send people down. That was the meaning of his life, sending people down. Everywhere he turned his eyes in the court you could see he was wishing he could stick someone in chokey. His filthiest looks were aimed at social workers and Probation Officers, he seemed to be thinking that twenty-five years apiece would be letting them off very lightly. While the solicitors were spouting he looked at them like he was trying to make up his mind between a tenner and a fifteener. He even glared at coppers as if he thought six months inside wouldn't do them any harm, either.

But after the prosecution had said their bit, which didn't last long, my mind was taken off the magistrates by the stuff my own solicitor started coming out with, in mitigation. I couldn't believe what I was hearing. It was everything I had told Pat I *didn't* want brought up in court – how I had been the child of a single parent till I was eight, and how my stepfather had mistreated me, and how I'd had to leave home at seventeen to get away from his violence – I just cringed, I thought I would rather get double whatever was coming to me, rather than have to listen to all this with Mum sitting no more than a couple of metres behind me. God, I tell you, that was the most embarrassing five minutes I have ever lived through. When Hugo's solicitor was speaking, sounding off about Hugo's previous unblemished record, all I could think of was what Mum must be feeling, and what might start going through her mind if I wasn't with her to cheer her up on the way back to Brighton.

There was a recess while Laurel and Hardy went off to decide whether we should just be hanged, or drawn and quartered as well for a bit of extra fun. Our lawyers come across and leaned on the dock, chatting to us. It was all I could do to be polite to mine, but I thought this wasn't really the best place to choose to pick a quarrel.

I twisted my head round and saw Mum sitting next to John, looking every bit the serious businessman in his dark suit. I smiled to them and they smiled back, but they were the hammiest smiles I'd ever seen. Then John leaned closer to May and whispered something to her which I saw really did make her smile, for a moment.

I turned back towards my lawyer and I thought: thank *Christ* John's here. If the worst comes to the worst Mum won't have to walk out of here on her own – John'll look after her, he'll know exactly what to say to reassure her.

And then I thought how sometimes I'd had real doubts about him coming all the way from Edinburgh to be there, wondering if he wasn't being – well, pushy, to be honest. Overdoing the 'I-am-a-caring-father' bit – showing off, in fact. And suddenly I felt dead mean, I realised it had been absolutely right for him to come, for Mum's sake more than mine. 'Cause she had no-one else she could turn to in this mess.

I felt a lump coming into my throat, and I thought, oh God, this is no time to start getting blubby – but fortunately for me, just at that moment we had to stand up again because Pearl and Dean were returning.

Hugo and me had to stay standing, of course, to hear our sentences. No need for a long story about that: he got a year and I got three months.

So when we turned to leave the dock it wasn't back towards the public benches, but to the entrance to the cells. And straight away I got a nasty surprise. During the case there had been a copper standing behind the dock. But suddenly he'd moved, without making a sound, to be inside the dock – the first sign to us that we were now prisoners.

* * *

I watched May at the payphone in the pub, talking earnestly. The conversation wasn't a long one.

'How did he take it?' I asked as soon as she came back.

'Very bravely, of course. He's been terrific right from the start. I tell you, Andy doesn't deserve him.'

'I don't think you mean that,' I said, with a slight smile.

'Oh yes, I do. Anyway, he reckons it's less than Andy thought he might get – he was afraid it would be six months or more. But he couldn't say too much, not with him being in the office.' May had arranged to ring Terry there in his lunch-hour if anything definite was known by then.

'Well, at least he was prepared for it.'

May sighed.

'I feel really sorry for Terry sometimes, honestly I do. His people sound *awful*. Not to mention very stupid. Apparently they haven't a clue about him being gay – unless he's wrong about that, of course.'

I remembered how Terry had spoken of his 'old man' that evening in Westhurst – it felt like several centuries in the past – and then also how he had exclaimed, 'Andy's Mum's great!'.

'Well, at least he's got you he can turn to,' I said, deliberately interfering in what, really, was none of my business. I was pleased to see May wasn't offended: 'You mean we can cry on each other's shoulders?'

'There's no reason for anyone to cry on anyone's shoulders. Andy'll only be inside for six weeks, with remission.'

'Assuming he *gets* remission. What if he gets into more trouble in – in there?'

'Oh, May, that's hardly likely, is it? He's not that stupid.'

'Isn't he?'

I knew this was no more than an expression of exasperation.

'Come on,' I said, finishing my whisky. 'Let's go back to Victoria and get something to eat.'

We had agreed, though neither of us was in the habit of drinking at lunchtime, that we needed a shot of alcohol after we came out of the court. The pub we were in was perfectly pleasant, and we could have had sandwiches there, but I was sure that May felt as I did – now we had had our drinks, it was time to get out of that part of London fast and put its associations behind us.

'I'm not hungry, John,' she said as she finished off her own gin.

'Yes, you are,' I insisted – and immediately wondered, as I had done when Andy first told me about his trouble, how it was I could so easily lapse back into the manner of a bossy schoolteacher. But damn it, I thought, sometimes you have to be a bit of a do-gooder, for other people's sake.

We didn't talk much as we walked to the tube, nor while it whisked us eastwards again. But once we were settled in a café crowded with London office-workers, inevitably we returned to the subject neither of us could forget for one moment.

'You say, "only six weeks", John,' May remarked, 'but this is going to be the longest six weeks of my life.'

And maybe of mine, I thought. But I felt I had to maintain the rôle I had undertaken: 'They'll soon pass, May.'

'I bet they won't for Andy.'

'From what I've read about prison, the first two weeks are the worst. After that, it's not nearly so bad.'

May looked at me oddly, and then, for the first time since we had left court, she smiled.

'John, I know you mean well, but I'm not sure that's terribly comforting. What do you imagine is happening to him right now?'

'You mustn't think like that,' I said at once, and much more firmly than I had spoken before. 'That's one thing you must avoid – trying to picture what Andy's doing at any given time. He'll get on alright, somehow – that's all you need to think about.'

May smiled again.

'You really are determined to make me cheer up, aren't you?'

This was true, but I wasn't going to admit it.

'No, I'm just trying to be sensible.'

'John, what would I have done without you today? You've been an absolute godsend, you really have.'

All my Scottishness flared up immediately: I was deeply embarrassed.

'Oh, nonsense.'

'It isn't nonsense at all. If you weren't with me right now I'd be sitting in a corner on my own somewhere, snivelling into my hanky.'

I wasn't having this: 'No, you wouldn't. You're a strong woman, May. You showed that twenty-three years ago.' I meant, by standing up to her mother on the issue of the abortion; but as soon as I had come out with the words I realised they could be interpreted quite differently. And instantly it was clear May took them that way: 'Did I? I haven't been much of a mother to Andy, have I?'

'What on *earth* do you mean by that?'

May looked down at the table.

'You heard what the solicitor said in court.'

Oh, God. I had been appalled by his mitigation speech; I knew May would brood on it.

'That was a defence solicitor talking,' I said – and suddenly, ten years after his death, I heard my father's voice echoing in my own. 'He was just doing his job – doing everything he could to get his client a lesser sentence. All that was meant for the magistrates' ears, and nothing else. You don't want to give it a second thought.'

May raised her eyes: 'Why not? It was true.'

'No, it wasn't. You know your husband wasn't half as bad as he was being painted today.'

May shook her head.

'I know you mean well again, John,' she said. 'But I'm not convinced.'

I leaned across the table: 'May, you mustn't start blaming yourself. I told you before – Andy's a grown man of twenty-three. At that age he has to take responsibility for his own mistakes.' May merely looked at me. 'Promise me you're not going to blame yourself.'

She shook her head.

'I'm sorry, John. I can't.'

I was about to protest further; but then thought, no, I've browbeaten her enough in this conversation. This is something she has to work through for herself.

Fortunately at that moment our order of soup and sandwiches arrived. I wasn't hungry, any more than May had said she was, but I set about the food determinedly, and was pleased to see May start to eat in the same spirit.

When we were at our coffees she glanced at her watch.

'I can get a fast train in half-an-hour. Good timing.'

I pondered the suggestion which had been in my mind since before I left Edinburgh.

'May – do you want me to come with you?'

She was astonished: 'Come with me? To Brighton?'

'Yes.'

'Whatever for?'

'Just so you've got some company.'

'But I thought you were going back to Edinburgh today?'

I'd already worked that one out: 'There's no problem. I can come down with you now, stay a couple of hours, and be back at Kings Cross in time for the last Edinburgh train this evening.'

She sat and gazed at me.

'John, it's very kind of you, but I really don't think . . . '

'There's no problem,' I repeated. 'It would just mean you wouldn't be on your own when you got back.'

Still she gazed at me.

'No, John,' she said eventually. 'It isn't necessary.'

'Are you sure? You've not exactly got some pleasant duties to return to.' We'd already discussed how she would have to write to Andy's office to inform them about what had happened.

'I know. But I can cope.'

'Are you sure?' I asked again.

She nodded: 'Yes. I've coped with worse things in my life.' She smiled: 'And what about you? You're going all the way home to Scotland – how are *you* going to cope?'

The idea had never troubled me. I shrugged: 'I'm used to being on my own. I've lived like that for years.'

'Well, there you are then.'

I didn't follow her logic; but before I could press her further she leaned across the table and took my hand. She smiled again: 'I guess we're just both very independent spirits – don't you agree?'

I grinned.

'I suppose that might be true.'

'Both bloody-minded members of the awkward squad.'

'Are we?' I wasn't certain I recognised myself in the description. But May nodded, smiling again: 'Oh yes – that's us, alright.'

Suddenly she started to laugh.

'No wonder we managed to produce such an *impossible* son!'

So in the end I saw her on to the Brighton train, collected my overnight bag from Left Luggage, and was at Kings Cross in time to catch the three o'clock train to Edinburgh. By nine I was sitting in my flat watching the evening News. It was just twelve hours since I'd met in May and Andy at Victoria.

Throughout the next six weeks I didn't take my own advice to May about not imagining what Andy was doing. Over and over again, as I talked to a customer in the shop, or drove through the Borders, or sat reading at home in the evening, I found myself trying to picture him. All my images came from tv documentaries, but I had little doubt they were mostly accurate. And they weren't comforting.

I made efforts to stop myself; when I caught myself at it yet again – 'he'll be being banged up about now,' as I crossed Princes Street on my way home at the end of the day – I deliberately switched to other thoughts. An early start tomorrow if I'm going to make it to Perth in good time. What a bore that old fellow was, wittering on about his rare editions of Stevenson. Must give Richard a ring about the set of school stories, he'll know if they're worth summat or nowt. I wonder how many guys he shares a cell with. What the hell do they *do* in the evenings?

Sometimes I was amused by my own conversion into an over-protective parent. For heaven's sake, I told myself, he's a man of twenty-three, not a nine-year-old boy in his first term at boarding school. If this was any other country in Europe he'd have had to do at least a year's military service when he was eighteen, and a year in the army is far worse than six weeks in a British jail. And he's not exactly a delicate flower with no street cred. He'll cope. He'll be coping. He'll be alright.

But at other times I was taken aback by emotions which swept across me without warning. I usually have Classic FM on the radio in the shop, but one morning it played the second movement of the *Unfinished Symphony* and I was almost in tears. After that I kept Radio Four on. Another morning a young man came in with a little boy – I suppose he was about three or so – who stood very patiently while his father looked along our shelves. But eventually he began to say, 'Have you got your book, Daddy? Have you got your book, Daddy?'. The young man ruffled his hair and laughed: 'Not long now.' 'Can *I* have a book, Daddy?' The man laughed again. 'I don't think any of the books in here would be of much interest to you.'

'Actually, there might be,' I interrupted from behind the counter, and produced a Thomas the Tank Engine book which was part of a job lot I was planning to sell on. I gave it to the boy: 'You can have it for nothing,' I said. The boy looked up at me with huge, shy eyes.

'What do you say?' his father prompted.

'Thank you.'

But I had simply wanted to stop having to hear that repeated 'Daddy'.

And one day, on a bus, I watched an even younger man cooing delightedly over a baby who gazed up at him with eyes which scarcely blinked, absorbing the mystery of his father's face and his father's voice. And beside them I saw myself as nothing more than an ageing and lonely man.

After four weeks a letter came in from Andy, on ruled prison notepaper and with his prison number written in by another hand at the top. He apologised for not writing earlier, but explained that he was limited in the number of letters he could send, and he had been keeping in touch regularly with his mother and Terry. Otherwise the letter told me very little, except that he was fine, and to confirm the date of his release.

I sat down to write back by return, scribbling at the shop counter while we were quiet. But I found I had hardly more to say to him than he had had to say to me. I was well, it was a mild autumn in Edinburgh, the shop was busier than usual for this time of year: as I posted it with its discomforting address – his number, his wing, 'HM Prison' – I couldn't imagine it bringing much brightness into his cell.

But at last the morning came when I could imagine a much happier picture: Andy leaving the prison and heading down to Victoria for the train home. Though what kind of life he was returning to – that I didn't dare imagine. I knew from May he was now, unsurprisingly, jobless.

CHAPTER FOUR

I'm not going to write much about my six weeks inside, 'cause the worst thing about it was that for most of the time I was bored out of my skull, and if it was boring for me to live through, it'd certainly be boring for you to read about.

I was in this London nick – I won't name it – which isn't the worst in England, but is certainly the dirtiest. Everyone's agreed about that, even guys who've done bird on the Island. It has a kind of clammy, sticky dirtiness you feel you can never wash off – and of course you don't get too many chances for that anyway. What makes it worse is that as a convicted prisoner you're not allowed to wear a stitch of your own clothing. Almost the first thing you do when you arrive in a prison is, you strip. After that, even your underpants are prison underpants. Not nice – take my word for it.

Because the nick I was in deals with short-term prisoners, like I was, there's a constant coming and going of blokes, with the result that half the time the screws haven't a clue who most of their charges are. They never get a chance to find out. I'd like to say we were just numbers to them, but I'm not sure we were even that, 'cause you'd have needed a portable computer to keep up with all the numbers that were arriving and leaving every day.

No – to the screws we were just bodies. That's what they call you, in their slang – 'a body'. 'I'm bringing down a body,' a screw calls out, and there you are standing right next to him, wondering if in the past second or two you might have died without noticing. But they don't mean any harm by it. They don't have *time* to do you any harm. They count you into your cell, make sure you're fed when you're hungry, see that your bucket's emptied when it needs to be – and that's about it.

I hardly saw Hugo inside. He was one of those who passed through our nick quickly, having at least six months to serve, and I learned later he'd soon ended up, as I'd hoped he would, in an open prison, where conditions were a lot easier than they were for us. The only time we got a chance for a brief chat we couldn't say much, but I could see he was coping better than I'd expected. Even so, it was strange to think of him as he'd been on that day when we met at R&R. He'd really fucked up his life, there were no two ways about it.

But as for me, I had to learn to live with being 'three-up' – sharing a cell with two other guys. And I'm not going to say too much about what *that* meant, when it come to the necessary. I don't want you heaving up if you're reading this on the tube or something.

Sex, oddly enough, was easier, though I need hardly say I kept my gayness well under wraps – in fact, when I had to, I did an impersonation of a randy het I can guarantee you'd have been very impressed by. But in a way I was lucky, 'cause the first few nights I was only sharing with one other guy, called Eddie. On the very first night he just sort of – well, he just got it out and started, while I was lying pretending to read a magazine, and blushing to the backs of my ears. I'm not exactly prudish – you probably gathered that some time ago – but even so, when you're lying scarcely two metres from a guy who's bashing his bishop for all it's worth – well, it makes you distinctly uncomfortable. If you're not involved yourself, I mean.

Eddie was soon finished, and cleaned himself, and nothing at all was said. But when it come to shy Andy – later that night I found I didn't even dare do anything under the blankets, in case Eddie woke up.

The next night the same thing happened. And once again I kept my eyes on my magazine, and when Eddie was done neither of us spoke a word about it.

But Nature will take its course, nick or no nick. The following night I was lying on my bed in a funny way, trying to hide that I had a stiffy like a bloody poker. For once I was grateful to the prison for giving me a pair of trousers that were too big for me. If I'd been in my own jeans, I'd have burst the seams. I'm not kidding.

Suddenly Eddie turned to me and grinned. He was just one year older than me, but already this was his umpteenth stretch, and he had taken to treating me as if I was a kind of learner-con. He was quite handsome, in a rough way, and bloody well-built – he did press-ups every night like they were his religion. In his underpants. Christ knows what he'd have done to me if he'd ever guessed what I was thinking about as I watched him, but I can tell you, I very much doubt if I'd be alive now to tell this story.

Anyway, like I said, Eddie grinned and nodded towards my middle.

'Andy, boy, you're not going to try and leave it alone for six fucking weeks, are you?'

'What?'

He grinned even more.

'For fuck's sake, Andy, there's no need to lie there in misery. Get it out and start rubbing, man.'

I didn't say a thing. I hadn't a clue *what* to say, to a remark like that.

Eddie's grin went.

'There's nothing in here more normal, Andy. Otherwise we'd all go mad.'

He turned on his side and made out he was reading a book.

And soon, very soon, I'd got over my shyness. Which was just as well. 'Cause Eddie was dead right – if I hadn't, I'd have ended up being carted off in a white van. And without knowing it, he was useful to me in another way – or should I say, 'handy'?

But what I don't think I can get across to you, as I said at the start of this chapter, is the boredom of it all – the sheer, unbelievable, tedious, bloody, unbearable boredom.

But at last my release date come round, and one morning early in December, just after eight o'clock, me and about twenty other guys stepped through the prison gate, and it shut behind us. All I had to wear was the clothes I'd gone in with – no coat or nothing (I hadn't thought ahead), so I was *freezing*. Thank God it was a dry day.

I set off walking down the street, by myself. I don't quite know how to describe that street. If I called it 'run-down'

I'd be paying it a major compliment. I remember thinking that if a street could look dismal to a guy who was getting his first sight of the outside world for a month and a half, then it didn't exactly have a lot going for it.

I'd walked a little way, quite fast, when I come across a café, and went in. I'd had my prison breakfast, of course, but I wanted to wash the taste of prison food – even just the memory of the taste of prison food – out of my mouth. So at the counter I ordered a big mug of tea.

And then something awful happened. The woman who served me gave me a dirty look when I placed the order, and a positively filthy one when she took my money. Now, I know that by London standards she was maybe being quite polite by not actually chucking the tea at me, but there was something different about this woman. Her attitude seemed really personal – she threw me the kind of look you'd get from someone who knew you well and disliked you a lot.

It wasn't till I sat down at a table and put my bag on the floor beside me that I understood. How many men walk down that road every weekday morning at that same time? How many of them call by that caff? She knew what I was. And as I sipped my tea, for the first time so did I. I was an ex-con.

I listened to the conversation of two boys at the next table. They couldn't have been more than twelve or thirteen, and they were talking about someone who'd just had an abortion. They only ever called her 'she'. 'She' was an alcoholic. They might have been talking about their sister, or even their mother.

I begun to get depressed. It was ridiculous. Here I was, out of jail, and I was getting depressed. But I realised that in a strange way I was missing the guys inside – I mean, knowing that everybody about you is just the same as you are. In the same bloody mess.

So I soon finished off my tea and set off walking quickly again, to keep warm, till I reached the centre of London, right in the middle of the rush hour.

It was the first time I'd been in London at that time in

the morning, and I can tell you, I'd never heard such a racket of traffic in my life. A block in the nick with two hundred guys all yelling at once was peace and quiet compared with this. I wondered how Londoners could cope with such a din day in, day out. But then, very few of them seemed to have time to notice there *was* a din. They were rushing out of the Underground, rushing into the Underground, rushing out of rail stations, rushing into rail stations, rushing onto buses, rushing off buses, rushing in and out among cars, falling over each other, getting in each other's way, shoving each other, sounding their horns at each other, doing everything to each other except talk – all of them on their way to work. I was back in the world of the free.

I walked across the centre of town in a kind of haphazard, zig-zaggy way. You know how it is in a city, you follow one road, and then another, just 'cause they look interesting, without any particular plan, and you let the city itself steer you, if you see what I mean, till you end up wherever luck takes you.

It's funny, but while I walked down all those long streets, with the high buildings on every side – they seem high when you're used to Brighton – I felt as if, instead of being locked *in* in London, now I was locked *out*. Maybe it was just that I was in a strange mood, with it being my first morning of freedom, and everything. But I kept thinking what I was to the people who were hurrying past me and around me and jostling into me – a bit of a yob from Brighton, badly spoken, poorly educated, and to cap it all, an ex-con. What would they have said if they'd known where I'd got out of bed three hours earlier?

I ended up in Trafalgar Square, with its usual collection of tourists, even in December, photographing the pigeon shit. From here I could have taken a bus to Victoria, but I wasn't in a hurry to get back to Brighton – Mum and Terry were both at work, of course – so instead I went east, towards Covent Garden.

I soon found the gallery where, over a year ago now, Caroline had had her exhibition. I hadn't been in touch with her for many months, since before the trouble begun, and I guessed I'd never hear from her again. And I certainly wouldn't be delivering legal papers to her office, or anywhere else.

I wished I hadn't come here after all, it was only making me sad. So I turned away and walked quickly through the bijou little streets in that part of town, till I found another café which looked nice and warm, and went in. It was several cuts above the dump I'd been in near the nick, so I sat down quite happy with tea and a roll. And then I nearly had a fit.

The walls were covered with posters. And right in front of me, opposite my table, was a poster with a photograph that I'd seen before. Dear God, I thought. Of all the cafés in all of London, I have to walk into this one . . .

I sat and looked at it, I couldn't very well avoid doing so. There was little Tommy grinning at me like he'd grinned at Caroline on that summer morning – years and years ago, it felt like.

Christ, but I'd screwed things up for myself since then. Jesus, but I had. No job and no chance of a decent reference from my last employers – what was I going to do with my life now?

Right from the day we were arrested I'd been certain I was never going to get into trouble with the law again. No, I'd made that mistake for the last time. But suppose I had no choice? Suppose the only way I could make any money was to get back into wheeling and dealing? It wouldn't be difficult, not in Brighton. And I'd picked up a good few tips inside which could turn out to be very useful.

But I didn't want to think about all that right now, not on my first morning out. So I just ate my roll and sipped my tea, with my own arse in leather to provide a little visual diversion. There was one thing I was sure of, though. Never again would I wear cuffs for anyone, for any reason, no matter how much they liked the idea. Somehow bondage isn't quite the same after you've been handcuffed for real in the back of a prison van.

I had lunch in a pub, and my first pint for six weeks, which was quickly followed by my second, and very soon my third, at which point I begun to feel a lot friendlier towards London and Londoners than I'd done for a long time, even the Londoners who packed out that pub something terrible. I stayed on till most of them had left – the free having to get back to their desks, of course – and then meandered around for an hour or so, dropping by a few posh shops, as I slowly made my way to Victoria, and my train home.

In Brighton I took a taxi from the station to Mum's place. She was already in, so immediately we had a soppy reunion – though it was only a couple of weeks since she'd visited me in the nick. But Mum made the most of it. You'd have thought I'd come back from ten years in the desert, you really would.

Almost the first thing I wanted to do after we'd talked and drunk a large gin each was have a bath. You cannot imagine what a luxury it was to jump into a bath and *wallow* – just wallow, with a hot tap to turn on again and again whenever I needed a top-up. I hadn't had a bath, as opposed to a shower, since I went down, and soon I was feeling really clean for the first time in six weeks.

So there I was, wallowing away, when Mum called up from downstairs: 'You've got a visitor' – and a moment later someone rapped on the bathroom door.

'Who is it?' I shouted.

'It's me, you idiot.'

Well, I was out of that bath in a microsecond and opened the door so fast Terry damn near literally fell into my arms. We hugged and kissed right there till he laughed and broke away, kicking the door shut: 'What will your Mum think if she sees you like that?'

'That I've grown up to be a big boy.'

'Oh, God! You haven't changed, have you?'

'I certainly hope not.'

He brushed himself down: 'Look what you've done to my suit!' He'd come on straight from the office. 'I'm all wet.'

I grinned.

'Well, why not get your birthday suit wet as well? The bath's big enough for two.'

'Oh, control yourself, man. We've plenty of time – I'm off now till Monday.'

'How did you manage to pull that?'

'Had some leave due to me, of course.'

'Great stuff!'

We looked at each other. Then Terry laughed again: 'Are you just going to stand around flashing?'

'Why not? It's what *you* usually do when you meet people.' He punched me in the ribs: 'You cheeky cunt! Put some clothes on, your Mum's getting dinner ready for us.'

I grabbed a towel and flicked it at him: 'Scrounging another meal off us, are you?'

We went on joking like that – yeah, I know it sounds puerile, but we were in a puerile mood – while I dried and got dressed. I had a change of clothing there, and what a pleasure it was to put it on – my own jeans, my own tee-shirt, my own sweater.

By the time we went downstairs there was a gorgeous smell coming from the kitchen. But it was quite a while before dinner was ready, and when I saw it, I understood why. God knows what Mum imagined I'd been fed inside, she must have thought I'd been on bread and water or something. She always does go in for large meals, but this was ridiculous. It was *huge*.

All the same, somehow we managed to find space for it, and then we sat and burped for an hour, with more gin in our hands. This was all very comfortable, but I was beginning to get worried. The evening was wearing on, and I had definite plans for young Terry before I sent him home to his folks.

But at last we got off – I nearly wrote, 'escaped' – and Terry drove me across to Hove. On the way I asked him when his people were expecting him back.

'They're not,' he said. 'I told you we had plenty of time.'

'They're not?' I exclaimed. 'What excuse did you give them?'

'Oh, they just know I'm going to be away for a few days.' He jerked his head to indicate the back seat. 'I've got a bag with me – I can stay with you till Sunday evening.' He paused. 'I mean, if you'd like that.'

'Well, of course I'd like it! But didn't they ask some awkward questions?'

'No more than usual.'

This was all very odd – I was going to ask him what on earth he'd say to them if he ran into them in the centre of Brighton – but for the moment I didn't care. The thought of having Terry with me for four nights in a row was fantastic. We hadn't had that many nights together on the trot since we'd been in Westhurst.

So when we got to my flat there was no need to rush after all. We were able to sit in the kitchen nattering with my flatmates for ages. Terry went into my room to change out of his suit, and come back in a sweatshirt and a new pair of jeans. Which certainly showed off what was ready to welcome me home.

By the time we were finally alone together I was horny as hell, as the Yanks would say. We were hardly through the door of my room when I was making up for six weeks of being surrounded by crotches I could hardly dare even glance at. I tell you, I groped that boy like he'd never been groped – in fact, I did a very good impersonation of Hugo. Terry laughed at my eagerness: 'I take it you like these jeans?'

'Did you buy them special?'

'Yes. I don't think I'll ever have the nerve to wear them in the street.'

'Why not?'

'In case perverts like you get all excited. Are you trying to pull my goolies off?'

I was revelling in it – feeling balls through denim again, and a dick other than my own.

'What are you wearing underneath?'

'Nothing.'

'And you call *me* a pervert!' I stepped back and looked at him. 'Strip off till you've just the jeans on.'

That only took a second or two, and then I was hugging him again and this time feeling his rear through the denim. I begun whispering the kind of patter I knew he liked: 'I'm going to shaft this bum for you tonight, my son. You'd better get ready for it. I'm going to fuck you out of your senses.'

'I was rather hoping for that.'

It was my turn to laugh. We went on hugging and kissing, and then tumbled on to the bed. Fortunately Terry had all the necessary with him in his bag. And I think I can safely say I lived up to my promise. 'Cause after six weeks of wanking, what I needed more than anything else was *arse*.

The next morning – late – I put my leather on and Terry drove me up to where the bike had been kept. There she was, safe and sound, and within thirty seconds I was hearing her sound too (sorry, I couldn't resist that) as the engine roared – I still hadn't fitted her with a new silencer. I rode her back to Hove, followed by Terry in his car. Then we discussed what to do about lunch.

'Why don't we go out into the country somewhere?' he suggested. It was a bright sunny day.

'On the bike? That's a great idea!'

'Certainly not! I meant, in the car.'

'But she needs a good run, to clear her out and warm her up.'

'Well, you can clear her out and warm her up some other time.'

I grinned.

'Why are you so stubborn about taking a pillion ride?'

'Because I have this strange, overwhelming desire to go on living.'

'Oh, crap!'

But he wouldn't budge, and the car it had to be. We discussed where to go: 'How about Westhurst?' Terry said.

'Westhurst?'

'Yes – we could go back to the pub and see if that miserable landlord's still there. Keep your leather on – it might wind him up again! And don't forget your driving licence, whatever you do.'

I patted my jacket: 'Yeah, it's here in my pocket.'

I can never see that licence, of course, without remembering how it brought me and John together. Suddenly I felt guilty, I hadn't thought about him much since I'd left the nick. I'd mentioned to Mum that he'd written to me inside, a chatty little letter telling me all he was up to in Edinburgh, but apart from that he had hardly crossed my mind. I felt a bit mean, after all the interest he'd taken in what happened to me. I must ring him, I decided. I'll ring him tonight to thank him again for looking after Mum on that awful day, and to find out how he's getting on.

So Terry and me headed off to Westhurst, and walked into the Royal Oak, and sure enough, there was the Laughing Cavalier himself behind the bar. But much to our disappointment he wasn't rude once, not even a little bit. There were no dirty looks at my leather, no demands to see my licence, nothing. If we'd known he was going to be like that we wouldn't have gone to all the trouble of driving out there. Honestly, you can't rely on anyone nowadays.

Maybe his good manners were due to the fact that the place was nearly empty, as you'd expect in a country pub on a weekday in December, and he couldn't afford to turn away any business. Terry and me got a seat easily at a table near the fire, with our chicken and chips and our pints. It was only then that I remembered to ask him the question I'd put to one side the night before.

'Where do your parents think you are?'

He laid down his knife and fork.

'They know where I am.'

'Sorry?'

'They know where I am – they know I'm staying a few days with you.'

I was gob-smacked. Until that moment I'd thought they didn't even know of my existence.

'And what do they make of that?'

He looked down at the table top.

'They're not very happy about it. But that's their problem.'

I couldn't understand this: 'What excuse have you given them for staying with me?'

He raised his eyes.

'I haven't given them any excuse. They know exactly why.'

I dropped my own fork on the floor.

'They know – ?'

'Yes, they know. Everything.'

'You mean . . . ?'

He nodded.

'Yup. I've come out to them.'

Well, part of me wanted to jump up and cheer, but another part – the more sensible part – knew straight away there might be a lot *not* to cheer about.

'How did they take it?'

'How do you think?'

'As badly as you thought they would?'

'Oh, no. Much worse.'

'*Worse*?'

'Yes.' Suddenly he smiled. 'But I'm afraid I wasn't very tactful about it. You see, they were going on at me one day about why was I moping about, and what was the matter with me, and what did *I* have to be such a misery about, and so on, and so on. Till I just exploded.'

'Exploded?'

'Yes. I turned round and said, "because my boyfriend's in prison".'

I stared at him. And then I buried my face in my hands.

'Oh, my God,' I said from between my fingers. 'Great coming-out lines of our time.'

I raised my head. We looked at each other. And the next moment – we both fell about laughing. I don't know why, it just seemed hysterical.

'You actually said that?'

'Yes!'

'It's a wonder your old man didn't have a heart attack on the spot!'

'Better if he had, if you ask me. Anyway, it means I'm now in the same boat as you – or I will be soon, at least.'

'Come again?'

He picked up his knife and fork: 'I can't stay in that

house, Andy. They're doing my head in. So I'm looking for a place of my own – a flatshare, I mean.'

He raised his eyebrows. I understood at once what he was getting at.

'You and me?'

'Why not?'

I didn't answer.

'Why not?' he repeated.

CHAPTER FIVE

Much to my pleasure Andy rang me only a couple of days after his release. He said he was fine, that apart from being very boring prison hadn't been too bad, and that he and Terry were now having a few days' break together. He told me they had taken a run out to Westhurst, and made me laugh with his account of 'old cheerychops'. But he didn't say anything about Terry and his family.

It was May who informed me about 'the ructions', as she called them. From her phone-calls I learned that Terry's people were being incredibly difficult; there were hints of some kind of ultimatum - I gathered May herself was in the dark as to much of the detail - along the lines of 'give all this up or never darken our door again'.

'I suppose things might improve with time, May. It can come as a hell of a shock at first to parents when they find out their son's gay.'

This wasn't, of course, the most tactful remark I could have come out with: 'Well, *I* didn't make such a total fool of myself when I realised about Andy . . . '

'No, May, I'm sure you didn't. But maybe Terry's people aren't quite so - so experienced as you.'

'What on earth do you mean by that?'

I pacified her in the end. After the call I put the phone in the fridge to cool down and laughed as I poured myself a whisky. The better I got to know May again, the more easily I could imagine what her mother had been like when she learned May was pregnant.

* * *

John rung me two or three times to ask about Terry, but I didn't say too much about it all, partly because there was also another problem which I certainly wasn't going to discuss with either him or Mum.

Terry was desperate to move away from home, which I understood easily. But I wasn't at all sure I wanted him and me to move in together, and this hurt him terribly. He accused me of letting him down when he most needed me, of not standing by him like he'd stood by me, of not really caring for him - we had such terrible rows I even begun to think we were going to break up. Time and again I told him I *did* love him, of course I loved him, it was just -

'Just what? Just what? You're always saying '"it's just" - you're always saying, "but", "but", "but"... '

'It's just – '

'There you go again!'

'Will you fucking let me finish? Fucking shut up and listen for once! I just don't think it'd be right for us to actually live together, that's all I'm trying – '

'Why not? Why not?'

'Because I like things the way they are. I think they work fine, I think we should carry on like this.'

'Why?'

'Because it means we don't get on each other's nerves, we're not in each other's way – '

'You mean, so you can hawk your arse around Brighton when I'm not here.'

'Fucking Jesus Christ! Fucking clear out of here right now!'

Of course, he was all over-wrought 'cause of the trouble at home, and I was still coming to terms with being an ex-con, and none of that helped. But me being on the dole was one of the reasons I couldn't go along with his idea. It meant that if we lived together, not only would Terry be paying his share of the rent while I got housing benefit, but also that I'd be stuck in all day while he was out working. And the idea of being a little house-husband did *not* appeal to me.

About a week before Christmas John rung me again. This time he said: 'I've been thinking about a present for you, Andy.'

Hell, I hadn't done a thing about my own Christmas presents.

'Oh?'

'Yes. I'd like to send you a cheque.'

'That's very nice of you. Thanks!'

'I'm thinking of' – and he stated the amount. And I damn near dropped the phone.

'*Eh*?'

He repeated the amount.

'But John' – I was gasping. 'That's – that's . . .'

'That's nothing,' he interrupted me. 'I want you to think of it was something to tide you over for a few months. Are you getting your full dole money?'

'Not yet, but I think I can sort it out . . . '

'Well, you might not – I know what the rules are when you've been dismissed from your last job. So this is to help top it up. And if you're still on the dole in a while, there can be another instalment.'

'But, John – '

'I'm not interested in "buts". Have you still got the Kawasaki?'

I was baffled by the change of subject: 'Yeah?'

I heard him laugh at the other end of the line.

'Well, it costs money to run a bike like that. And I don't want you wondering if you might have to sell her. I couldn't bear to think of you selling the Kawasaki.'

I was speechless. I heard him laugh again: 'So if you like, regard the money as a subsidy towards the bike. But just one thing, Andy.'

'Yeah?'

'Not a word to your mother about this – OK? You can tell her you got some money from me for your Christmas, but there's no need to go into detail. This can be just between us, Andy.'

Well, if ever I was flummoxed in this life, it was then. But of course I agreed, and put the phone down still with my jaw hanging open. I was suddenly a lot less hard-up than I'd been five minutes earlier.

* * *

I'd thought very carefully about that payment to Andy. But I've quoted *A Christmas Carol* before, and I'll quote it again: 'a great many back-payments were included'. It wasn't that

I wanted to play the philanthropist, or anything disgusting like that, but the plain fact was that my grandfather had worked hard to put my father into the Bar, my father had worked hard to establish his career, and I had worked hard to build up the shop. As a result I was now in a position to help my son when he needed it. I was certain it was the right thing to do, even though I had the uncomfortable feeling that Mrs Thatcher would have made a political parable out of the whole story.

* * *

Before Christmas Terry and me begun to patch things up again. He calmed down a lot, and admitted he could see my point that maybe we got on best as we were, meeting up every weekend but having time to ourselves in between. We ended up sort of agreeing that after New Year he'd look for a flatshare of his own, rather than the two of us trying to find a place together.

He wasn't looking forward to Christmas at all, which wasn't surprising. And then a thought come to me. I rung up Mum: 'Mum, how would it be if I invited Terry to spend Christmas Day with us? Would that be possible, or is it too late now?'

'Do you mean, have we got enough food in? Well, our turkey will certainly stretch to one more person, and I'd have no problem getting a few extra trimmings. But do you think Terry's people will be happy with the idea?'

I was certain they wouldn't be. But I didn't give a fuck.

'That's fantastic!' Terry exclaimed when I put it to him. 'Thanks!'

'How do you think your folks will take it?'

'Who cares?'

Well, when he went home and said what he was planning to do, all hell broke loose. He was told it was the last straw, what were they supposed to say to all the family who were coming to Christmas dinner and would be wanting to know why he wasn't there, it showed just how much he cared for them, was this all the thanks they got, if he preferred the company of crooks and swindlers at Christmas that was up to him, but he needn't think he could come running back the moment it suited him, he had made his bed now and he could lie in it –

'That's exactly what I mean to do,' he interrupted them.

The upshot was, him and me went round to Mum's place Christmas Eve and stayed there till the day after Boxing Day. And the bed he lay in was my old single bed in my old room – which in a way was a bit frustrating, 'cause though it was very sexy we were both of us too shy to do anything, with Mum just the other side of the wall.

But we had a great time on Christmas Day. We forgot all our troubles, we drunk and ate and drunk again till we were well past half seas over – three-quarters, more like. After the Queen's Speech (Mum has a soft spot for the Queen – I think it has something to do with knowing what it's like to have difficult children) Mum said: 'Let's phone your Dad, Andy, to wish him a happy Christmas. Do you know he's on his own today?'

'On his own?'

'Yes. He says he doesn't mind at all, but it must be *awful.*'

So she dialled Edinburgh, and sure enough he was in, and after all the usual Christmas stuff she begun asking him what kind of a day he was having, and had he had a nice dinner, and so on. I couldn't stop myself grinning, I could picture his face at the other end of the line. Then she told him how Terry was with us, and I heard her add, 'Yes, Terry.' And then, 'No, everything's fine,' and she went on quickly: 'Oh, John, it's a pity we couldn't all be together today. Next year you must come down to Brighton and be with us. No, really, you must. Anyway I'll let you have a word with Andy' – she handed the phone to me and said, 'Here's your Dad.'

I took the phone off her: 'Hi, Dad. Happy Christmas!'

It was a couple of moments before he answered: 'And the same to you, Andy!'

'You having a good time? I hear you're by yourself?'

'Oh, don't *you* start,' he said, and I hooted with laughter.

'I'm perfectly happy, but I'm damned if I can get your mother to believe me.' I laughed again. We chatted on a while, till he said: 'I gather you've got Terry with you?'

'Yeah.'

'Is he there right now?'

'Yeah. You like a word with him?'

'Just briefly – I don't want to be running up your Mum's phone bill.'

'OK, here he is. Bye for now, Dad.'

Once again he took a moment to reply: 'Bye, Andy. See you again before too long, I hope.'

I handed the phone to Terry, who took it and said a little shyly, 'Hallo, John. Happy Christmas.' Then he laughed and looked at the two of us: 'Yes, it's a bit like that. They're feeding me up fit to burst.'

When he gave the phone back to Mum she said: 'Now, remember, John – next Christmas you're to come down to Brighton. I won't take no for an answer, so you can book your flight tomorrow. Yes, I certainly hope so too. Cheerio for now, John. Take care.' She put the phone back on the hook: 'Poor man! He's putting a very brave face on it.'

It wasn't till we were in bed that night that Terry remarked: 'You've started calling John "Dad" now, I noticed?'

I was astounded: 'I've what?'

'You've started calling him "Dad" – you said it to him twice today.'

'Did I?'

He laughed: 'Yes, you did. Didn't you realise?'

'Christ, no. It must have slipped out 'cause of the booze.'

'Well, that's a nice thing to say!'

'I didn't mean it like that – I meant . . .'. But I didn't know what I meant. Of course I probably wouldn't have called John 'Dad' if I'd been sober, but on the other hand, I'd become very fond of him and maybe that was why, because I wasn't sober, I'd . . . Oh hell, I was too pissed to work it out.

But afterwards I wondered if I hadn't created a problem for myself. 'Cause if the next time I spoke to him I went back to calling him 'John', wouldn't that sound rude now?

* * *

He'd said it not once, but twice: 'Dad'. When I came off the phone I turned up the tv again and poured myself another glass of the port I only drink at Christmas. And I must own that after I'd been sitting for a few minutes, not paying much attention to the film, I had to wipe my eyes. Dear God, I thought, what a sentimental old queen I'm turning into. And what an odd thing for an old queen to become sentimental about.

When I next spoke to May we were both a good deal more sober. She was able to explain why Terry had been at her house at Christmas, and told me it had proved the end of the road for him as far as his family were concerned, at least for the time being. He'd moved out, into a room in a flat in Kemp Town – 'and you wouldn't believe what he's having to pay,' she added.

I rang Andy a few nights later. After a while I noticed he was avoiding calling me either 'Dad' or 'John', and guessed that since Christmas Day he had become embarrassed about the matter. I wondered if I should say something along the lines of '"John" is still OK by me,' but I couldn't think of any way of putting it which wouldn't sound patronising.

'I'm looking around really serious for a job now,' he told me. 'Now that the holiday's past.'

'Any luck?'

'Nah, nothing yet. But it's early days.'

'Couldn't you find something as a courier again? Maybe with a despatch firm this time?'

'It's funny you should say that, 'cause I've been looking into that idea, in London.'

'London?'

'Yeah – Brighton's too small for that.' He paused. 'But there's problems with London.'

'You don't want to move?'

'No, I don't. Though there'd be nothing to prevent me coming back down at weekends to stay with Tel. But the despatch rider scene in London – well . . .'

I guessed straight away what he meant: 'Yes, I see.'

'And it's not just that – Mum's dead against the idea. And Tel too, though maybe not quite so much.'

'Why?'

'Cause of the danger. It's not like biking around Sussex – sooner or later you're going to have a spill. It happens to them all.'

'Well, in that case I entirely agree with your mother and Terry!'

He laughed: 'There doesn't seem much chance of it anyway, so you don't need to worry. But come the spring the seasonal jobs'll start, so I guess I'll be able to pick up something then.' He laughed again: 'Taking the money off the dodgems at Peter Pan, or something like that! Maybe selling balloons on the Pier.'

'Well, listen, Andy. If you want a break some time, you're very welcome to come up here for a few days.'

He was obviously surprised: 'You mean that?'

'Of course I do. I can make up a spare bed in my front room. The only thing is, you'd have to look after yourself during the day, when I'm working.'

'I might hold you to that – it sounds a great idea!'

'There you are, then. And don't concern yourself about the ticket – it would be on me.'

'Nah, I couldn't let you do that.' Before I had a chance to insist he went on quickly: 'Anyway, I'd come on the bike.'

I was aghast: 'From Sussex?'

'Yeah!'

'Are you sure?'

'Yeah!' he repeated.

'Well, in that case let me give you a word of advice – don't even think of coming up here before Easter. Because believe me, no-one in their right mind travels to Scotland between September and April in a car, let alone on two wheels.'

He laughed: 'Bad as that, eh?'

'Oh yes!'

* * *

I didn't have much luck with my job-hunting. It wasn't that my old employers were awkward – I had to get in touch with Gordon, the Office Manager, to ask if he'd give me a reference, and he told me he wouldn't say anything about why I'd left the firm, he'd make out I'd gone of my own accord. He was decent that way, Gordon, though I suppose he was maybe inclined to stand by a fellow gay man as well.

Not that it made much difference, 'cause in three months no-one took up my references anyway. I didn't have so much as sight of an interview. I'd joked to John about looking for summer work on the Pier, but by the end of March, when the seafront was being all tidied up and sorted out again ready for Easter, I begun to think it really was going to come to that. Not that I was sure I'd be much better off – it'd get me off the dole, of course, but it'd also get me off housing benefit. In fact, I might even be *worse* off.

And Christ alone knew what kind of long-term prospects I had. What was my future going to be? Stuck forever in a series of dead-end jobs, never able to get away from the fact I'd once done bird? Sometimes I got dead depressed about it all, when I was bored out of my skull on a winter's afternoon, nothing to do but watch crap telly, not even enough dosh in my pocket to go out and get pissed – 'cause I didn't want to spend the money John had given on me on booze, I kept it for luxuries the dole didn't stretch to, like clothes and heat.

If it hadn't been for Terry, I don't know what I might have done. I don't mean I'd have taken a one-way ride up to Beachy Head or anything like that, but I might have decided to quit Brighton altogether – maybe moved to London whatever Mum said, and got myself into the despatch rider set-up somehow. Or sold the bike and gone abroad, drawn the dole somewhere else in Europe, and at least been warm while I was bored.

You can see how much I was becoming a dreamer. 'Cause how the hell could I have got a job abroad? I can't even speak English properly, never mind any foreign lingo.

And then, as I can imagine John might put it, 'fate played a hand'.

CHAPTER SIX

When Andy rang me and said he'd like to take up my offer to come and stay in Edinburgh for a few days, my first reaction was sheer delight.

'Terry's going on this training course in Glasgow,' he told me.

'*Glasgow*?' I exclaimed.

'Yeah – there's some kind of centre there.'

'It's a hell of a way to come from Brighton, isn't it?'

'I dunno. Anyway, it's residential, for three days, so I thought while he's there, maybe I could visit you? And pop across and see him when it's over.' He hesitated. 'Is it far?'

'About fifty minutes by train.' I laughed. 'Or fifteen minutes on the Kawasaki – I take it you still want to come by bike?'

'Natch!'

'I could easily put Terry up as well, you know. If he had a day or two free at the end.'

'We'll maybe take you up on that!'

But as I sat and thought about the practicalities, my feelings changed. And by the next morning, when I told Sandy about it in the shop, the prospect had begun to terrify me.

'What am I going to *do* with him?' I exclaimed.

'"Do" with him?'

'Yes – how am I going to entertain him? He'll be bored stiff.'

'Why should he be bored?'

'Staying with me? You know what a quiet life I lead.'

'Well, it'll just have to be a bit less quiet for a week.' Sandy grinned. Of the two of us he's much the more outgoing; he's never allowed middle-age – he's only a year younger than I am – to restrict his social activities. 'We'll see you in the gay bars at last.'

'Oh, God forbid.'

'Will he be here over the weekend?'

'Yes.'

'That's perfect, then! You can take him to the gay ceilidh next Friday.'

'*You* can take him, if you like.' Ceilidhs are not, shall I say, 'my thing'.

'Ach, lighten up, man! Anyway, I should think a young man of his age should be able to make his own entertainment.' He grinned again. 'Will you be providing him with a double bed?'

'Yes, my sofa bed in the front room.' Now it was me who grinned. 'I'd thought of that for myself.'

But I remained nervous about the idea of having to look after Andy for a whole week, even though I knew I certainly wouldn't be visiting Edinburgh's gay scene with him. After all, who goes trolling with their *father*, for God's sake?

* * *

I was knackered when I got to Edinburgh, I can tell you – it's a hell of a long ride from Brighton. I'd set off early on a beautiful sunny morning – we'd been having a superb spring, more like an early summer, on the south coast – but about two minutes after I crossed the Border the rain come on. Hullo, I thought. So it's true what they say about Scotland. I stopped and dug my over-trousers out of the pannier, and then a few miles further on I had to stop again and dig out an extra sweater, the temperature was about twenty degrees below what I'd been used to for the last fortnight.

By the time I reached Edinburgh the rain was coming down in sheets, and the little map John had sent me to help me find his place got all wet as I stopped and pored over it. While I was trying to work out where the hell I was, a voice beside me said: 'Caan Ah help ye, son? Arrre ye lost?'. (OK, I promise not to take the piss out of Scottish accents. But just this once . . . Besides, that's what it sounded like to me.)

It was this little old guy, with a cloth cap.

'Yeah, I'm trying to find' – and I named the street where John lives.

'Oh, you're frae England, are you?'

I owned up I was.

'Well, we'll no hold it against you!' – and he started chortling away. I tried to smile as the rain dripped off my visor.

'Let me hae a wee look at your map.'

So I let him hae a wee look, and he showed me exactly where I was and explained how to get to the New Town – 'though you'll find the traffic's *terr-rrible*' he added, making the word last about a minute and a half. But bless him, what would I have done if he hadn't stopped to help me? I'd probably have been going round and round the centre of Edinburgh till midnight. As I rode off he called after me: 'Take care, son!'

I wondered if anyone in Brighton would have helped a stranger like that. And I didn't even have to wonder about London, I knew from experience.

John's flat is in what they still call the 'New Town', though in fact it's about as new as the United States. And it's very, very grand. When I finally drew up outside his place the only thing that was stopping my jaw from hanging open was my helmet. It was in this great long row of stone houses, facing a kind of private park.

I was just clambering off the bike, all stiff from the ride, when John opened the front door.

'I thought I recognised that silencer!' he said with a grin.

He helped me unload my bags from the panniers and led me upstairs to his flat, which was on the first floor. And now my jaw very nearly did hang open. I'd known he was well-off, but I'd never imagined anything like this. You could practically have fitted our place in Hove into his front room.

He showed me the sofa which opened up at night into a bed, and drawers he'd cleared out for my clothes, and so on. Then he said: 'If you want to change out of that lot I'll leave you in peace for a few minutes. Would you like a drink? Or maybe something hot?' He laughed. 'Or both?'

I asked for coffee and he went off into the kitchen, which I suspected was probably about half a mile away. By the time he come back I was in jeans, and looking around me a bit.

'I see you bring your work home,' I said. He burst out laughing. There were books everywhere – shelves and shelves of them, filling two walls, and piles of them in corners and on tables and behind the furniture.

'Sometimes,' he admitted. 'But you look cold – draw up near the fire.'

So I did, and soon I begun to warm up, and soon we were chatting away.

* * *

Andy was shy a little, that first evening. And since I was still shitting bricks, as he might put it himself, about entertaining him for a week, I guess we were both glad of the large glasses of whisky I poured to welcome him to Scotland. Not being sure of his exact time of arrival I hadn't tried to prepare a meal, so we ate out in a little place I know in Stockbridge which I thought he would like. Much to my relief I saw I was right; he began to relax there.

When we were back at the flat I offered him a copy of *Gay Scotland* and a map on which I'd marked the locations of the bars and clubs.

'Only don't ask me what any of them are like, because I haven't a clue!'

I saw in his face an embarrassment which I instantly understood. Who wants to imagine – or even *can* imagine – their father's sex life? Yet we were both gay men, and in other circumstances the age gap between us wouldn't have been unbridgeable; certainly I have had men as young as him in recent years. But I meet them off the scene, since I long ago gave up on the bars as noisy hellholes, and a man of my age hanging around a disco looks as pathetic as he is ridiculous.

'Here's the spare keys,' I went on quickly, 'so you can come and go as you please.' I smiled, to cover an embarrassment which was the mirror-image of his; now I was in the awkward position of sanctioning my son's sex life. 'If you want to bring someone back, there's no difficulty about that, and I always go to bed early . . . '. He laughed and shook his head: 'Me and Tel are still being faithful.'

'Oh?' Privately, I was relieved: 'I hope that won't prevent you going out and enjoying yourself, though?'

He laughed again: 'Nah, I want to see what you Scots get up to.'

'Well, I'll let you get on with it. But I've taken the day off tomorrow, so I can show you some of the tourist sights, and give you an idea of the city. After that, I'm afraid you'll have to look after yourself a lot.'

'No problem!'

* * *

The next day I learned something important about John – if he says something is 'easy walking distance', it's nothing of the kind, and if he just says 'walking distance', it's bloody miles away. The man's a walking fanatic. Apparently his idea of a relaxing Sunday is to pop down to Yorkshire and back. I was damn near dropping by the end of the afternoon, but I have to admit I'd got to know Edinburgh – in fact I knew every bloody paving stone of the Royal Mile. Fortunately it was a dry day, and much warmer than when I first arrived.

We started by going up to the Castle and all around it. We looked at the dinky little Crown Jewels they have there, the Scottish Crown Jewels, though I didn't have to ask to know I was supposed to be dead respectful and not point out that one crown and one sceptre doesn't exactly put the Tower of London in the shade. Then we went down to Parliament House, where they don't have a parliament, but they used to when Scotland was a separate country. Nowadays it's their main courthouse. There we saw something really weird – the advocates, as they call them, walking up and down this great long hall, from one end to the other and back again, deep in talk.

'Why do they do that?' I asked.

'So that they can discuss a case without being overheard. It's a tradition of the place.'

'Did your dad do that?'

'Oh yes, any time he was appearing in court here.'

Now I know where he gets it from, I thought.

There was a break when we had lunch in a pub, but afterwards we walked all the way down to Holyroodhouse. I silently thanked God when John told me he didn't think it was interesting enough to be worth doing the guided tour, till a few moments later he suggested we go and have a look at his shop.

'Is it far?'

'Oh, no – walking distance.'

And bloody uphill, too.

When we got there his partner Sandy was behind the counter. He's a tall, thin man with reddish hair, big thick glasses, and a great sense of humour. I soon found that out because the shop was empty and we had plenty of time to talk.

'John, I've got excellent news for you,' he said, and you could tell from his eyes he was getting ready to take the piss.

'What?' John asked, looking nervous.

'I've managed to get two extra tickets for the gay ceilidh – very difficult this late in the day, I can assure you. It's on Friday,' he added, to me.

'What's a "cay-lay"?' I asked – I'd never heard the word before.

'A kind of public torture,' John answered. Sandy started to laugh: 'Don't listen to him. It's an evening of traditional Scottish music and country dancing – eightsome reels, and so on.'

'That's what I said.'

I gathered they'd had this argument before: 'You *must* come this time,' Sandy insisted.

'Don't you like that kind of thing?' I asked John.

He shrugged: 'I've nothing against it. It's just that I'd rather be penetrated by a red-hot spit and roasted alive over an open fire.'

Sandy burst out laughing: 'Don't pay any attention to this old fogey! The ceilidhs are one of the highlights of the gay year here. They're enormous fun.'

'Well, maybe Andy'll enjoy going. Who's the other ticket for?'

'You, you miserable old bugger.'

'I am *not* going to a ceilidh.'

'Oh yes, you are. Now' – he stepped back and looked at me – 'I wonder if I could lay my hands on a kilt for Andy.'

'A *kilt*?' I exclaimed. John roared with laughter: 'Sandy, for heaven's sake! The boy's only been in Scotland for twenty-four hours and already you're trying to turn him into a walking cliché.'

'Do you *have* to wear one?' I asked.

'No,' Sandy said. 'But you've got the height and the build for it' – he turned to John: 'You know, Andy's very much the same build as Chris – I wonder if I could borrow something off him? He's not able to make it on Friday.' He turned back to me: 'I might be able to get you a kilt and a sporran and a sgian dhu.'

Christ, it was worse than being abroad: 'What's a "skeean do"?' I had to ask.

'It's a little dagger you tuck down your sock,' John explained. 'You carry a sgian dhu to persuade your opponent to sgian don't.'

'There you are, then,' Sandy said. 'I'll speak to Chris tonight, and that'll be you both fixed up nicely.'

'I am *not* going to the ceilidh!' John repeated.

The next day he had to work, so I was free to wander round Edinburgh by myself, and what a relief *that* was. I found out about something John didn't seem to know existed – buses. But I wasn't entirely lazy, I climbed all the way to the top of Arthur's Seat, this big hill that's right in the middle of the city, and looked down on it from high up. There was a Force 25 gale blowing, but apart from that I was happy – more than happy, even. I'd already decided I loved Edinburgh, it was an incredibly beautiful city. I was up there for ages, looking across to the Castle, and the Forth Bridges, and beyond them, far away, mountains. I made up my mind that before these few days holiday were over, I'd take a run west and north on the bike, and see at least a bit of the Highlands.

When I told John this, back in the flat, he said: 'You don't have to do that. I'm off on Monday, I'll take you out for the day in the car.' He grinned: 'We really *are* making a little Scot out of you, aren't we? I have instructions to tell you that Sandy's got hold of the Highland dress for tomorrow night. If you call round the shop towards the end of the afternoon, he'll have it ready for you.'

'How about you? Have you changed your mind about tomorrow night?'

'*No*!'

Later, as I was chatting to him while he was cooking dinner, I brought up a subject which had been troubling me a little during the day. It was slightly embarrassing: 'John . . . '

'Yes?'

'What should I wear *under* the kilt?'

He nearly fell into the saucepan laughing.

'Rugby shorts,' he got out eventually.

'Listen, I'm serious!'

'So am I! No, what you want is . . .' Now *he* looked embarrassed. 'Normally, do you wear – er, shorts or briefs?'

'Either.'

'Well, you want to choose a tight-fitting pair of briefs. For, er . . . '

I couldn't help smiling at his awkwardness: 'For support?'

I saw that he understood my amusement: 'Yes, exactly. Or even a plain pair of swimming trunks. Otherwise' – he was embarrassed again.

'Otherwise everything's a bit – wobbly?'

'That's one way of putting it.'

Well, I didn't have any swimming trunks with me - I wasn't *that* naive about the Scottish climate – but I did have some briefs, of course. Which I'd originally bought for the benefit of Hugo Thomson. So he turned out to be some use to me in the end.

The next day was sunny and almost warm, though not quite, and I took a long run on the bike south of Edinburgh, on John's advice, into some fantastic scenery. I was amazed there could be so much empty countryside so close to the city. This was nothing like Sussex, with villages all over the place – I rode for mile after mile hardly seeing another soul. I could get to like this, I thought as I rolled along without a care in the world. I could get to like this a lot.

When I arrived at John's shop he was out on business, but Sandy was there, and he had the goods ready for me in a bag.

'You'll need to try it on,' he said. 'Come through into the back while we're quiet.'

Well, first of all I had to take my jeans off, of course. Then in order to show me how to fasten the kilt Sandy had to spend a remarkable amount of time fussing around my waist and my knees. Then he fixed the sporran, which for some reason involved a whole load more fiddling at my waist. Finally he was very concerned that the kilt hung right on me, and to make sure it did he kept smoothing it down at the back. Over and over again. Just to be certain the pleats were straight, you understand.

When he finished he stood back a little and looked at me.

'You'll be a sensation tonight!' he said.

If you haven't worn my bum away, I thought. But I didn't say anything about this when I got back to the flat, I just asked John if he'd changed his mind.

'Certainly not!' he said. 'I am *not* going to a ceilidh.'

* * *

As I walked into the ceilidh beside Andy I saw that he produced an effect almost instantly. I wasn't surprised. When he had come into my front room after changing, with a self-conscious smile, I could scarcely credit how stunning he looked. Sandy had understated the case when he judged that he would suit the kilt.

But after a few minutes, once we'd got drinks and found a seat at the one of the tables round the dance floor, I began to wonder whether to be outraged, flattered, or just amused, by the glances I was attracting myself. I felt like having a public announcement made: 'John Paterson is *not* the sugar-daddy of the amazingly handsome boy he's with.

He's his *real* daddy.'

But, no, perhaps not.

It wasn't long before Sandy joined us, resplendent in Highland dress himself, together with Paul, a publisher from Glasgow we both knew. Sandy merely grinned at me.

'One word from you,' I said, 'and I'll disembowel you with your own sgian dhu.'

He sat down: 'It's a fine thing when a man has to be dragged to a gay ceilidh by his son. And an Englishman to boot.'

'Son?' Paul asked. So I had to explain who Andy was; and since Paul knew Brighton well, having once lived there himself, they were soon deep in conversation about groynes – the breakwater type – and other features of the English seaside. As I listened to them I realised for the first time how oddly Andy's accent went with the way he was dressed; I was so used to his voice I hadn't, till then, registered the incongruity. Paul had: 'There's a tune called "Cockney Jocks",' he told Andy. 'We should get them to play it in your honour.'

'I'm not a Cockney!' Andy exclaimed.

'At this distance,' Paul said, 'no-one will notice the difference. Are you dancing? There's about to be a "Dashing White Sergeant".'

Andy looked shy – a rare expression for him: 'I don't think I can – I don't know any of the dances.'

'Oh, it's dead easy. I'll tell you what to do as we go along.' He stood up. 'You can't come to a ceilidh and not dance!'

'I hope you heard that,' Sandy remarked as they made their way on to the floor.

'Don't push your luck.'

And in fact I didn't dance – I really do hate all that – but sat and drank slowly as I watched Andy dancing with a whole series of men who were astonishingly willing to educate this kilted visitor in reels and 'Strip the Willow' and what have you. He'd arrived wearing a simple sweat-shirt as his top, but, unsurprisingly, that soon came off; and soon afterwards he had to roll up the sleeves of the white shirt I'd loaned him. His inexpertness at the dancing didn't matter; a fair number of the Scots hadn't much of a clue either; and in the wild muddle of an eightsome reel he looked totally at home, clapping and hooching along with the best of them.

I realised Sandy was beside me again.

'Sitting this one out?' I asked.

'Aye, I'm feeling my age.'

After a while he said quietly: 'He really is the beau of the ball, isn't he?'

I turned sharply.

'Yes,' I said after a moment. 'He is.'

'He's won a few hearts here tonight, I can tell you. Biggest sensation in Edinburgh since Bonnie Prince Charlie.'

I laughed: 'Shut up, you old daftie.'

He spoke quietly again: 'You're incredibly proud of him, aren't you?'

The moment Sandy spoke the words I felt a lump come into my throat. Oh, damn you, I thought.

'Why should I be proud of him? He's an unemployed ex-con – or have you forgotten?'

'You don't fool me, John Paterson. I've known you for twenty years – or have *you* forgotten?'

It was several moments before I answered.

'You're right,' I said. I hoped the noise of the band would cover the thickness in my voice. 'I am incredibly proud of him.'

CHAPTER SEVEN

Well, I didn't half enjoy the ceilidh. But I must say I found out why the Scots drink so much – dancing a reel is a heck of a lot easier when you're pissed. In fact, I very much doubt if you could do Scottish country dancing at all if you were sober.

I soon gathered that my accent caused great amusement, coming from a guy dressed like Rob Roy. Not that people were nasty about it in any way – quite the opposite, in fact. They kept telling me how sexy it was. Never happens to me in Brighton. And I lost count of the number of times someone said to me, 'So you're English, are you? Well, we won't hold it against you!' – chortle, chortle.

I fell in with a crowd of guys about my own age. One of them, called Ally (or Sally, depending on who was talking to him), had obviously taken quite a shine to me. Which was a bit of a problem for me, 'cause I could easily have taken a shine to *him*. He was in a kilt too, and short and dark, with very sexy grey eyes. And great legs.

Anyway, as the ceilidh was coming to its end, at gone midnight, I was invited to go back to his place with him and some of the others, 'for a few more bevvies'. I wanted to go, of course, but I didn't want my reasons to be misunderstood. At least, I didn't think I did. I wasn't sure. I toddled over to John and had a word with him, and said I might not be home till morning. He laughed, and told me to enjoy myself.

We all tumbled into a taxi, nearly literally, and went back to Ally's flat, about half-a-dozen of us. He was a student – of law, would you believe – and the rest were a mixture of students and guys on the dole. Ally turned out to have near enough 'bevvy' in his place to have got the entire ceilidh roaring drunk, never mind just us. And that's what we proceeded to do. And Christ, but those guys were a laugh with the booze inside them.

I woke up next morning beside Ally with the mother and father of a hangover, and the son and daughter as well for that matter. I was in my underpants. I couldn't remember how I'd got out of my kilt and sporran, but I knew I wouldn't have had a clue how to undo them when I was drunk. I had to suppose Ally had helped me.

But my underpants were round my waist, so obviously I'd behaved myself. But it hadn't been out of virtue. To judge from the state I was in, I wouldn't have been capable of shagging Keanu Reeves, never mind someone as pissed as I was myself.

I got out of bed, stumbled to the bog, and come back to find Ally sitting up. To my amazement he was bright as ninepence: 'Fancy making up for lost time?' he asked, turning back the duvet.

I explained that, being a mere Englishman, I was suffering more from the drink than he was. He was understanding about it.

I picked up my clothes and fumbled about till Ally burst out laughing: 'Do you need a hand?'

'Yeah, I'm afraid I do. I can't remember where this bit goes.'

So he jumped out of bed and come across to help me. And he certainly wasn't a shy lad. Unlike me he'd taken off his underpants, always assuming he had any on in the first place. What a time to find yourself with a thumping hangover, I thought, when there's a ballock-naked Scot fiddling with your sgian dhu.

Maybe it was just as well I'd been totally rat-arsed the night before, or that Ally had been wearing a kilt that hid what he had to offer. 'Cause if I'd seen what I was seeing now as a bulge in a pair of jeans, I knew I would not have been a good boy. Good head, more like.

There was another guy who'd stayed over, called Brian, and him and me breakfasted on coffee and a couple of bowls of paracetamol, while the amazing Ally – in jeans now it was too late to matter – tucked into cereal. By this time it was nearly midday, and I realised I had a problem.

'How am I going to get home?' I asked. 'I'd better call a taxi.'

'Why?' Brian asked.

'Well, I can hardly get on a bus dressed like this, can I?'

'Why not? But if you prefer, you can always walk.'

'Walk?'

'Yes. You're staying in the New Town, aren't you? That's on my own way home. I'll come with you, as far as Princes Street. The walk'll do us both good, it'll help to clear our heads.'

'I'll come along as well,' Ally said.

'It's alright for you two – you're both in normal clothes.'

They roared with laughter: 'Ach, give Edinburgh another chance to see your legs!'

'Well – is it far from here?'

'Not at all. Walking distance.'

Oh, God.

So we walked – miles, I need hardly say. With about a million shoppers giving me funny looks all the way. At the corner of Princes Street we stopped to take our leave of each other, and Brian and Ally told me to be sure to look them up the next time I was in Edinburgh. I was in the middle of saying I certainly would when two large middle-aged men with cameras come up to us.

'Hey, you guys, pardon us for interrupting, but we would just *love* it if you could just pose for us for a moment with the Castle there in the background, we really would appreciate it, we wouldn't take a moment of your time but that really would be fantastic, hey, thanks, guys – no, sorry, we just meant the guy in the kilt, no offence intended, do you know you look real swell in it, by the way we're from Omaha, Nebraska, you ever been there?'

By now I had been shepherded to one side to stand beside a railing: 'No, I haven't.'

'Well, we just *love* Edin-boro and Scot-land, hey, that's fantastic, can we just take another, we're sorry we're taking up your time here, hey, this is real swell of you.'

'No, it's OK.' I was having to keep my eyes off Ally and Brian. They were doubled up with laughter.

'Hey, you're not from these parts, are you?'

'No, actually I'm not.'

'You sound English, hey, did we get that right?'

'Yes, you did.'

They both chortled huge American chortles.

'Well, hey! But we won't hold that against you.'

Oh, good grief.

At last I managed to get away, and said cheerio to Ally and Brian. Then I walked on as fast as I could, in case there were any more Americans who just *loved* Scotland lurking at street corners.

John was out, at work. He'd left a note about finding stuff for lunch in the fridge, but I didn't bother. I got the clobber off, lay down on the sofa, and fell fast asleep.

* * *

Andy and I had a quiet Saturday evening. He went out to a bar after we'd eaten, but was home before I'd gone to bed. I wasn't entirely surprised. He hadn't needed to tell me he'd had just a wee drop after he left the ceilidh.

The next morning was sunny and warm, the first time the weather had been half-decent since he arrived. I was up before him, and was out in the street polishing the car when he appeared at the front door, smiling.

'So, what are your plans for today?' I asked him.

'I dunno. What are yours?'

I shrugged.

'I've nothing definite.' Then I summoned up my courage: 'Andy . . .'

'Yeah?'

'Would you mind if I had a little shot on your bike?'

He was very obviously taken aback.

'The bike?'

'Yes. You see, I've been admiring her while I've been at this, and thinking – it'd be great to have the feel of a bike again, just for a couple of minutes. Nothing more than that. I'd only go to the end of the street and back. If you're happy with the idea,' I added.

'Well – I don't suppose there's any problem. You know how to handle a bike this size?'

'She's a bit bigger than the 400-4 I had, but . . . I wouldn't be going more than a few hundred yards.'

'If you think you can manage it . . . '

'Don't worry, I'll be very careful.'

He relaxed: 'OK, then! You want to borrow my helmet?'

I grinned.

'I won't need to.'

After all these years, I'd never thrown out my biker's gear – I suppose it was a souvenir to me of my lost youth. So, to Andy's visibly growing astonishment, I produced a helmet and gloves and boots from the back of a cupboard. And when I put them on I thought his eyes were going to pop out of his head.

Back in the street I felt the sensation of sitting astride a bike for the first time in ten years. And then the thrill of her starting to roar at the press of a button. And then the familiar motions of holding in the clutch and clicking down into first. And then the gentle release of my left hand and the simultaneous twist of my right – and smoothly I pulled away, and smoothly I clicked her up into second, and along the street I rolled, and turned, and rolled back, and stopped, and clicked her down into neutral.

I hadn't forgotten a thing. I repeated the exercise two or three times before I drew up beside Andy again, and pushed up my visor.

'This is amazing!' I said. 'I feel as if it's ten minutes since I last rode a bike, rather than ten years.'

He laughed: 'It's all coming back to you, is it?'

'Yes, it is! Would you mind if I took her a slightly longer run this time – round the block, so to speak?'

'If you're confident enough . . . '

'I think I am.'

I shut the visor and rolled off again, but now at the end of the street I turned left, went uphill, and came back in a long rectangle. After I'd done this several times I headed in the opposite direction. With each circuit I became more and more aware that I didn't even have to think about what I was doing – my feet and hands moved in the correct pattern as if the sequence of actions was engraved somewhere in my brain.

It was nearly an hour before I returned Andy's bike to him. By then I'd been along Princes Street, up Lothian Road, past the Meadows, and down the Bridges. Three times.

Over lunch we discussed what to do with the afternoon.

'It's a lovely day,' I said. 'Why don't we go somewhere on the bike?'

Andy burst out laughing.

'You've really caught the bug again, haven't you?'

'Not a bit of it. I just think it would be a waste of a sunny day to drive around in the car.'

'Where would we go?'

'Well, we could take a run across to Stirling. It's only forty miles or so – a nice distance on a bike.'

He nodded: 'OK, if you like. I take it you want to be in front?'

'Me? Oh, heavens, no – I wasn't thinking of that at all.'

He grinned: 'But you know the way – I don't.'

'Yes, but all the same . . .'

'I don't see why not. You looked perfectly OK with her.' He laughed. 'Besides, I'm on holiday here. I rather fancy riding pillion for a change.'

I needed a bit more convincing: Princes Street was one thing, the M9 quite another. But Andy can be very persuasive when he wants to be. And so about an hour later we rolled off with me in control and him behind me.

I was determined to take things easy. After all, we weren't in any hurry; we were just out for a Sunday afternoon jaunt. As it happens, the western exit from Edinburgh is a route where you can rarely travel fast at any time, so the question of accelerating didn't arise till we reached the motorway itself. Here I settled down in the inside lane at a steady sixty which put no strain on either the bike or its rider.

But then, damn me if I didn't find myself behind a driver who was carrying his Sunday afternoon relaxation just a shade too far for my taste. So I had to pull out and overtake.

And then I felt it – the thrust of power that a large bike gives you in response to the twisting of your right wrist. As the petrol surged through the carburettor, the adrenalin surged through me. And in an instant I was hooked again. I was hooked as hopelessly as I'd been twenty-five years ago, in Sussex.

I opened the throttle further, and further, and further again. We were doing seventy, seventy-five, eighty. And all my old confidence as a biker came back as if I'd last ridden like this the day before.

It was the fast lane from then on, and get out of my way if you were anywhere inside the speed limit. We rocketed past Linlithgow Palace. We raced between Falkirk and the oil refineries at Grangemouth. We were at the turning off for Stirling disappointingly soon, and I had to slow down again and behave myself as we rolled by the field of Bannockburn, where I thought it would be tactless to stop and offer Andy a guided tour, and so into Stirling, and up to the Castle.

I parked on the esplanade, and we clambered off. Andy took off his helmet and looked at me with the strangest look I had ever had from him. It was as if he couldn't make up his mind whether or not to be hugely amused; and yet I thought I also saw affection there, an affection for me which he had never before made obvious.

'Well!' he said. 'Now I know where I get it from.'

I simply grinned.

We went into the Castle, and from its western rampart looked out across the Carse of Stirling to the great line of the mountains. There was still snow lying in their high gullies.

'Jeez, what a view!' Andy exclaimed. 'Jeez!'

'This is just a taste,' I told him. 'Tomorrow I'll take you across the Highland line.'

He walked up and down the rampart as if he was entranced: 'Christ, but this is a beautiful country!' he said, not once but several times. I watched him with growing surprise; I had never expected him to react like this.

'I suppose it is,' I said.

'Suppose? Why do you waste your time going on holiday in Sussex, when you've got all this on your doorstep?'

I laughed, as much to hide my puzzlement at his

enthusiasm as out of genuine amusement.

'You know,' I said, 'it's not uncommon for English people who come up here to turn more nationalist than the Scots are themselves.' I paused. 'But it usually takes longer than three days.' The irony was lost on him; I wasn't sure he'd been listening.

We looked round the Castle itself, had tea in the café, and ended up back on the esplanade beside the bike.

'You like to go in front again?' Andy asked.

'May I?'

He grinned.

'Well, I wouldn't want to deny an old man his bit of fun in life.'

'You cheeky little sod!'

But the old man had his bit of fun again. We were at the outskirts of Edinburgh in half-an-hour.

Back in the flat, I laid down my helmet and gloves.

'Thank you, Andy,' I said. 'I enjoyed that. I really did.'

'Yeah, so I noticed. You want to have another ride on her before I leave? It wouldn't be any problem.'

I shook my head, smiling: 'No, I don't think so. It was a great little fling – but enough.'

'Why?' he asked as he undid his own helmet. 'Why don't you buy a bike for yourself?'

'Buy a bike?'

'Yeah – you can afford it, can't you? Then you could go hurtling up to the Highlands whenever you fancied.'

I shook my head again, laughing now: 'Andy, Andy! I don't think you should make suggestions like that.'

'What's wrong with it?'

I sat down: 'Because I'm far too old to be "hurtling" anywhere, as you put it.'

'Rubbish! I think it's a brilliant idea.'

'And I think it's nuts,' I said, as I struggled to get my boots off.

* * *

The next day John drove me, in his car, on a huge run to

places with the strangest place-names I'd ever heard – 'Yetts o' Muckhart', for heaven's sake – and the most unpronounceable place-names I'd ever tried to get my tongue round. He had a whale of a time taking the piss out of me: 'Say "Auchterarder", Andy'; or, 'Andy, it's "Loch Venachar", not "Lock Vinegar"'; and when we passed a sign to 'Crianlarich', I flatly refused to try.

But he'd been right the day before when he said that the view from Stirling Castle was just a taste of the scenery we'd pass through as we drove up to Crieff and then to Lochearnhead and down to Aberfoyle, in the Rob Roy country. It was amazing, totally amazing – in my wildest dreams I'd never imagined Scotland was as beautiful as this. John even seemed to get quite worried about how I was going on about it. If I'd listened to John, I'd have believed that by sheer good luck we'd hit the Trossachs on the one and only day in the year when they weren't either under five metres of snow – he made out the winter lasted about ten months – or invaded by giant midges and overrun by a billion tourists.

'Well, aren't we tourists?'

'Certainly not. We're visitors.'

It was a fantastic end to my holiday. 'Cause by then Terry was in Glasgow, and the next day I went through there, till the end of the week. And now my trip to Scotland was for business, not pleasure.

* * *

Andy and Terry had decided to stay on in Glasgow for a couple of days after Terry had finished with BT – though why anyone would want to spend longer in Glasgow than they had to, I couldn't imagine – and were to come back to me on Friday for the weekend, before making their separate ways home. Sure enough, the car and the bike arrived about tea-time, and now I had two young guests to entertain rather than just one. But Andy's visit had been such a success I was no longer fearful about the prospect.

'I'm afraid I'm working tomorrow,' I had to tell Terry.

'It's the busiest day of the week in the shop.'

'Oh, that's OK,' Andy said at once. 'I'll show Tel round Edinburgh.'

For some reason this remark seemed to amuse them.

In the evening, however, I took them to dinner in a tiny, crowded restaurant near Bruntsfield Links which I'm particularly fond of. We had placed our orders, and I was just pouring wine, when Andy spoke words I'd heard once before.

'John, there's something I got to tell you.'

I nearly dropped the bottle.

'Oh, my God! What *now*?'

He laughed: 'No, it's good news.' He turned to Terry: 'Will you tell him, Tel?'

Terry smiled a little shyly: 'The thing is, John – I haven't actually been on a training course in Glasgow.'

I put the bottle down: 'Yes?'

'I've been checking out a possible job – a transfer up here.'

'A transfer?' I exclaimed.

'Yes. The chance came out of the blue, at work, a couple of weeks ago. I'd never even thought of such an idea till then, but I decided I had to look into it.'

I stared at him.

'You mean you might be moving to Glasgow?'

'No – I *am* moving. I've been offered the place. They liked me' – he blushed slightly – 'and I needed to know, of course, if it would suit me.' He smiled again. 'And I think it does. So I've accepted the offer. It's similar work to what I do in Brighton, but one grade higher.'

I still hadn't taken it in: 'You mean, you're leaving Brighton?'

'Yes.'

I looked from Terry to Andy.

'And what about you?'

He was grinning: 'Me, too. I'm coming with him, of course.' He became serious: 'That's what I've been doing this week. I've been sussing out whether there's any chance of despatch rider work. And I think there is, I've been round quite a few firms.'

'My God,' I said softly.

I thought for a few moments. Then I asked the first question that came to me: 'Does your mother know about this?'

Andy looked down at the table.

'Yeah, we talked about it before I left. And I was on the phone to her yesterday.'

'And how does she feel about it?'

He very slightly shrugged.

'Well, she's not over the moon, of course. But she's being very brave about it' – he raised his eyes. 'You know Mum, you know what she's like.'

I nodded: 'Yes, I do. But doesn't this mean she'll be left on her own in Brighton?'

To my surprise Andy grinned.

'Maybe not, as it happens. There's a new bloke in her life.'

'Really?'

'Yeah, but it's supposed to be dead hush-hush at present.'

'Have you met him?'

'Yeah, a couple of times. He's a definite improvement on Bowman, I can tell you.' I saw he wanted to get back to the main subject: 'But you see, the point is' – he tailed off, and appealed to Terry with his eyes.

'The point is, John – it solves a lot of problems. It gets me away from my family, and right now that's what I want more than anything else. Having a place of my own has made a hell of a difference, of course, but they're still on my back – as long as I'm in Brighton they're just too fucking close', he finished with an unusual vehemence for him.

I nodded, as if sympathetically. But I couldn't help thinking this was a rather drastic solution to his difficulties.

'And it'll be good for Andy, too. He's not had any luck finding work in Brighton – we're hoping it'll be easier in Glasgow.'

'A kind of clean break,' Andy put in. 'A way of putting the past behind me.'

I nodded.

'I mean, I'll always have my record,' he went on. 'I can't change that. But up here nobody knows me – I don't have the feeling it might be thrown in my face at any moment.'

I could see the logic behind all this. But my doubts were growing and growing. I had to ask: 'Are you *sure* you can find work in Glasgow? There's very high unemployment.'

'There's very high unemployment in Brighton, too,' he said, a little sharply. 'But even if I can't get courier work, not at first – there's bound to be a better chance of something else. If just because Glasgow's so much bigger than Brighton.'

I turned my head from one of them to the other. They were brimming with youthful enthusiasm for their scheme; their eyes were shining; they clearly hoped for, or even expected, my endorsement. I wished I could have given it; or at least, that I could have done so more wholeheartedly.

'But do you think you'll *like* Glasgow?' I asked. They exchanged what I immediately thought were significant glances.

'Well,' Andy said. 'It's different from what we're used to.'

'What an understatement!'

At that moment the waiter arrived with our first courses. I took the opportunity to withdraw into my private reflections.

And tonight, as I finish off this book – on St George's Day, which may or may not be appropriate – the same doubts are with me. The boys are back in Brighton now, preparing to move to Scotland; but I have a suspicion that by the time this book is in the shops they may already have left again.

I've discussed it with May, of course, several times. As Andy said, she's facing the prospect of his moving so far away with her usual spirit. But I can hear her underlying sadness when she talks about it, and I try to cheer her up by joking about how on earth the boys will cope with Glasgow.

And it's not entirely a joke. I find it hard to imagine that after being used to the south coast climate – and enjoying sunbathing in the nude! – they'll be able to tolerate the dismal Scottish excuse for a summer. Once they've discovered how rarely it's warm and dry here, nostalgia for sunny Brighton days may overwhelm them. And what will they make of Scotland's limited gay scene? How can it compete with the opportunities open to them in Brighton, or make up for the nearness of London?

But they have each other, of course. So perhaps I'm being over-cautious – perhaps I'm letting the cynicism of middle-age get the better of me. Certainly, that evening in the restaurant they were bubbling with cheerfulness: 'Just think of it!' Andy said to me. 'You're going to have a son not fifty miles away.' He added with a slightly self-conscious archness: 'Dad.'

I grinned.

'Oh, yes? And how often will I see you?'

'Regularly!' he exclaimed. 'We'll come through and see my old man, won't we, Tel?'

'Less of the "old man"!' I protested. 'No, I can see it now – I can hear myself complaining to Sandy: "That son of mine, he's just the other end of the M8, and do you know how long it is since he last came to visit me? *Well* . . ."'. The boys roared with laughter.

'Never mind,' Andy said. 'If you get that bike, you can come and visit *us*. It wouldn't take you ten minutes,' he added, with a slight emphasis on 'you'.

'Listen, I keep telling you – I am *not* buying a bike. My mind is made up.'

'That's what you said about the ceilidh.'

At the end of the meal I ordered glasses of the finest malt for all of us. The boys sniffed at theirs a little suspiciously, while I showed them how to add just a touch of water to release the fragrance of the whisky.

I raised my glass to them.

'Slainte mhath,' I said.

'You what?' Andy asked. He mimicked the pronunciation: '"Slanjy-va"?'

I grinned, and repeated: 'Slainte mhath. It's Gaelic for "good health".'

They still looked blank. I burst out laughing.

'Oh, God,' I said. 'I see I'll have to give you both a crash course in how to be Scots.'

Written in stages and finished in Stepps
St George's Day, 1995